PRAISE FOR *NEW YOR*
TODAY BESTSELL
ANNE FRASIER

"Frasier has perfected the art of making a reader's skin crawl."

—*Publishers Weekly*

"A master."

—*Minneapolis Star Tribune*

"Anne Frasier delivers thoroughly engrossing, completely riveting suspense."

—Lisa Gardner

"Frasier's writing is fast and furious."

—Jayne Ann Krentz

PRAISE FOR *THE BODY READER*

"Absorbing."

—*Publishers Weekly*

"This is an electrifying murder mystery—one of the best of the year."

—*Mysterious Reviews*

"I see the name Anne Frasier on a book and I know I am in for a treat . . . I thought it was a very unique premise and coupled with the good characters, made for an almost non-stop read for me. I highly recommend this."

—*Pure Textuality*

"*The Body Reader* earned its five stars, a rarity for me, even for books I like. Kudos to Anne Frasier."

—*The Wyrdd and the Bazaar*

"A must read for mystery suspense fans."

—*Babbling About Books*

"I've long been a fan of Anne Frasier, but this book elevates her work to a whole new level, in my mind."

—*Tale of a Shooting Star*

PRAISE FOR *PLAY DEAD*

"This is a truly creepy and thrilling book. Frasier's skill at exposing the dark emotions and motivations of individuals gives it a gripping edge."

—*Romantic Times*

"*Play Dead* is a compelling and memorable police procedural, made even better by the way the characters interact with one another. Anne Frasier will be appreciated by fans who like Kay Hooper, Iris Johansen and Lisa Gardner."

—*The Best Reviews*

"A nicely constructed combination of mystery and thriller. Frasier is a talented writer whose forte is probing into the psyches of her characters, and she produces a fast-paced novel with a finale containing many surprises."

—*I Love a Mystery*

"I couldn't put it down. Engrossing . . . scary . . . I loved it."

—Linda Howard

"A deeply engrossing read, *Hush* delivers a creepy villain, a chilling plot, and two remarkable investigators whose personal struggles are only equaled by their compelling need to stop a madman before he kills again. Warning: don't read this book if you are home alone."

—Lisa Gardner

"A wealth of procedural detail, a heart-thumping finale, and two scarred but indelible protagonists make this a first-rate read."

—*Publishers Weekly*

"Anne Frasier has crafted a taut and suspenseful thriller."

—Kay Hooper

"Well-realized characters and taut, suspenseful plotting."

—*Minneapolis Star Tribune*

PRAISE FOR *SLEEP TIGHT*

"Guaranteed to keep you awake at night."

—Lisa Jackson

"There'll be no sleeping after reading this one. Laced with forensic detail and psychological twists."

—Andrea Kane

"Gripping and intense . . . Along with a fine plot, Frasier delivers her characters as whole people, each trying to cope in the face of violence and jealousies."

—*Minneapolis Star Tribune*

"Has all the essentials of an edge-of-your-seat story. There is suspense, believable characters, an interesting setting, and just the right amount of details to keep the reader's eyes always moving forward . . . I recommend *Play Dead* as a great addition to any mystery library."

—*Roundtable Reviews*

PRAISE FOR *PRETTY DEAD*

"Besides being beautifully written and tightly plotted, this book was that sort of great read you need on a regular basis to restore your faith in a genre."

—Book of the Month, Lynn Viehl

"By far the best of the three books. I couldn't put my Kindle down till I'd read every last page."

—NetGalley

"A mix of dark humor, wit, psycho, suspense, paranormal, and a delicious crime thriller."

—*Judith D Collins Must Read Books*

"An adrenaline rush."

—*Lyon Editing Reviews*

"My favorite book from the Elise Sandburg series. Once again Anne Frasier kept me captivated from the beginning to the end."

—NetGalley

PRAISE FOR *HUSH*

"This is by far and away the best serial killer story I've read in a long time . . . strong characters, with a truly twisted bad guy."

—Jayne Ann Krentz

"Enthralling. There's a lot more to this clever intrigue than graphic police procedures. Indeed, one of Frasier's many strengths is her ability to create characters and relationships that are as compelling as the mystery itself. Will linger with the reader after the killer is caught."

—*Publishers Weekly*

PRAISE FOR *THE ORCHARD*

"Eerie and atmospheric, this is an indie movie in print. You'll read and read to see where it is going, although it's clear early on that the future is not going to be kind to anyone involved. Weir's story is more proof that only love can break your heart."

—*Library Journal*

"A gripping account of divided loyalties, the real cost of farming and the shattered people on the front lines. Not since Jane Smiley's *A Thousand Acres* has there been so enrapturing a family drama percolating out from the back forty."

—*Maclean's*

"This poignant memoir of love, labor, and dangerous pesticides reveals the terrible true price."

—*O, the Oprah Magazine Fall Book Pick*

"Equal parts moving love story and environmental warning . . . B+."

—*Entertainment Weekly*

"This is one of the loveliest books I have ever read, it reaches into the very heart of the word love and exemplifies its meaning with an unbelievable depth of understanding."

—*Cover Me*

"While reading this extraordinarily moving memoir, I kept remembering the last two lines of Muriel Rukeyser's poem "Kathe Kollwitz" ("What would happen if one woman told the truth about her life? The world would split open"), for Weir proffers a worldview that is at once eloquent, sincere, and searing."

—*Library Journal* Librarians' Best Books of 2011

"An unforgettable story beautifully told."

—Skokie Public Library

"A brilliant memoir."

—*The Local Social*

"This story of hardship and suffering, and love and hope pretty much stole my heart. An unforgettable story."

—*Rhapsody in Books*

"She tells her story with grace, unflinching honesty and compassion all the while establishing a sense of place and time with a master storyteller's perspective so engaging you forget it is a memoir."

—Calvin Crosby, Books Inc. (Berkeley, California)

"One of my favorite reads of 2011, *The Orchard* is easily mistakable as a novel for its engaging, page-turning flow and its seemingly imaginative plot."

—Susan McBeth, founder and owner of Adventures by the Book (San Diego, California)

"Moving and surprising."

—The Next Chapter Fall 2011 Top 20 Best Books List

"Searing . . . the past is artfully juxtaposed with the present in this finely wrought work. Its haunting passages will linger long after the last page is turned."

—*Boston Globe* Pick of the Week

"If a writing instructor wanted an excellent example of voice in a piece of writing, this would be a five-star choice!"

—*San Diego Union-Tribune* Recommended Reads

"Mesmeric."

—*San Francisco Book Review*

"Her subtle exposure of our antiquated notions of 'family farming' in America will leave you disquieted."

—Zomppa

"*The Orchard* is one of the most pivotal books I've ever read, irrevocably changing my view of the world."

—*Book End Babes*

"A stunning memoir, ripe with victory and defeat."

—*Raleigh Examiner*

"The truths she lays bare about the life of a farm and the farmers who work it are both simple and, dare I say it, profound."

—Madison Public Library

"This book produced a string of emotions that had my hand flying up to my mouth time and again, and not only made me realize, 'This woman can write!' but also made me appreciate the importance of this book, and how it reaches far beyond Weir's own story."

—Linda Grana, Diesel, a Bookstore

"*The Orchard* is a lovely book in all the ways that really matter, one of those rare and wonderful memoirs in which people you've never met become your friends."

—Nicholas Sparks

"A hypnotic tale of place, people, and of midwestern family roots that run deep, stubbornly hidden, and equally menacing."

—Jamie Ford, *New York Times* bestselling author of *Hotel on the Corner of Bitter and Sweet*

TRULY DEAD

ALSO BY ANNE FRASIER

Hush
Sleep Tight
Before I Wake
Pale Immortal
Garden of Darkness
The Body Reader

The Elise Sandburg Series

Play Dead
Stay Dead
Pretty Dead
Truly Dead

Nonfiction (as Theresa Weir)

The Orchard: A Memoir
The Man Who Left: A Memoir

TRULY DEAD

ANNE FRASIER

THOMAS & MERCER

Published by Thomas & Mercer, Seattle
www.apub.com

ISBN-13: 9781477819920
ISBN-10: 1477819924

Cover design by Cyanotype Book Architects

Printed in the United States of America

TRULY DEAD

PROLOGUE

Savannah, Georgia

The construction worker hefted the mallet, the momentum of his swing punching a hole in the wall, sending a shower of debris to the floor. He swung again, harder this time. One firm tug and a large section of drywall fell away. As the chalky dust settled, he peered inside the gap, looking for the copper pipes he'd been hired to remove, along with anything else of value that could be salvaged and sold before the house was torn down.

"Gimme that flashlight," he said, hand held out to his assistant, face in the dark gap. "Think I see something."

The flashlight was slapped into his palm, and his fingers closed around it. He flipped the switch and shot the beam inside the wall. It illuminated what appeared to be a grotesque mask until he panned the light down. Gasping, he stumbled backward, tripped over the mallet, and crashed to the floor, crab-crawling away in horror.

Tremain had done to her. But sex with a stranger was stupid. She knew that.

Her phone buzzed. Relieved by the interruption, she pulled it free of her pocket and checked the screen. The call was from Savannah medical examiner John Casper.

"Got something going on down here you might find interesting," he said. "A body has been found in a house scheduled for demolition."

"Tremain?"

"I wish, but no." His voice dropped. "I didn't think about that being the first conclusion you'd draw. Sorry. No, the body was identified as Zane Novak."

She hit "Speaker" to include David in the conversation. "The boy who disappeared a few months ago?"

"Yep. And this isn't for public consumption, but the MO matches those child killings in Florida you've probably heard about."

"Asphyxiation as well as the method of disposal?" Elise asked.

"Yep."

"Possibly a copycat?" David asked, thinking aloud.

Or worse. "Maybe the Florida killer has moved to Savannah," Elise suggested.

"I had both thoughts," John told them. "Another thing that's probably just a weird coincidence—the house where the body was found used to belong to Frank J. Remy. Know who I'm talking about?"

"The name sounds vaguely familiar." Elise glanced at David. He was drawing a blank too. "But no. Not really."

"Convicted killer. Died in prison thirty-six years ago. And get this. Your father was behind that conviction."

Jackson Sweet? Now that *was* an odd coincidence, but then everything connected to her father was odd in some way or another.

"What does Homicide say?" she asked.

"Not much. No surprise, but I think Avery's in over his head. And Lamont . . . You know how he is. Doesn't listen to anybody but Lamont.

Come home and I'll update you on everything. I'd feel better if you and David were around. I could really use your input."

Not their case, but, like John, Elise didn't have much faith in Lamont, the ex-FBI agent who'd taken over her position and had most likely been behind her and David's firing.

Not that being fired was a bad thing.

She could see David was thinking what she was thinking. "We'll be back today," she told John. "See you soon." She ended the call.

David braked for a signal. "Come on. Admit it," he said, focused on the red taillights in front of them. "You're relieved."

"About what?"

"About another postponement of our vacation."

He understood her more than she wanted him to. She'd had this idea that if she got far away from everything, then maybe she could put the stuff that had happened with Tremain behind her. In a completely different setting, somewhere unfamiliar, maybe she and David would have a chance. But time and time again she'd discovered that she couldn't run from her own life. She couldn't run from the life she'd created. She had to face it head-on. Yet sometimes she just wanted to run, and sometimes she just wanted to give in and be vulnerable.

David took the hotel exit. "Know what I think?" He sounded a little sad. A little hurt. "I say we forget it completely. A vacation together was a bad idea. Kind of a pipe dream for both of us. You wanted a beach; I wanted . . ." No need to spell it out. Sex. A future?

"Maybe I want what you want."

"Think so?" He didn't sound at all convinced, and his voice held an unfamiliar distance.

"I don't know." Was that fear in her voice? "I don't know if I'm ready." Yeah, fear. Had he heard it? She hoped not.

"When you figure it out, *if* you figure it out, let me know."

CHAPTER 2

Once the plane made contact with the tarmac of the Savannah / Hilton Head International Airport, Elise turned on her phone, getting a tone that indicated a message. She thumbed the green icon and let out an involuntary gasp as she read a cryptic text from her daughter.

He made me go with him.

Her heart slammed—one of those deep and unnerving movements that felt like something was living in her chest. Had someone abducted Audrey again?

"Call her," David said, reading over her shoulder. The seriousness in his voice made her heart pound even harder.

Audrey didn't pick up, so Elise tried Sweet.

"Didn't want to tell you this until you got home," her father said, "but your ex-husband was here. He took Audrey back to Seattle with him."

Elise's relief at discovering Audrey was safe was quickly replaced by anger. Someone *had* abducted Audrey. "You let her go with him? Without contacting me first?"

"He had a court order filed by Child Protective Services."

That was insane. "Thomas wouldn't do anything like that."

"I'm at the airport," Sweet said. "In the waiting area. I'll explain more when you get off the plane." He disconnected, and Elise quickly related the news to David.

"That makes no sense. Has this ever come up?"

"No." She thought back to Chicago. They'd been so busy, so involved in the case. She was always careful to check for anything from Audrey or Sweet, but had she gotten a few messages from Thomas she hadn't read? *Yes.*

In unison, she and David unbuckled their seat belts as the plane approached the Jetway, the aircraft coming to a complete stop with a final jerk, engines shutting down.

They'd flown first class, courtesy of the City of Chicago as thanks for a job well done, so they were among the first passengers to disembark. Shouldering their laptop bags, they hurried up the walkway, passing the departure desk, sidestepping the retractable belts. Practically running, they moved past security, through the checkpoint exit, and into the brightly lit public lounge and atrium.

Sweet spotted them and pushed himself out of a rocking chair. Dressed in jeans and boots, with his gray hair tied back, he waited and watched as they approached.

"It happened a few hours ago," he said. "I rode to the airport with them. And the dog. They took the dog." He seemed almost as upset about that.

"You were supposed to be watching her," Elise said. The man who claimed to have no qualms about killing people was saying he'd just let his granddaughter leave Savannah to live with her father in Seattle? "Taking *care* of her."

Without comment, he handed her two envelopes. The first one contained a court order stating that Audrey would have to either go into temporary foster care or move in with her father. After reading the official document, she passed it to David and opened the second envelope.

Thomas was filing for full custody.

"As you can see, there was nothing I could do," Sweet said. "It was either that or foster care."

"Nothing you could do? Did your bout with cancer turn you into a coward?"

"Jesus Christ, Elise." The words came from David. She wasn't scoring any points with him today. She'd feel ashamed of her harsh comment to Sweet later. That's how her relationship with her father worked.

"I didn't want to make it any worse," Sweet said.

Without discussion, all three of them moved toward the down escalator and baggage claim while Elise opened her message app, then searched for and found Thomas's name.

"We'll fight it," David said.

He said "we" as if they were a unit, a family. His inclusive choice of words, along with the shedding of his earlier distance, reassured her. Elise scrolled through pages of text, catching words and phrases like "concerned for Audrey's safety." She slowed to read an entire message from Thomas about how she'd allowed Audrey to hang around undesirables like Strata Luna, owner of the Savannah brothel, Black Tupelo.

> You, rushing off to Chicago to leave our daughter in the care of Jackson Sweet, a liar with no morals, putting her life in danger once again. After she almost DIED!

True. Every word. How many times had she silently criticized herself for her parenting decisions? Maybe that's what this was really about. Maybe she was transferring the anger she should have directed at herself to Sweet. "I'll never win," she said with dawning realization. Thomas was a model citizen with a perfect family and perfect job. She, on the other hand, could only give her daughter a life of danger, chaos, and, like Thomas said, questionable company. "There's no way I can get her back."

And did she deserve to get her back? Really? How telling it was that her first thought upon receiving Audrey's message was about her daughter being abducted. Again.

The undeniable truth was that her job put Audrey in constant danger. She'd hoped that would change now that she no longer worked for Savannah PD. But would it, especially with media attention stronger than ever? Either way was a no-win. If she didn't fight for custody, Audrey would hate her. If she fought and won, her daughter would continue to live in danger. And resent her.

Why had she taken the Chicago job? Why had she left Audrey in the care of a man with a disturbing past and dark reputation? What kind of parent did that?

A bad one.

Like father, like daughter.

At the carousel, she felt David's hand on her shoulder and looked up to catch his silent nod, directing her attention to her father, who was moving toward the exit. David, acting as her conscience. And he was right.

She ran after Sweet, catching up to him outside, body-shocked by the blast of smothering heat, surprised by the sharp rush of bittersweet nostalgia carried to her heart by the scent of pine trees. But along with that nostalgia, she felt a sharp stab of unfounded fear she shoved away. "I'm sorry." She caught her breath. "I shouldn't have said that to you. There was nothing you could have done."

He watched her with unreadable eyes. "You're wrong. I could have done something. I could have stopped him, but I'm sure you would've liked that even less." He smiled a smile that made her scalp tingle, his face shifting and changing until it seemed she was looking at another person altogether. The transformation reminded her that the persona he presented most of the time, even to her, was a false one. In that moment, she believed all he'd told her about being an undercover operative for the FBI, a man who tortured and broke people. Killed people.

"Since Audrey is gone, I'll be leaving," he said. They both knew the only reason he'd stuck around was to keep an eye on his granddaughter.

"You don't have to." But after that smile, she wasn't sure she wanted him to stay. Sharing a house, just the two of them . . . The thought made her uneasy.

"What do you know about someone named Frank J. Remy?" she asked, taking advantage of his presence in case he slipped away and she never saw him again.

Something darted across his craggy features. A flicker that was almost a flinch. It happened fast, and then he was just an old man again. If Sweet had been anybody else, Elise would have thought he was hiding something. But hiding something was Sweet's whole existence, so how did you get a read on that?

"Why do you want to know about him?" he asked.

"I'm not at liberty to say. But I can tell you I've come by some interesting information."

He thought a moment, then seemed to decide to share at least a little with her. "He was given the death sentence before you were even born."

A strange way of putting it. *Before you were even born.* Odd that her birth was even on his timeline.

"I heard you brought him in," she said.

"That's right. He got the death sentence, but he died in prison before it was carried out. Too bad, because I wanted to watch his face as they delivered the lethal injection."

"Why?"

"He hurt children. Very young children. Remy taught piano to kids. They trusted him, and he violated that trust."

"Is that your calling? Protector of other people's children?"

He let out a snort. "I'll always be the bad guy, won't I? No matter what I do."

Behind them, the sound of automatic doors could be heard. David appeared, dragging two suitcases.

Her phone vibrated. It was Audrey.

"Sorry, Mom," Audrey said, talking fast. "I had to come to Seattle with Dad. If I didn't, they were going to put me in foster care!" Her rush to explain things to Elise demonstrated how far their relationship had progressed in just a few years. Not that long ago, Audrey wouldn't have bothered to call at all and wouldn't have cared if her mother was worried. This new thoughtfulness made the current situation even harder to bear.

"It's okay, honey," Elise said. "We'll do whatever we have to do to get you back." A promise she maybe shouldn't be making.

"You're not mad?"

"Not at you."

"At Grandpa?" Audrey knew Elise's relationship with Sweet so well.

"Is that your mother?" Thomas's voice, in the background. "Let me talk to her."

Suddenly Thomas was on the phone, tripping over his words, trying to explain himself. Thomas was not a brave person, and when faced with Elise's wrath, he always backpedaled. That alone explained why this had happened when she was gone. He would never have tried it if she'd been home.

A cab stopped at the curb. David and her father helped the driver load the suitcases into the trunk.

"I've got to go," Elise told her ex. "Tell Audrey I love her." She wasn't yet certain about the truth of her next words, but she wanted to make him sweat. "You'll be hearing from my lawyer."

After telling Elise he wouldn't be heading to her house, Sweet left the airport in a separate cab. Elise and David shared a ride, with David getting out first at his apartment at Mary of the Angels, giving Elise a look she couldn't read before turning to pull his dark suitcase behind him up the sidewalk. It seemed like they'd been gone months, but she knew in a day or so it would feel as if they'd never left.

In the heart of the Savannah Historic District, Elise paid the cab driver, dropped her suitcase inside the front door of her Victorian home, closing and locking the door behind her.

The odor of her own house seemed foreign the way it always did when she'd been gone more than a few days. Even though it had been recently renovated, she could still detect the old wood, now mixed with the scent of newer materials. Beneath that was a little bit of dog and something floral, maybe the shampoo Audrey had used that morning.

Under other conditions, it might have felt good to be home, but not now. Not with Audrey gone. The only reason she'd finished the renovation was because of her daughter. Elise didn't care about homemaking or cooking or anything domestic—another indication that she was an unfit mother. Now the house itself mocked her.

She kicked off her shoes and headed to the kitchen in her bare feet. She wasn't much of a drinker, but she felt the need for something to reset her brain or maybe even numb it for a few minutes. She dug out a bottle of vodka and poured herself a couple of inches.

After surviving a three-day nightmare with Atticus Tremain, she'd prided herself in her ability to maintain. So far she'd done okay, and when the department psychologist had suggested drugs for possible PTSD, she'd passed. She'd needed a clear head. She'd needed to be there for Audrey. But now . . . Did it matter anymore, what crutch she reached for?

Not fond of the taste of vodka, she slammed the liquid down like someone taking medicine or someone who was way too into the drama of her own life.

She'd been hard on Sweet, and now she mentally flogged herself. No matter how she tried, she lost all resolve whenever a situation with her father moved beyond the ordinary. One step outside their established boundaries, she reverted back to the resentful child. Especially annoying, since she was a detective, someone who should always have a cool head. It would probably be best if Sweet *did* move out, because it was beginning to look as if she'd never be able to completely forgive him for abandoning her and her mother and setting her life on such a strange and dark path.

Slightly buzzed, she took the stairs to Audrey's room, where she found the bed unmade. Elise stripped the sheets and carried them downstairs, stuffing them into the washing machine, adding detergent, turning the machine on, listening to the water, experiencing a blow of sorrow. She had the urge to pull the sheets from the machine and put them back on the bed, still smelling of Audrey's shampoo and lotion rather than clean and fresh and awaiting her daughter's return.

In the kitchen off the laundry area was an empty spot where Trixie's bowls had been. Above that, the leash hooks were empty. As if everyone in her life had vanished while she'd stepped away for a few moments. As if she were being punished for leaving, and punished for the choices she'd made.

She headed back to the living room, pulled her laptop from her messenger bag, sat down on the couch, and began searching for any information she could find on Frank J. Remy. Cops called it "open-source intelligence." Funny, the descriptions they had for basic things. It was the same Google search engine everybody used.

Remy's history was old and not much came up because the Internet hadn't kicked in until after his arrest, incarceration, and death. She took a couple of screen grabs of his image and e-mailed them to herself so she'd have them on her phone. Fifteen minutes later she sent an e-mail to her information broker, a specialist outside the police department she sometimes used for research.

"I need anything you can dig up on Remy," she told him. "Especially anything that might be connected to Jackson Sweet."

Short conversation over, she set her laptop aside and dropped deeper into the couch, covering herself with the colorful throw her aunt Anastasia had crocheted while doing time in the Georgia State Prison. She'd made a lot of throws. She was still making throws while hoping her good behavior resulted in a reduced sentence and possibly parole.

Elise dozed until a sound like fingernails tapping against glass roused her long enough to reawaken the stab of fear she'd felt earlier, and long enough for her to identify it as the patter of live-oak leaves hitting the windows. Then she was asleep again . . . until she heard a faint crash of glass from somewhere outside.

Savannah was never quiet, and night noise was commonplace, but a check of the front-door peephole revealed a shrouded form on her porch. She hit the light switch—nothing happened.

In the darkness, as she watched, the person walked backward, away from the house, the face remaining hidden beneath a hood. Size and movement suggested a male. Reaching the middle of the street, he tossed something into the air, creating a cloud that drifted to the ground. Then he turned and ran.

With no time to analyze the event, Elise grabbed her gun, along with the flashlight she kept in a basket near the door.

Outside, the street was empty except for the far-off sound of the street sweeper and a few distant voices. She directed the light beam toward her feet and spotted glass shards, looked up, noted the shattered bulb, then looked back down to study the mess in front of her.

Mixed with the shards was a pile of gray powder.

Elise crouched to examine the material in the additional light cast from the open door. She noted the grittiness of the powder and recognized it for what it was. Cremains. She could even make out small pieces of bone. Along with the cremains was dirt, maybe even graveyard dirt—goofer dust. And judging from the odor, the potion also contained a large measure of sulfur.

Gonna sprinkle goofer dust all around your bed; wake up in the morning and find your own self dead.

The media attention around the Chicago case made it easy for anybody living in Savannah to know she was home.

Exhausted and unalarmed, she nonetheless knew better than to completely dismiss the curse as just Savannah being strange. She straightened and looked down the street shadowed by moss-draped branches.

Welcome home.

CHAPTER 3

Early the next morning, after toast and coffee, Elise scrolled through her contacts and called Strata Luna. The Gullah woman confirmed Elise's suspicion about the powder left on her doorstep.

"A killing spell," she said, alarm in a voice that was typically deep and smooth. "You've been throwed. Clean it up. Right now. An' make sure nuthin's been buried on your property. Check under the steps. Check 'round the house. In the backyard. Gonna need a purification ritual too. I can do that."

"No purification ritual."

"A killin' spell ain't nuthin' to mess with, darlin'."

"Who's that?" The voice belonged to Jackson Sweet, and it was coming from somewhere in the room with Strata Luna. Elise felt an unexpected pang that took her a moment to identify. Sadness over the loss of their short-lived family, dysfunctional though it had been.

"Somebody's just messing with me," Elise said. "Trying to get my attention. It's only bones and dirt." Spells didn't worry her. People worried her.

Strata Luna clicked her tongue.

She and Elise had argued over the topic of spells so many times it had become tedious, with Elise vacillating between full denial and faint belief, depending upon the circumstances and how they might impact her. And if she hadn't believed at least a little, why had she called Strata Luna? And why had she gotten so upset the time she found out Strata Luna had given David a mojo to make Elise fall in love with him?

Whatever Elise's murky and confused position on the issue, there was no denying that spells could have a powerful impact on someone who believed. Elise called it the placebo effect, and it was why belief was at the core of all rootwork and mojos. And there was no denying that it was a practice deeply ingrained in low-country culture.

They discussed Audrey.

"He did what he had to do," Strata Luna said in defense of Sweet. "Man had no choice. But don't worry. Strata Luna's gonna make you a 'come back to me' spell. That girl'll be home in no time."

Elise didn't mention her concerns about Audrey's safety if she returned. Instead she told the woman good-bye. Moments after she ended the conversation, her landline rang. It was David.

"Got a call from John Casper," he told her. "Crime scene status was lifted from the Remy house, and demolition restarted. And guess what? More bodies. John is on-site and would like our input. I'm heading there now." Without waiting for a response, he finished: "I'll swing by and pick you up."

Before David's arrival, Elise returned to the front porch with a broom and dustpan, cleaning up the glass and powder, dumping it and zipping it into a clear storage bag rather than tossing it in the trash.

She considered calling the police to file a report, but all she could share was a vague description and some ground bones. More of the very thing she didn't want associated with her name. And maybe that's all this display had been about. She was a local celebrity, and there was a whole underground scene of people who thought she should be doing more to embrace her heritage. No, a call to the police was something she wanted to avoid unless the behavior escalated.

***

The Remy house was located in the Starland District, an area of Savannah once known for high crime but currently in the process of gentrification. Gentrification was not always the best thing for neighborhoods, but if it meant fewer homicides, Elise was for it. Disturbingly—and something David probably wasn't even thinking about—the location wasn't that far from the house where Atticus Tremain had left his mark on her. It seemed all roads led back to hell.

At the scene, a bulldozer and crane waited to raze the only home left standing on the block. A billboard on the corner displayed an architectural drawing of plans—apartments for SCAD students, a coffee shop, pizza joint, and green space. Marring the vision of progress were a white coroner van, local forensics, plus a forensic team sent down from Atlanta, cop cars, and yellow crime scene tape.

It was no surprise to find Detective Avery along with Victor Lamont, the guy who'd replaced Elise in Homicide, at the scene. Avery was glad to see them, shaking David's and Elise's hands. "Great job in Chicago," he said. "I followed your progress the whole time." He shifted from foot to foot in his excitement. "Wish I could have been part of it."

Lamont worked his way into the conversation, addressing David, refusing to make eye contact with Elise. "It was a media circus. You apparently didn't learn anything about decorum while working for the FBI."

Someone—maybe the project manager—appeared and passed out white hard hats before being pulled away by one of his crew.

David stared at Lamont. "If decorum is code for screwing your partner's wife, then no." He slapped the hat on his head. "Guess I didn't."

"Show some respect for your line of work," Lamont said, ignoring the bait, probably because the argument over David's ex was one he'd never win. "You're giving us a bad name. And I doubt the photo that's gone viral will get you any private detective jobs no matter how much the mayor of Chicago praises you."

"Photo?" Elise asked.

Avery pulled out his phone, scrolled, and turned the screen around. Elise and David leaned in close. She'd almost forgotten about jumping on David's back in front of city hall yesterday. It already seemed ages ago. The image was electric, both of them laughing, caught up in the excitement of the moment. Below the photo was the caption *Homicide power couple.*

David smiled. Elise frowned.

Lamont had a point. The photo was unprofessional and undignified. But what struck her was the expression on her face. She looked happy.

Staring at the picture, she noted details that had gone unremarked in real life. How long David's hair had gotten—over his ears and collar—how it was a few shades lighter than hers. How her arms were locked almost intimately around his chest, how his hands supported her legs. She thought about their bodies beneath their clothes. His, hers, along with the knowledge of what her clothing hid from the world. The scars. The tattoo—the signature of Atticus Tremain—a permanent stain on her skin.

It came to her that things weren't right in her head. She understood that now, in this moment. While in Chicago, she'd been able to put the creeping unease aside, but coming back had reawakened what had lain dormant.

In Savannah, after her ordeal, she'd become desensitized to familiar and painful places. But going away, returning, had reset her brain, taking her to square one, returning her to the day she'd escaped from Tremain. Only back then she'd had the euphoria of her escape and something similar to the fog of fresh grief to protect her. Now she was naked, vulnerable, shaking inside, but hopefully cool and calm outside.

Avery stuck the phone back in his pocket. "It's everywhere. Facebook, Twitter, blogs."

"Go big or go home," David said.

Lamont grunted his disgust.

Elise shook free of her navel-gazing and steered the conversation back to the crime scene. "I'm surprised the building was released so quickly."

"We'd finished our investigation," Lamont told her. "The construction company was losing money every day the project was delayed." Defensive, as usual.

Seeing her doubt, he added with insistence, "We were thorough."

"Apparently not thorough enough," David said.

"One more comment like that and you're going to have to leave," Lamont told him. "I only agreed to allow you on-site because Casper requested it. But this is *my case*, and your presence alone, thanks to your newfound obsession with media whoredom, is already creating a spectacle."

Elise knew David had no reservations when it came to public displays of anything. Normally laid back, he'd been known to exhibit a lack of control around Lamont. And the detective was right. They had no reason to be there other than as a favor to John Casper. Without saying it, John hoped they might spot something Lamont had missed. The subtext was that nobody had much confidence in Lamont. That had to rankle.

She put a hand to her partner's chest. He might have been wearing his affable expression, but his body was tense and his heart was pounding. "Let's go inside the house." She spoke in a low voice meant just for him. "That's what we're here for."

He blinked and nodded.

"Inside" wasn't really the right word. The roof had been removed. Some of the walls were gone, exposing two-by-fours, studs, and wood turned black from age. That was where they found John Casper.

Wildly curly dark hair, red sneakers, coroner jacket. She hadn't seen him since his wedding a month ago in Wright Square. She and David took turns giving him a hug. John was the good kind of family. The kind that wasn't blood.

"I'm getting fat, right?" he asked, mistaking the intensity of her gaze for something other than happiness to see him. "You know how Mara loves to bake. Speaking of food, you're both invited to our new place on Johnny Mercer Day. We'll have all the appropriate fare for both vegans and carnivores."

The first Johnny Mercer Day was getting a lot of buzz, and the city hoped for something on par with their Saint Patrick's Day festivities, which brought thousands of people into town. Elise internally shuddered thinking about the crush of drunks, but the event would be a financial boost for the city.

"Love to," she and David said in unison.

None of them thought it odd that they were catching up in the middle of a crime scene. It was what they did.

"Over here." John motioned for them to follow him toward a set of stairs.

"The first body was found in a wall on the ground floor," he explained. "Not making excuses, but it didn't occur to us to look further. Nobody was expecting more."

Upstairs, he led them down a hallway to a small bedroom. Even though the house had no roof, the wallpaper with giant flowers overwhelmed the space.

One area had been stripped of plaster and drywall, revealing studs spaced a couple of feet apart. Beside her, David let out a small sound of dismay. Between every set of studs was a body wedged into the space, some of the bodies held in place by strategically placed nails and ropes.

David hung back but Elise stepped closer, careful not to touch anything, scanning the bodies and the crevices they were wedged into. "Did you see this?" She pointed to gouges in the wood.

John nodded, his face grim. "That's one of the reasons I called you. Look under the fingernails."

"Wood?"

"Pretty sure of it. I'll know when I do the autopsy."

"My God. This means at least some of them were alive when they were put here. Either by accident or design."

"Yes."

She could feel David behind her, reluctant to step closer.

She understood his reaction. The presentation was horrible enough, but the most horrifying and inhuman? All the bodies appeared to belong to children.

"How long have they been here?" Elise asked. Judging from the clothing, the shrunken and dehydrated corpses had been there a very long time.

"Decades, possibly."

Remy died thirty-six years ago. She thought of what her father had said yesterday. *He hurt children. Very young children.* "Didn't think I'd be saying this," Elise said, "but we need to get Jackson Sweet in here."

CHAPTER 4

"How did you know about the children?" Elise asked.

She and Sweet stood in the upstairs bedroom of the half-demolished house. She'd asked that they be allowed to visit the room without anyone else present. Knowing Sweet, he'd be more willing to talk with no audience. Surprisingly, Lamont had agreed to give them five minutes.

"I researched his case," Elise went on. "He was convicted for the murder of a neighbor. An *adult* neighbor. This"—she swept a hand in front of the death wall—"doesn't appear to be the work of the same man. But yesterday you said Remy killed children."

"Remember how I told you I sometimes did what I had to do to make sure the guilty paid for their crimes?" He gave her a look that said he expected her to understand where he was coming from. "You have to know what I'm talking about. You deal with this stuff all the time. You know someone is guilty, but you don't have enough evidence to convict him."

"Are you saying you framed him? With the neighbor's murder?" It wouldn't surprise her. During a previous conversation, Sweet had admitted to meting out a form of justice that had nothing to do with any law but his.

"Just leave this alone, Elise. Walk away. Leave it in the hands of Lamont."

"Who'll never solve it?"

He raised his eyebrows. *Hopefully.*

"I can't do that."

"Then I'm going to have to disappear again."

Always a runner. "That would break Audrey's heart. It would break Strata Luna's heart."

"What about you?"

How *would* she feel about it? Relieved? Sad?

When she didn't answer his question, he said, "They'll get used to it. I haven't been back in their lives that long."

She noted the hardness of him, the conviction, the will to do whatever it took to uphold that conviction, and also whatever it took to keep himself safe. "Did you kill these children?"

He recoiled, and she immediately felt bad for suspecting him.

"Good God, Elise. I *protect* children. Don't you get that?"

"It's hard for me to grasp such behavior, since I was never one of those children you protected."

"For somebody who is so independent, you seem to harbor a lot of resentment toward people you claim weren't there for you."

"Are you talking about you? Or David?"

He laughed. "Both of us."

"I don't resent David."

"Come on. I know you partially blame him for what happened with Tremain."

It was true. Unfair of her, but true.

They heard a sound on the stairs. Lamont. No doubt coming to tell them their time was up, to gloat, to do all manner of irritating things Lamont did.

Sweet was still staring at her.

"If you leave, don't come back," she told him. "If your cancer returns and you're sick and need us to change your diapers and feed you baby food, don't come back."

He smiled his brittle smile, basking in the cruelty of her words. And then he said something that put a crack in her heart. “If you need me, I’ll come.”

He smiled his lovely smile, basking in the [illegible] of [illegible] words. And then he said something that [illegible] stuck in her heart. "If you need me, I'll come."

CHAPTER 5

John and I were able to extract DNA from beneath the fingernails of some of the cold-case victims before they were taken to Atlanta," Mara, John Casper's new bride, told Elise and David two days later in the morgue office. She was perched on the edge of the desk, her long dark hair shining, skin glowing, the hem of a floral skirt just visible beneath her white lab coat. Her pose might give the casual visitor the impression of noncommitment, but nobody was more committed to dead bodies than Mara. And nobody was more committed to John Casper.

Elise wasn't surprised to hear that the old bodies found in the Remy house were gone. Georgia Bureau of Investigation had much better equipment for dealing with crimes that required intricate analysis. The downside was they were always backed up, and bodies dead for over three decades would not be a priority. If Elise had been in charge, she'd have pushed to have the bodies remain with John and Mara as long as possible.

"It didn't match anything in our database, so we tried to find DNA on Remy." John munched one of the ginger cookies Mara kept on hand for anybody who might be feeling queasy after a visit to the autopsy suite. "There is none. Not surprising considering the date. From 1970 to 1991 the state of Georgia did enzyme typing only. Not that it would have mattered, because nothing was collected from Remy—not uncommon back then with a case that was considered open and shut."

"Where's Remy buried?" Elise asked.

"Laurel Grove."

Laurel Grove—a recurring theme in their lives. It was where Elise had been abandoned as a baby on the grave of Lavinia Lafayette, a voodoo priestess. Later, to Elise's mortification, someone turned the grave into a shrine. Laurel Grove was also the place where David had been shot by Lamont. They might as well buy a couple of plots and set up some lawn chairs.

"I called Lamont," John said. "He filed an exhumation request. It's been approved. I'd like for you two to be there."

Elise took a sip of coffee and thought about the detective's reaction to their presence at the construction site. "Lamont won't like that."

"Keep a low profile and maybe he won't find out."

That seemed unlikely.

David scooted his wheeled office chair closer and grabbed a cookie from the tray on the desk. "Nothing like a good exhumation."

CHAPTER 6

Elise learned long ago that the dead and buried of Savannah didn't always stay that way. She'd once worked a case in which victims were given a drug that mimicked death, and poor John Casper had almost cut open a living person on his autopsy table. But there were more common reasons for the deceased not remaining six feet under, one being robbery. Not even the dead were safe from crime.

Bodies were regularly pilfered by criminals looking for anything of value. Caskets were dug up, the vault's gummy seals broken and pried open with crowbars, bodies stripped of fancy funeral clothes and polished shoes, teeth containing gold and diamonds yanked out with pliers. Hard to say if it was worse for a family member to come upon a desecrated grave containing the stripped corpse of a loved one or to come upon an empty coffin, the mark of another kind of thief, a wannabe root doctor or shady purveyor of ingredients to be sold as goofer dust. And then there were the plain old exhumations, sometimes of victims—sometimes, like today, of prosecuted and processed criminals.

"Haven't decided if it feels good to be home or not," David said from where he and Elise stood in the shady area they'd staked out earlier. A diesel truck with a winch was parked next to Frank J. Remy's grave, hole already dug with a backhoe and shovels. Two men inside the pit attached chains to lift the cement vault that held the coffin.

Elise crossed her arms and shifted her weight. "I know what you mean."

She and David were partially hidden behind a curtain of Spanish moss, observing from a distance, trying to avoid attracting the attention of Detective Lamont. Since this wasn't their case and they weren't on-site in an official capacity, no work clothing was necessary. David wore a gray T-shirt and jeans, his hair damp from the shower he'd probably taken after his morning run. Even in Chicago he hadn't given up those daily jogs. It helped keep him level, he said, helped keep him sane. In contrast to David's casual attire, Elise wore her usual black slacks and white top, thrown on in that brief moment after waking when she forgot she wasn't heading downtown to the police station. Unlike David, she wore a gun at her waist. Too hot for a jacket.

The exhumation was an affair heavily attended. No surprise, because news had hit online networks in ample time to draw a crowd big enough to require traffic police. Earlier a pile of tamales had floated past, the tray held aloft by a woman in a brightly colored skirt as she proclaimed the meal to be 100 percent pork and the best in Savannah. Food aside, the event had also brought the mayor and his entourage, not to mention the swarming media. The residents of Savannah loved local stories, the darker the better.

Elise wouldn't have contacted the media, but Lamont seemed to be working on building a public résumé. He'd often made it clear he hated Savannah, so he'd probably cause all the strife he could, then move on to what he would consider greener pastures while leaving a mess for everybody else to clean up. "Shitting his nest," as David put it.

The morning was already smotheringly hot, with June clouds racing across the sky. Near the grave stood John Casper. He wore a shirt that said "Coroner" in large letters across the back. Not far away were Avery and Lamont. And damn if Elise's father wasn't there too. At whose request, she didn't know. Maybe the mayor's. Maybe Lamont's. So much for Sweet's threat to leave town.

Elise tried to contain the irritation that would always be present whenever her father walked down the red carpet that seemed to unfurl before him wherever he went. And yet she knew he couldn't help it. He *was* larger than life. People ate that up.

She caught a whiff of boiled peanuts. "You'd think this was the state fair or Saint Patrick's Day," she said with annoyance. A cemetery wasn't a place for celebration.

With what seemed ridiculously like sleight of hand, David produced a small, grease-soaked paper bag and offered it to her. Boiled peanuts. "Caviar of the South." At her questioning expression, he nodded in the direction they'd come. "Kid was selling them at the gate while you were scoping out a place for us to hide. Thought I might as well embrace the party mood."

She gave up. "Cajun spice?" Like half the people in the low country, Elise was addicted to boiled peanuts.

"Yup." David tossed a shelled peanut in his mouth while she dug into the bag.

"We just need hot dogs and beer," she said.

"And vomit." He bounced a few peanuts in his palm, chewed, and watched the events unfolding in the distance. "Doesn't it seem like Lamont is going out of his way to rub this in our faces? Turn it into a spectacle to make sure we don't miss his super sleuthing skills? Show us and the mayor and the city that he's really on the ball?"

David was sensitive when it came to Lamont, but making the exhumation so public just when she and David were back from a case that had garnered them national and international attention did smack of face-rubbing. And Lamont *was* an ass. Nobody would argue with that.

It felt weird to be watching everything unfold from the sidelines. She didn't like it. "Let's leave," she said, tossing peanut shells aside. "I don't think we should be involved in this." What she really meant was she didn't like being a bystander in something that would normally have been her case.

"Wait." David rolled down the top of the bag. "I think we're about to see some action."

Clichés became clichés not because they were bad descriptions, but because they were good enough to be overused. "A hush fell over the crowd" would aptly describe the immediate dialing down of voices, like someone hit the mute switch and the mob stopped breathing all at the same time.

The waiting truck's engine turned over with a deep rumble, the sound disturbingly loud in the newly formed silence. The scent of diesel drifted across a carpet of live-oak leaves and the dirt road that separated David and Elise from the crowd. The men inside the hole climbed out, tossing shovels aside and pulling up ladders. A leather work glove was raised—a signal to the winch operator. A second motor kicked in, and the chain that had vanished inside the pit went tight. A pause, a check to make sure everything was as it should be, and then the cranking resumed. Moments later the cement container that held and protected the casket appeared, the crowd letting out a collective gasp of approval.

As the audience watched, transfixed, the vault continued to rise in the air until it was free of the ground, dirt and roots clinging to rough edges, the container bobbing as the winch operator slowly pivoted away from the hole, lining up with a second truck, this one with dual wheels and a red flatbed. The vault swung precariously in the air for a moment as the operator positioned it above the waiting vehicle. Then, with another hand signal, the vault dropped, the truck bouncing from the weight, dirt and dust flying. A cheer went up.

Three men climbed onto the bed. With a rattle of metal against metal, chains were unhooked and removed, tossed aside, the corpse now ready to be given a ride to the coroner's office on the outskirts of town.

Maybe it was because Elise was tired after the Chicago case. Maybe it was preoccupation with her father and worry over Audrey. Or maybe she'd lazily allowed herself to fall into observer mode. Whatever the reason, she'd failed to take note of anybody suspicious.

Without warning, the air exploded.

Bullets chewed up the ground, mowing through the crowd of press and cops alike. Screams of pain and terror followed. Bystanders dove behind tombstones or stood numbly in place, too shocked to move, while fire was returned from the area where Avery and Lamont had stood.

Seconds after the eruption, two masked men waving semiautomatic rifles jumped into the cab of the truck, vault on the back. Tires spinning, engine laboring from the weight, they sped away.

CHAPTER 7

Weapon pulled, Elise ran after the truck, hesitating long enough to brace her arm on a tombstone, concerned with accuracy in such a populated area. Holding her breath, she managed to fire three rounds before the truck turned a corner. She straightened as David appeared beside her. Breathing hard, they stared at the cloud of dust where the truck had been.

"Did not see that coming," David said, echoing her earlier thoughts.

She holstered her gun, truck forgotten as cries for help reached them. David turned and ran toward the victims while Elise pulled out her phone, moving at a fast walk.

With no access to the internal emergency line any longer, she called 911.

"Gunshot victims. Several people down. We need ambulances. We need patrol units. Perps heading toward Victory Drive at a high rate of speed. Armed and dangerous. Escape vehicle is city owned, white with a red flatbed."

"Who am I talking to?" The operator sounded bored and suspicious, possibly suspecting a prank call.

Elise prided herself in believing everybody was equal. Even during her brief stint as head of Homicide, she'd rarely pulled rank. Today? Now? "Who are you talking to?" Different day, different story. "Elise Fucking Sandburg."

A gasp from the other end of the line, followed by the frantic clicking of keys. "I'm dispatching now!"

Elise ended the call, pocketed her phone, and raced to the grave site, where the injured and uninjured littered the ground. Like a jerky camera, her gaze jumped from one victim to the next, searching for John Casper, searching for Detective Avery, searching for her father. She spotted John and Avery, but there was no sign of Sweet even though she rapidly combed the area.

Pushing thoughts of her father aside, she caught up with John, finding him bent over the body of a man. Elise dropped to her knees, close enough to see a gaping chest wound and John's blood-covered hands. She knew he hated working on living people. He hated being responsible for a life.

She quietly spoke her friend's name.

Without looking up, he said, "Dead."

Heart pounding, she looked from the chest to the face.

Victor Lamont. Jesus.

"You okay?" she asked.

John nodded. "Blood's all his."

She got to her feet as emergency vehicles sped down the dirt road, pulling to hard stops, dust drifting over the scene. EMTs bailed out, running toward the wounded with gurneys and med kits.

Avery spotted Elise and shouted.

She hurried to his side, freshly shocked to see Mayor Chesterfield on the ground.

"I don't think the bullet hit anything vital," Avery said. A jacket was bunched under the mayor's head. Avery's face was flushed, his freckles bright red.

"What the hell happened here?" Elise asked.

"Don't know. There was no warning. Nothing out of the ordinary." Avery told her how he'd heard the first shots, pulled his gun, and pushed the mayor to the ground. He flinched at the memory. "I might have been a little rough."

The mayor groaned, his eyes squeezed tightly shut.

Does he know? she mouthed to Avery.

About Lamont? Avery mouthed back.

She nodded.

"Not yet."

The last time she'd seen the mayor had been in his office, when he'd fired her.

Five minutes later she found David on the ground next to a female reporter who'd come for a story but instead had ended up part of the bloodbath. A familiar face on the evening news, the young woman was one of those dark-haired pageant beauties who never had anything out of place. Even now her lipstick was perfect as she rested against a tombstone, a sheen of perspiration on her face, her breathing shallow, a hand pressing a T-shirt to her bare thigh. Nearby a young man stood shirtless, watching with big eyes.

"How many injured?" David asked.

"Five? Six? I'm not sure." Elise paused, lowered her voice. "Lamont's dead."

In a smooth motion, David stood and faced her, disbelief in his eyes. "Avery?"

"Rattled, but okay. The mayor was hit. Avery managed to push him to the ground, probably saved his life."

"Your dad?"

The big question. Sweet was the one person on the scene who'd had a connection to the deceased. "Gone." With her forearm, she pushed a strand of hair from her face. "I couldn't find him anywhere."

"Okay, I can see where you're going with this, but stop."

Two female EMTs appeared, crouched over the reporter, and started an IV. With a nod, Elise motioned for David to follow so nobody could overhear what she was about to share. Once they were out of earshot, she said, "Sweet warned me to leave this case alone."

"Sweet's not involved in this, Elise."

"Are you sure? Everybody acts like they know him, but nobody knows him. Nobody. Not even Strata Luna. We all just opened our arms and our homes to him, welcoming him back like a hero."

"He *is* a hero. He saved Audrey's life."

"I know, and I owe him everything for that. Everything. But a bad man can still love. A bad man can still do the right thing sometimes. And I gotta tell you, sometimes when he and I are alone together he gets this expression on his face that makes my hair stand on end. Suddenly he looks like a different person. *That's* the person who saved Audrey. I know it is, because I've seen that man and know that man is capable of things someone his age in his condition shouldn't be able to do."

"I hope you aren't talking about rootwork or spells or crap."

She remembered the goofer dust on her doorstep. At the time she'd thought it had been left for her, but what if it had been left for her father? "I'm talking about something that lives inside him. Something frightening and powerful. Call it soul, call it essence, call it intellect, call it vital force. Whatever you want. He's a helluva lot more than the old fart sitting on the couch eating popcorn and watching *Clueless* with my daughter."

"Are you saying that's an act?"

"All I know is that he was here when all hell broke loose, and now he's gone."

Someone shouted at them, and a second later Avery sidestepped through the controlled chaos of cops and EMTs, out of breath, sweating, face still red. "The truck's been found, abandoned," he told Elise. "Sounds like you might have hit the fuel tank."

She pulled out her keys and pointed. "My car's over there."

The three of them moved quickly toward the cemetery gates. Then David said what they were all thinking: "Just like old times."

CHAPTER 8

The detectives piled into the car. Doors slammed, seat belts were latched, tires spun. Elise drove while David entered the location of the ditched truck in his phone's GPS. Time had gotten weird the way it always did in an adrenaline-driven situation, but Elise figured the vehicle was at least ten minutes away.

"Turn on the AC," Avery whined from the backseat. Elise lowered windows, and David fiddled with the dashboard knobs.

"Can't believe Lamont's dead." Avery had to shout to be heard over the roar of the car engine, the wind, and the hot air blasting from the vents. "Feels weird 'cause I don't know how many times I wished he'd never shown up in Savannah. Know what I mean? But I didn't want anything *bad* to happen to him. And asshats never die, never go away. Take my ex-mother-in-law, for instance."

Elise risked a glance in the mirror. Avery had blood on his face.

Following the directions of the woman's voice on the GPS, Elise took a sharp corner, then blindly reached into her bag, groped, pulled out a package of premoistened disposable cloths, and held the packet over her shoulder until Avery grabbed it with a blood-encrusted hand.

Behind her, the container popped open.

"I've been working out." Avery's voice was muffled as he cleaned the blood from his face. "Either of you notice?"

"Good for you," David said. "Hand me one of those." Avery tugged a cloth free and passed it over the seat. "I thought you'd dropped a few pounds."

Elise heard Avery's seat belt release. Then the detective leaned forward, head between the front seats so they could hear him. "This sounds crazy, but I met a girl I really like, and she's into fitness."

Avery was wired. Wired about the murder of Lamont, wired about still being alive, wired about saving the mayor's life, maybe even wired about the three of them being together again. It had probably been lonely for him downtown.

"Somebody who's into fitness?" Elise couldn't imagine Avery exercising or eating healthy. "That doesn't sound like you."

"I know, right?"

They weren't in an unmarked car with a siren. Elise was forced to stop at a red light. Behind her Avery shifted nervously. He couldn't hold still.

"She meditates," he told them, elaborating on his new friend. "Jogs. The works. I was looking for somebody who was a cop. Hell, I would have been okay with a mall cop, maybe even a meter maid, someone who at least had a small understanding of what we go through, but Lucille invited me to take this yoga class, so I did. At the time, I didn't realize she was really asking me on a date."

Elise spared half a glance over her shoulder. Avery did look better. Healthier. Happier. She was glad to hear he'd met somebody, even if she did feel a little wary about the news, considering the difference in lifestyles.

The temperature roaring from the vents was tolerable now. She hit the switches on the door, raising the windows, cutting the interior noise in half. "Lucille. That's a name you don't hear every day."

Light turned green. Elise's ears picked up the faint sound of sirens. She took off, took another turn too fast. They all leaned into the curve.

"We went for coffee a few times. Then she invited me to jog with her. Jog. Me. Can you imagine? I'll admit at first I just did it so she'd like me. Hell, you should've seen me puffing and panting like some idiot.

But now I'm finding it's good for my head. And I'm up to five miles. Not only that—I'm going to run in a half marathon pretty soon." He nudged David with the side of his hand, an action meant to support his next words. "You should do it. Bet you'd be good the way you love to run."

"I don't really run for the challenge," David said. "Not my thing. Running just happens to work better than drugs."

"I get that, but think about it. The event's called Run for the Animals. Lucille and I are a team. Hey, you and Elise should both do it. You could be a team too."

Elise shot David a look of horror. In that fraction of a second before she looked back at the road, she saw a glimmer of interest in David's eye. Not in a *Good idea* kind of way, but more like something designed to drive her nuts. "I can't run a mile," she said, "let alone twelve miles or whatever a half marathon is."

"A little over thirteen." Avery shifted his weight and leaned closer in an attempt to transfer some of his enthusiasm to the one person in the car who wasn't on board with his idea. "You don't have to do the whole thing. And you can even walk."

David slapped his hands against his legs. "I'm in."

"Just a moment ago you said it wasn't your thing," Elise reminded him.

"Changed my mind." After seeing the horror in Elise's face, it was obvious he'd decided to *make* it his thing. *Their* thing. "What should we call our team? Gould and Sandburg? Sandburg and Gould?"

"There's no team." Had he forgotten about her old injuries? Her wrecked body? "I was still using a cane not that long ago."

"I could pull you in a wagon. You could just sit there drinking beer from a to-go cup."

He was baiting her. Even though she knew it, she couldn't ignore him. Maybe this was what passed for sex between them, pathetic as that sounded. "Nobody's pulling me in a wagon. Look, why don't we all just go somewhere to eat?" She shot the next words over her shoulder at Avery. "Better yet, you and Lucille can come to my place, and we'll cook out." Problem solved.

"That'd be great," Avery said. "You'll really like her once you get to know her. But I still think you should do the marathon."

The phrase "once you get to know her" made Elise uncomfortable. She was ready to ask what Lucille did other than yoga and running, when the sirens grew much louder. David shut down the squawking GPS as Elise tracked the sirens, taking a right turn quickly followed by a left, pulling to a hockey stop behind a cluster of police vehicles. Lights flashed, radios squelched, cars were parked haphazardly in a way that looked chaotic but served a specific purpose—to block traffic and contain the scene.

They bailed from the car, doors slamming, slipping past the police cruisers to jump into the heart of the scene. A female first responder broke away from a huddle of officers, looking pleased and surprised to see them. But she had a special smile for Avery he didn't seem to notice. The officer was blond, a little on the heavy side, with a kind face. Was this the jogger? No, Avery said Lucille wasn't a cop.

"Good to see you back," the woman said.

Elise checked her badge. Jo Palmer.

Elise and David had left Savannah almost immediately after being fired. Their sudden departure hadn't allowed for good-byes, or sympathy, or gloating from anybody in the Savannah PD. They'd just packed their bags and boarded a plane to Chicago. Until this moment, Elise hadn't thought about how their sudden absence might have impacted people in and out of Homicide, but now she knew they'd been missed, at least by a couple of people. "Thanks, but we're just tagging along."

"I wouldn't call it tagging along," Avery said. "Elise fired the shots that hit the gas tank."

"Did anybody get a look at the perpetrators?" David asked. It was hard, if not impossible, for him to take a backseat, badge or no badge.

"No, but we're canvassing the area, trying to find witnesses. Perps seem to be two men, but we aren't even positive about that." The conversation continued as all four of them moved in the direction of the flatbed. "Offenders were gone by the time patrol units caught up with the vehicle." Palmer pointed to the river of liquid darkening the street, silently motioning for them to watch their step. It wasn't hard to identify the overpowering scent of spilled diesel, a cleanup that would involve a toxic-waste crew.

"You've got a good footprint here." Elise noted that the diesel print hadn't been left by a regulation sole, which meant it shouldn't belong to any of the cops on-site. She pulled out her phone and took a photo. "You might not have a description, but somebody's going to smell strongly of fuel. Get a media warning out to people in the neighborhood," she continued, hardly noticing that both she and David had dropped into their old roles. "Residents need to be told to lock their doors, stay inside."

"I don't get it," the officer said. "What do you think they wanted?"

"That." Avery pointed to the cargo on the flatbed truck.

She rolled her eyes, annoyed by his implication that she might be too dense to figure out the obvious. Romance over. Sometimes things could be a little tense between Patrol and detectives. *"Why?"* she asked.

Elise moved toward the truck. The lid to the vault was askew, the gummy seal broken loose, possibly occurring when the vault had been lifted from the ground.

Using the metal step under the truck's license plate, David climbed onto the flatbed, extended his hand, and pulled Elise up behind him. While Avery waited below, she and David examined the vault. With no crime-scene team in sight, David said, "Toss me some gloves."

From the ground, Palmer pulled out a pair of black exam gloves and handed them to him. He snapped them on.

Bracing himself, he shoved the heavy lid of the vault aside, levered it, and jumped away as it crashed against the metal flatbed cage that protected the truck's back window.

Elise stepped closer, shooting him a silent question. Why was he actively proceeding? They were here to watch, nothing more.

"Aren't you curious?" he asked. "Don't you want to know what they were after?"

"I'm betting drugs or money."

"That doesn't make sense." He was bent over the vault, looking at the casket inside, hands on his knees, hair hanging over his forehead. "Why would it still be here? Why not dig it up years ago?"

"Too risky? Forgotten until now? Whatever they were after, it has to be valuable. Nobody kills a detective and wounds the mayor unless the stakes are high." But there were other things that might be considered just as valuable as drugs and money. The ground bones and organs of certain people could be worth a fortune. Elise knew that all too well. But the body of Frank J. Remy? Were the bones of killers now a commodity?

"Ready?" David asked.

Elise nodded and watched as David lifted the lid of the cheap pine box, revealing the contents.

No money. No packages of white powder. Instead they were looking at a man dressed in a too-large vintage suit, lying as he should be, on his back, hands resting on his abdomen, eyes closed and held in place with a large amount of glue, out-of-date dark hair slicked to one side while the overpowering stench of embalming fluid wafted from the box. David blinked and recoiled.

Elise turned her head, pulled in a breath, then went back to staring at the corpse as Avery clambered up beside them and peered in.

Three living people, hands on hips, stared at a well-preserved dead man who'd been buried decades ago.

Avery, bless his heart, said what David and Elise were both thinking. "Who *the fuck* is that?"

CHAPTER 9

It wasn't Remy. This man and Remy were both white, but that's where the similarity ended. Remy had been robust, with a face that made Elise guess a Scandinavian heritage. This guy was thin, with dark hair, possibly some Italian in his genes.

"That blows our drugs and money theories," David said.

"They were pretty weak anyway."

"Agreed."

Elise asked the obvious question. "Does this mean Frank J. Remy is still alive?" And if so, had her father known they wouldn't find Remy in the coffin?

From ground level came a familiar series of clicks. Elise looked down in time to see a female reporter wearing a *Savannah Morning News* press badge on the lanyard around her neck, her face half-hidden by a thirty-five-millimeter camera.

"Don't say anything else." Elise had distrusted reporters *before* meeting the man who'd almost killed her daughter, but she really distrusted them now. Not her case, but nobody would want this odd twist hitting the press until the PD was ready to release the news.

The woman lowered her camera and looked up at them with sober intent. A vaguely familiar face, someone Elise had clashed with in the past. Tall, close to forty, light hair parted in the center and pulled back in a severe ponytail, big black sunglasses resting on top of her head, no makeup, dressed in jeans and a vest with a multitude of pockets. She projected that specific attitude seasoned reporters had. Elise guessed it came from years of insinuating themselves into situations where they weren't welcome. It was marked by a bold defensiveness, a drive to get the story no matter who was mowed down, all in the pursuit of what the reporter claimed as truth when in reality most of them were after one thing—a byline. There was a good chance any story having to do with Elise and David would be big news and of interest beyond Savannah.

From the flatbed, Avery said, "Hey, Lucille."

Oh, *that* Lucille.

Elise looked at David. David looked at Elise.

Oh yeah. He knew how she felt about reporters, and she was sure he could read her dismay at discovering *this* reporter was the very woman she'd invited to dinner minutes earlier—Avery's girlfriend and yoga pal. Instead of shooting Elise the look of sympathy she expected, David smirked, then actually laughed out loud.

The woman on the ground took another photo.

Pretty soon there would be enough documentation of David's inappropriate behavior to fill an entire scrapbook.

CHAPTER 10

All three of them back on terra firma, David couldn't help but notice that the presence of two fired homicide detectives was making some officers uncomfortable, most of them probably wondering if someone should tell them to get the hell out of there.

Not David and Elise's case.

David was good at multitasking, and he had the ability to pick up distant conversation while engaged in something else entirely. As he listened to one of the first responders, he kept an eye and ear tuned to the exchange taking place a few yards away. Avery was introducing Lucille and Elise. This would typically be Elise's cue to tell the reporter to stay out of the way. She didn't. Instead she just kind of stared while trying to keep a pleasant expression on her face. He knew that pleasant expression. He'd been on the receiving end of it.

"We've been invited for a cookout," Avery told Lucille. "At Elise's."

The reporter shot him a look of surprise. Even she knew things were suddenly weird. For a detective, Avery could sometimes be oblivious to what was going on right in front of him, especially where women were involved.

Elise backpedaled as best she could. "Once we get settled. We just returned to Savannah."

Lucille pulled out her tablet, and Elise stiffened and dropped the pleasant façade. "This isn't an interview," she said, glancing at the press

ID around the woman's neck. David looked too, getting a full name. Lucille Bancroft. Now he recalled seeing her byline. Funny how a last name fleshed things out. "Our personal lives aren't for public consumption," Elise added. David liked that she said "we" and "our." Did she realize she was doing that? Probably not.

He couldn't deny that he got a kick out of tormenting her, and he knew his actions were similar to those of a grade-school kid with a crush. He was unable to make an adult move, so he pulled her pigtails just to hear her scream. But right now he was feeling a little sorry for her. She knew how to boss people around and put people in their places, but when it came to the normal things people did, she was at a loss. He could see her struggling for a way to extricate herself from the awkward exchange. It was especially hard when their days now loomed before them with no real direction. She couldn't just say she had to get back to the office. Or she had detective stuff to do. Or her mom wouldn't let her. The unfocused thing wasn't the best for him either. He needed structure, or he risked falling back on bad habits. Sex, drugs, and very little rock 'n' roll.

The conversation with the first responder over, David broke into the threesome. "I need to get home." Simple as that. The damsel was saved. He and Elise excused themselves and headed for her car.

Moments later Elise was behind the wheel and he was in the passenger seat, AC cranked, windows down. Rinse and repeat and hello to the sweltering summer heat.

They were halfway to Elise's when her phone rang. Without looking at it, she passed it to David. The screen read *Office of the Mayor*. He hit "Answer." "Gould here."

The call was from the mayor's assistant, a woman normally humorously deadpan. She wasn't deadpan now; instead she spoke fast, her voice barely recognizable. "The mayor is at Saint Joseph's/Candler," she said, "and would like to see you and Elise immediately, before he goes into surgery."

David knew where this was going. Lamont dead, Homicide short on officers. He was half tempted to say he couldn't come because he was getting a manicure, but that would make him the asshole. "Be there in fifteen minutes." He ended the call and stuck Elise's phone in the compartment between the seats. "Head to Candler."

She raised the windows and picked up speed. "Mayor Chesterfield isn't dead, is he?"

"Worse. He's alive and wants to talk to us."

She didn't laugh or chastise him. Her hands gripped the steering wheel so tightly her knuckles were white. "Sucked right back in," she said.

Then he noticed something else. "Are you shaking?" Elise rarely lost her cool.

She held up a hand, giving it a quick glance. "Yeah." Surprised, yet not surprised.

"Pull over. I'll drive."

"I'm fine."

"Shaking isn't fine."

She ignored him and merged onto Harry S. Truman Parkway. "Sweet knows something," she said. "I want to see his face when I tell him the body in the coffin didn't belong to Remy. I'm betting he won't be surprised. And we need to get the name of the mortuary that handled the embalming. Talk to the person who did it, if he's still around and still alive."

She seemed to suddenly realized what she was saying. "What am I doing? This has nothing to do with us." Traffic slowed. She hit her blinker and pulled into the left lane, passing a string of cars, somebody's shrunken mema leading the pack.

"You're already involved," David said. "*We're* already involved. Mayor or no mayor."

"You think Remy might have faked his own death forty years ago?"

"That seems the most obvious theory," he said.

"Consider the timeline for the disappearance of Zane Novak. He vanished a few months after my father returned to Savannah."

"You aren't saying your dad is behind the boy's murder?"

"Why am I always being accused of blaming him for everything?"

"Uh, because that's your MO?"

She veered back into the right lane. "What I'm *saying* is what if Remy was living in Florida, continuing to commit murders, he reads about my father's return from the dead, and decides to come back to Savannah. Maybe to enact some form of revenge."

"I'll buy that. I'll totally buy that. But why the shootout at the cemetery? The guy would have to be pretty damn cunning to have escaped prison the way he did, and today's stunt seems a bit extreme and reckless. Why not just stay under the radar and let the body switch play out?"

"Whoever stole the vault didn't want anybody to know Remy might still be alive, but the question is, why?"

David turned down the AC a notch. "The obvious answer is because a manhunt would be launched."

"Exactly. Makes me wonder if he's been living fairly visibly. Didn't want his cover blown."

He riffed on her idea. "He could even have a wife and kids. Some serial killers do. He definitely has to have a lot at stake if he was the one behind today's stunt. Maybe he didn't want your dad to find out he's still alive."

"That could be it. Which is why we've got to find Sweet."

"We might have a problem if he doesn't want to be found. He's pretty good at lying low. I mean, he vanished for decades."

"Lamont was a kill shot," she said, returning the conversation to the immediate case. "I have no doubt about that. Why take out Lamont?"

"To weaken Homicide?"

"And maybe the bullet that hit the mayor was meant for Avery?"

"Maybe."

At the hospital Elise parked in the adjoining garage. Inside the lobby David punched the elevator button. While they waited, he said, "I was kidding earlier in the car. You know that, right? About the mayor?"

"No need explain yourself."

"It was kind of a shitty thing to say."

"But funny."

They entered the elevator, and Elise pushed the button for the second floor, where the mayor was being held pre-op.

"Sometimes I get a little carried away," David said.

"I can't imagine you any other way."

"Is that a weird compliment?"

"Pretty sure it's not."

"O-kay."

Upon exiting the elevator, a nurse led them to a private room. Hard to miss the two male cops standing on either side of the door, fig-leaf pose. Both gave the detectives a somber nod.

Up until this point, David thought the mayor had simply been in the line of fire, an unfortunate victim of collateral damage, but was it possible that he, along with Lamont, and both been deliberate targets?

The man who'd always come across as a good ol' southern white boy, kind of reminding David of President Bill Clinton, was pale, his face tight, IV needle taped to the back of his hand in preparation for surgery. His wife had "trophy" written all over her—it was another shitty thought David regretted as soon as it entered his head. It was a good thing no one could actually read his mind. He'd have to go into seclusion simply out of shame.

Mrs. Chesterfield excused herself, leaving them alone with the mayor.

"Thanks for coming." The mayor stoically bit out the words as he attempted to remain as immobile as possible. "I've got a damn bullet in me, and it hurts like a son of a bitch." He hardly seemed to breathe. "Guess you two know the feeling."

"It'll be better once they get that metal out," David said. They were probably all thinking about the last conversation they'd had. Not a pleasant memory.

Elise stepped closer. "We're glad you're alive. Glad you're going to be okay."

"They say I'll be fine, but all surgery comes with risk. I didn't want to be put under until I talked to you two. And I'm guessing you know what I'm going to say." He paused, pulled in a shallow breath in preparation for his next words. "You need to come back."

Didn't get much more direct than that. David thought he would have given them a soft sell, then reeled them in. But the clock was ticking. He tried not to feel annoyed by the mayor's phrasing, which made it sound as if they'd left of their own free will.

"My assistant's on the way," the mayor said. "As you're aware, this kind of thing typically goes through the board, but in cases of urgency I can make an executive decision. We'll get the papers signed and notarized so it's official. Get you sworn back in. Follow up on anything that needs to be done later."

"No." The word came from Elise.

Both men stared at her in surprise.

"I can't come back," she said. "I'm willing to consult, but I can't come back to Homicide."

Elise could hold a grudge. David wasn't sure she'd ever forgive her father, but he didn't think this was about their being fired. Well, not completely. It probably had more to do with Audrey and with Elise's need to distance herself from danger, as well as the long hours that would keep her away from home.

"Elise, think about it," David said. "If we don't sign up in an official capacity, we won't have access to the databases and assistance we're going to need. We won't be able to make an arrest. You know how it was in Chicago."

As welcoming as Chicago had been, they'd experienced frustration when their investigation was blocked and they had to rely on other people to get information to them. And if those people didn't want to share . . .

Elise gave him a hard look, silently signaling her disapproval of his position on the situation. Why hadn't she said anything before they'd stepped into the room? Had she suspected he'd try to talk her out of it?

She frowned, the harshness of her expression one she hadn't aimed at him in a while. "You want to go back to work for the people who fired us?" she asked, as if the mayor wasn't in the room.

"No."

"Did you forget about us? Gould and Sandburg Investigations?"

"Sandburg and Gould is fine."

She rolled her eyes.

"Did you think I was going to say no too?" David asked.

"Yes."

He motioned toward the door. "Let's step out a minute."

"I don't have much time," the mayor reminded them.

A knock sounded, and the mayor's assistant stuck her head inside the room. "I have the paperwork and my notary seal."

The detectives moved into the corridor, out of earshot of the two cops. "Elise. I know you're thinking about Audrey . . ."

"I'll never get her back this way."

"You will. We'll figure it out."

"You don't know that. The only chance I have is to settle down. Be a normal mother. Be home. Not put my daughter in danger." She leaned her back against the wall, shoulders sagging, eyes suddenly red-rimmed and glistening. "Damn it. Why didn't you support me in there?" She pressed a hand to her mouth, and to his horror, she let out a sob. She suddenly seemed fragile, not the Elise he knew.

He reached for her, grasping her gently by both arms, bending to look into her eyes. "You okay?"

She nodded, pulling herself together. He could see she was embarrassed. He straightened and let her go.

She wiped at her face with the back of her hand, more like a kid than an adult. She was shaking again. Not very much. Probably nothing anybody else would notice, but David caught it. And yet hours earlier she'd pulled her gun and fired with precision.

Was her protest just about Audrey? Or was there more going on? She'd been remarkably cool since the Tremain incident. Maybe too cool. Her breaking down like this, her shaking, her never seeming to have dealt with Tremain, had the hallmarks of PTSD.

"This sounds crazy, but what if this was all orchestrated?" she asked. "What if we're doing exactly what the shooter or shooters want us to do?"

"What are you talking about?"

"Think about it. We just got back to town. Maybe the shot that killed Lamont wasn't as random as it seemed. And maybe Avery and the mayor were also targets. And now the mayor wants us to come back. A logical progression of events."

"That's paranoid."

"Is it?"

He stared at her, thinking. "Maybe not." Damn, it *could* make sense. He didn't want it to, but he had to remain open to the possibility. No sense stepping into the middle of a trap. No sense putting their lives in danger. He'd had enough of that for a while.

They'd both seen what had transpired in the cemetery and knew what the perpetrators were capable of. It could have been a slaughter.

"So we tell him no," David said, decision made. "We tell him no, and we take the next job offer we get, hopefully somewhere other than here, hopefully looking for some rich widow's estranged son who went off to join a commune but doesn't know his mother is dying and wants to leave him her estate and her five yappy dogs."

Elise pulled in a breath. "I'd be happy with any kind of cold case as long as it doesn't involve Savannah, my father, and serial murders."

"Let's go break the news to the mayor." He spun on his heel, stopped when he felt her hand on his arm. Not a grip, but a gesture that said, *Wait.* She rarely touched him. If she did, it was almost always an accident. If any touching was done, it was done by him. Friendly, reassuring—hold the longing.

She looked into his eyes, driving her resolve home. "We go back in and take the position."

What the hell? "But—" He gave his head a shake that felt cartoony. Even though he disagreed, he was supporting her. That's what she'd said she wanted. "The danger. The possible plot to drag us back to Savannah PD—"

"We take it."

She didn't elaborate. She didn't have to. He got it. Refusing, standing on the sidelines while at the same time knowing they could help . . . It wasn't them. He let out a resigned sigh and nodded.

Her hand dropped away, but he could still feel the imprint of it on his skin. He imagined taking a marker and drawing a line around the sensation, wondered if it would look like a hand.

She straightened and squared her shoulders. "Just for now. Just for this case."

But he could sense her defeat. He felt it too. How could it be so hard to set your life on a new track? He envied those people who somehow pulled it off. "Let's do it."

Back in the privacy of the hospital room, the mayor told them to raise their right hands; then he recited the oath. They answered in the affirmative, papers were signed, and it was done. "Press conference is scheduled for later today." Mayor Chesterfield sank into his pillow and closed his eyes. "Talk to Avery about it," he whispered hoarsely. "I want both of you there, especially since you were in the cemetery when it went down. And honestly"—he opened his pain-edged eyes—"Avery isn't the best when it comes to dealing with the press."

And so here they were. As though they'd never left.

The assistant pulled out two familiar leather cases. She passed them to the detectives. Elise opened the case and gave her old badge a glance. With a flip of her wrist, she slapped the case closed and looked at the mayor. "This is temporary. I want you to know that."

He gave her a slow blink, but who really knew what the guy was thinking? He'd fired them without remorse. He could probably find some loophole to keep them breaking rocks for him until they were old and arthritic and blind.

"We'll get a composite artist to age Remy," Elise said. "Then get the image to media outlets. The body from the cemetery should have arrived at the morgue by now. I'm hoping the autopsy will lead to an ID." Elise, the pro, confident and on top of her game.

"We'll talk to the prison," she said. "We'll talk to the mortuary where the body was processed. See if we can figure out how and when the switch took place."

The door opened, and the mayor's wife appeared. "He needs to go to the pre-op area."

Two nurses came in and began readying the bed in order to wheel the mayor from the room.

Chesterfield looked from Elise to David. "Thanks." He meant thanks for coming back even though he'd treated them so poorly. "I can go into surgery knowing Savannah is in good hands."

"Good luck," David said.

The bed was wheeled away.

They were leaving the building when Elise reached into her pocket and pulled out her phone. She checked the screen and answered the muted device while they walked through the parking garage. "I'm sorry," she told the caller. "We're not going to be able to take the case." That was followed by a few suggestions and names; then she disconnected and looked at David. "A parent in Portland wanted us to investigate her daughter's cold case."

The perfect job. A cold case would have been something that wasn't dangerous. It would have been something with regular hours. And Portland wasn't that far from Audrey and Seattle.

Neither of them mentioned any of that.

Instead they got in the car and headed to the outskirts of Savannah and the morgue. Hopefully John Casper would be ready to examine the corpse with no name.

CHAPTER 11

The morgue was on the outskirts of Savannah, away from the curious and the morbid, the nondescript flat-roofed building made impenetrable with cement block walls. A big plus: it was blessed with a generous parking lot. Selfishly, Elise often wished it were closer to downtown and the heart of the action. That was never going to happen. There was a strong push to eventually relocate the police department to the suburbs, where they could all do their part in perpetuating urban sprawl.

The morgue might have been city property, but it wasn't a place that welcomed the casual citizen, especially since it protected evidence every bit as important as that in the evidence room at the Savannah PD.

Mara Casper answered the buzzer and let Elise and David in the back door. "I'm so glad to see you both."

Kind words, but Elise noticed Mara wasn't her typical happy self. She had worry lines between her eyes, and she seemed distracted as the detectives stepped inside. They knew the way, but with heels clicking on the white linoleum floor, Mara escorted them beneath rows of fluorescent lights to the prep room adjacent to the autopsy suites. "John and Detective Avery are already with the body."

Mara normally either suited up in order to assist or returned to her office. This time, for some reason Elise hoped would soon be revealed, she remained in the prep room, hovering nervously while repeatedly tucking a strand of straight dark hair behind her ear, even going so far as to bring that hair to her mouth for a couple of chews before realizing what she was doing.

David noticed too, and Elise could see he was forming a comment, possibly something about her vegan diet.

"I never thought of this job as dangerous," Mara finally blurted out. "We deal with the *aftermath* of crime, not the crime itself. Not the criminals."

Ah, there it was.

"I love my job," Mara said. "I love working with the dead, discovering their secrets, but John could have been killed today."

A lot for a new bride to deal with. A husband caught in the middle of what could have been a massacre. Elise attempted to reassure her, knowing the truth of her words wouldn't bring as much comfort as simply the passage of time. "What happened today was highly unusual."

"It might have been unusual, but he's always at crime scenes. He's the one processing the dead body." She looked from Elise to David. "I don't know how you do it. How you put your lives in danger every day. And when we hang out, you act like it's just a normal day." She fake laughed. "It *is* a normal day for you."

"You get used to it." David pressed one finger against Elise's shoulder, silently urging her to turn around so he could tie her disposable yellow gown. When he was done, she did the same for him while he snapped on blue gloves.

"I'll *never* get used to it." Mara shook her head and stared at something in her own mind, a look of horror on her face. "I don't *want* to get used to it. Right now all I want is for John to come out of that autopsy suite so I can hold him. Just hold him."

As she tied the last bow on David's gown, Elise considered offering a different reassurance, yet she knew it wasn't unheard of for a medical examiner to end up dead due to a case. It was rare, but it happened. The ME wasn't out there pounding the streets or knocking down doors, but he dealt directly with evidence that could convict the perpetrator. So to say John wasn't in danger would be a lie. "I'm sorry," she said. "I know it's hard." Pathetic words.

The snap of David's gloves seemed to punctuate the scene, drawing attention away from Mara's plight. "See you inside." He gave Elise a look of commiseration. With his surgical mask still around his neck, he opened the door to the autopsy suite. Her back turned to Mara, Elise mouthed the word *Chicken* to David, meaning his escape into the suite.

He nodded agreement before spinning away. Once the door slammed, Mara asked, "What if it had been David? What if *David* had been hit today?"

"He wasn't. John wasn't," Elise said. "I don't allow my mind to go to the what-ifs. It serves no helpful purpose to worry about something that'll probably never happen. And if I allowed myself to dwell on those possibilities, I'd be unable to function. Cops can't obsess about those things. The very act of cluttering up my head with such thoughts puts lives in danger." Harsh words, but Mara needed to hear them. And Elise doubted John would lay it out for her.

"You can't be serious when you say it'll probably never happen." Her voice rose. "That's *denial*."

"Call it what you want. I do what I have to do." Elise's sympathy was fading fast.

"You and David have both been shot. You've been kidnapped, raped." Mara's eyes got big, and she put a hand to her mouth, realizing she'd just revealed something she'd been told in confidence. "Oh my God. I'm sorry. John told me. And I think David told him. You know what good friends they are. They tell each other things."

Elise was surprised to hear anybody knew such details about her ordeal. She'd not shared them with anybody, not even the department psychologist. Somehow David must have figured it out, filled in the blanks.

"It's over," Elise said. "Done. That door is closed. I don't look back." Damn David, but at the same time nobody would assume she'd been treated to sweet tea and scones during those three days spent with Tremain. The shock of their return to Savannah had Elise finally admitting that she'd been blocking what had happened, and now she was worried that it was coming back to haunt her. A person could only ignore that kind of thing so long.

"So you never think about it?"

"Not unless someone brings it up." She managed to hide her annoyance this time and instead said it with a gentle humor. But it wasn't enough to stop Mara from continuing to press her.

"Not even in your sleep?"

"No," Elise lied.

"You know what I think? If anything happened to David—I think you'd break."

The words made Elise's heart slam and her mouth go dry. And then she blocked *those* thoughts, abruptly excused herself, and joined David, Avery, and John in the autopsy suite, relieved to be standing over a dead body instead of hanging out in the prep room.

David glanced at her, his white mask now in place. "You okay?"

Avery and John were on the opposite side of the stainless-steel table, the exhumed body between them, exhaust fan on high to keep dangerous formaldehyde fumes to a minimum. It was uncommon to see a fully embalmed body in an autopsy suite.

"You've seemed a little off since we were at the cemetery," David said. She knew he was talking about her shaking hands and the uncharacteristic tears at the hospital.

"It's the heat."

"I heard we're supposed to hit over a hundred tomorrow," John said. "And with this humidity . . . It's already brutal out there."

It was probably sixty-five degrees in the autopsy suite, the temperature low due to the bodies.

"Congratulations on your return to Homicide." Avery was blissfully oblivious to how Elise and David might feel about being back.

David straightened him out. "I'm thinking your heartfelt sympathy might be more appropriate."

Avery laughed, and Elise glared at him above her surgical mask. "You forgot to mention that your new girlfriend is a reporter for the *Savannah Morning News*."

"Okay." John clicked off the recorder with his foot pedal. "I'll just wait for the chitchat to wind down. No need to have a record of this."

"I know how you feel about reporters," Avery said, shifting uncomfortably. "I was hoping to bring that up under better circumstances."

"I doubt there would have been better circumstances."

"Does that mean we're no longer invited to your house?"

She wanted to say Avery was, Lucille wasn't. Instead she asked, "What about that officer at the crime scene this morning? The blonde?"

"Palmer? What about her?"

God, he could be thick sometimes. "Never mind."

"Hey, look at me! I'm a medical examiner!" John raised his doubled-gloved hands in the air, then flexed his arms—visual cues to get them back on track. When no one protested his interruption, he moved forward with the autopsy, turning the recorder back on. Easy to see why Mara was so crazy about him.

"Okay." John exhaled. "As you can see, I've already removed his burial garb and laid it out over there." He pointed to a table covered with a suit, dress shirt, shoes, underwear. "It came off pretty easily because funeral directors often cut the back of the clothing to get it on the body. So for anybody who's thinking they're going to run around in the afterlife in a snazzy suit—they'd have to stitch the back side closed first."

Unlike Mara, John didn't appear upset by what had happened at the cemetery. As always, he seemed like a kid who'd consumed too much sugar, although he was a little more amped than usual. Not uncommon following a close call. Adrenaline was high, and the people who survived often felt superhuman until they came down.

Elise had been in on a few exhumations, but none involving bodies that had been in the ground this long. The nameless corpse didn't look too bad considering decades had passed since the burial. The skin was leathery, the body somewhat shrunken, with evidence of actual decay to the fingers and toes. But the clean-shaven face wasn't too skeletal, and the lips and cheeks still revealed rouge applied in the mortuary.

Astounding.

David must have been thinking along the same lines. "Well pickled."

"You'd think Remy would have opted for cremation just to make sure this day never came," Avery said.

Elise agreed. "It *is* odd."

When you really thought about it, embalming was an unnatural process, draining the corpse of blood and bodily fluids to replace those fluids with a preservative that could keep someone looking pretty much the way he'd looked when lowered into the ground. Elise, for one, would prefer to rot. "In this case, embalming worked in our favor. An embalmed body might still give up clues."

"It would be cool if you could lift DNA that triggers a CODIS match," David said. "I'm also hoping you can determine cause of death."

"CODIS is a long shot." The fumes in the room seemed especially strong, and Elise adjusted her mask before continuing. "The database was just getting off the ground when this person died, and those early entries were exclusively sex offenders. I honestly think our best chance is uploading a photo, along with an aged image, to the police-department website so the media can grab it." As much as she bitched about reporters, they were often essential players when it came to catching criminals.

"Is that a knife wound?" Avery pointed to an area near the clavicle that had been stitched closed.

John shook his head. "Incision made by the mortician to reach the common carotid artery."

Avery stared at the corpse's chest. Under his breath he muttered, "Sweet kitty."

"I can already tell you the probable cause of death." John stepped to a laptop covered in soft plastic, hit some keys, and brought up a series of digital images he then navigated. "I X-rayed the body." He enlarged a JPEG of the skull. "He's got a broken neck. And without even cutting him open I noted signs of blunt-force trauma." He returned to the table.

David pointed, drawing their attention back to the body. "His fingernails look well manicured. I mean, as much as I can tell in his present condition."

"Good catch," John said. "I noticed that too, and I think you're right."

"If someone were just looking for a body, any body, to take the place of Remy," Elise said, "I'd think they would have targeted a homeless person. And the suit he was wearing doesn't appear to be high quality. That doesn't really fit with the manicured hands."

"The suit's too big," John said. "Probably something the funeral home picked up or had around."

"Or meant for the larger Remy." Avery squeezed the metal nose clip on his surgical mask. "Anybody else's eyes burning?"

"He's leaking formaldehyde," John told them. "You don't want to breathe too much of that stuff. I'll probably grab goggles and a respirator before I cut him open."

Elise took a step back. "I don't think we need to see anything else."

They all agreed, although John seemed sorry to see them go. He clicked off the recorder. "We need to get together. Don't forget about Johnny Mercer Day. You're all invited," he said, including Avery. "Significant others too, if you're so inclined. Our place is small, but it has a nice courtyard."

David pulled his mask below his chin. "Let us know if you find anything unusual once you cut him open."

"Will do."

In the prep room, they snapped off gloves. Elise was relieved to find no Mara in sight.

Avery tossed his gown in the biohazard container. "Gotta head back downtown and prepare for the press conference. The mayor wants you both there. Those were his last orders before being taken into surgery. And you know I'm not great when it comes to answering questions."

True. Avery wasn't good at speeches or good at planning or even good at bossing people around. His strength was thinking fast in the field. That was an important quality, like today when he'd saved the mayor's life.

"Who's in charge here?" David asked. Not such a weird question, all things considered.

Avery shrugged. "I think I am." Then he nodded as if agreeing with himself. "Pretty sure I am, but I'm open to any and all suggestions." His phone buzzed. He pulled it from his pocket, read a text, and tucked it away again. "Mayor is out of surgery. Everything went smoothly. Right now I think you should both go to the mortuary. Research was able to dig up information. Looks like the body was embalmed at Hartzell, Tate, and Hartzell. And, as we all know, they're still in business. See if you can pick up any details. We need to determine where Remy's trail ended. I've also got someone checking prison records to see if we can pull anything together."

"Good ideas," Elise said. "I'd also suggest searching Chatham County news archives for anybody who went missing just before Remy's burial."

Avery agreed.

It had to be strange, telling her what to do when she'd been bossing him around barely a month ago. But that role hadn't suited her any more than it suited Avery. Or maybe it hadn't suited her mind-set at the time, just coming out of her encounter with Tremain, a big reason she'd been forced to slam and lock that door and never open it again. The head of Homicide couldn't indulge in meltdowns. She still felt resentful about that sometimes. But she'd done okay in Chicago. It had been good to drop into a new location, meet new people. It helped her forget.

Coming back made her remember.

She and David left the morgue. It was probably 120 degrees in the car. Simultaneously they lowered the windows while the AC blasted hot air in their faces.

David slipped on his sunglasses and rested his arm in the open window. "This day sure went to hell fast. Six hours ago we were heading to Laurel Grove to take in an exhumation from a safe distance. Just one of many curious bystanders. Now here we are." He pulled out the leather case that held his badge and tossed it on the dash.

Elise was having a hard time figuring out his take on returning to Homicide. Part of her suspected he was enjoying this, which was something he knew she wouldn't want to hear.

She pulled onto Abercorn to head for the funeral home. "For a while back there in the hospital I got the sneaking suspicion you might be happy about the turn of events."

"I hate that the mayor was shot, but I gotta admit I didn't at all mind seeing him grovel."

"I mean being back, regardless of the mayor."

Like a kid with ADD, or more likely desperate for a way to evade her question, he suddenly took note of something beyond the interior of the car and beyond their conversation. "Hey, pull over." He pointed to a food shack she'd never noticed before. "This place is supposed to have good barbeque. I haven't had anything to eat since those boiled peanuts."

"That seems a lifetime ago."

"Back when we were carefree and unencumbered kids."

CHAPTER 12

Hartzell, Tate, and Hartzell Funeral Home, with its green awning and ornately carved door, was located off Montgomery Street, between Laurel Grove Cemetery and the old Candler Hospital.

"Brings back fond memories," Elise said.

Inside, their feet sank into red carpet as they located the office. They flashed their newly returned badges, the woman behind the desk frowning at David's unprofessional attire of jeans and a T-shirt.

Elise could see the second she recognized them, because her demeanor changed—became friendly, a little awe filled. Being in the public eye opened doors even a badge couldn't. Elise noted the nameplate on the woman's desk. Camilla Bowen. "By now you've probably heard about the shooting at Laurel Grove," Elise said.

"Yes." The woman's expression went sad. "So awful."

David didn't tell Camilla about the body not belonging to Remy—that wasn't yet for public consumption—but he let her know they needed to see the records from the Remy burial.

Somewhere below their feet, a motor kicked in and Elise felt a blast of cool air from a nearby vent. "We especially need to know who was in charge of the embalming and burial."

"That could take a while." Camilla got to her feet. "All records that old are in a storage area. The business was bought out over twenty years ago. Those old files were just kind of shoved in a corner." She made an apologetic and slightly embarrassed face. No surprise. Hartzell, Tate, and Hartzell had a history of losing things, even bodies.

"Maybe we can help speed up the process," Elise said.

Camilla reached for the phone. "I need to call my supervisor. This might require a search warrant."

David did one of the things David did best. Flirt.

He looked into the woman's eyes. "This is a matter of urgency. Life or death. The mayor has been shot. I'd hate to see the investigation delayed with a phone call and a warrant request. At this point you can just plead ignorance if your supervisor ends up unhappy with your decision. Make the call, and all of our hands are tied."

She was about twenty years older than David. Not old-old, but past the turning-head stage. Probably some gray under her dyed hair. Maybe single. Maybe married.

In that second, Elise saw him through the receptionist's eyes. His dark hair hadn't been cut for a while, and he had those areas that always bleached out a little from the sun. Once he got a trim, the light hair would be gone, only to appear again over time.

There was a sexuality to him, but that wasn't what made David so appealing to women. It was the sexuality combined with what she considered David's exclusive brand: a charming sense of tragedy.

Elise hadn't responded to Mara's comment about how she'd feel if anything happened to him. They'd become such a team, two halves of a whole. With shock, she realized losing him would be unthinkable. In the pyramid of those most important to her, Audrey and David took the top spots.

The woman caved. Of course she did.

She smiled, and David smiled back. "I don't think it would hurt," she finally admitted.

"It'll only help. And believe me," he said with sincerity—it was the sincerity that always got them—"you'll be doing the city of Savannah a great service."

Camilla led them down a set of ancient stone steps, through a narrow tunnel, to a dark storage area of crumbling stone walls and a damp floor of tabby cement. It was a place Elise had been before. Not the exact room, but one not far away. Like many old buildings in Savannah, the mortuary had a tunnel, this one leading to the old Candler Hospital and Laurel Grove Cemetery.

It seemed the receptionist wanted to stay and either watch or help, but she reluctantly excused herself. "I need to get back to my desk."

"Camilla grossly downplayed the condition of their filing system," Elise said once she and David were alone.

The room had suffered water damage, and many of the cardboard containers at the bottoms of the stacks had collapsed, crushed by the weight of the ones above.

David surveyed the mess. "At least the dates are readable."

Thirty minutes into their search Elise tugged out the year they were looking for. She placed the box under a bare lightbulb, opened the lid, and riffled through the contents. Ten minutes later they had the file containing receipts and the signature of the mortician who'd handled the body. A man named Abraham Winslow, the previous owner of the funeral home.

Elise's phone buzzed. She checked the screen. *Audrey.* "I have to get this." She hit "Answer" and remained in the basement while David carried the file upstairs to the receptionist's office.

"Mom. Are you okay?" Audrey was talking fast. "We just heard about a shooting. The news is saying you and David were there and that you caught the guy."

"I'm fine. David is fine, but Victor Lamont is dead and the mayor has a nonlethal injury. The perpetrators are still at large."

Audrey's voice lost clarity as she addressed someone else in the room. "She's okay."

"Give me the phone."

Elise recognized Thomas's voice. She heard footsteps; then Thomas was speaking to her, asking his version of the same questions. "Are you okay?"

"I'm surprised you care."

"Of course I care." His voice caught. "How could you think otherwise?"

She felt a rush of sorrow for the loss of those days when they'd been a family. Thomas was a good man, and a good father. He just hadn't been able to deal with her long hours and the constant worry. He'd wanted her to quit Homicide, but she'd refused. And now he had a lovely wife and twin boys, along with Audrey. "I'm fine," she managed, her ears tuned to her own voice, hoping she hadn't revealed any of what she was feeling.

He let out his breath in relief. "You sure?"

"Positive."

"We were all worried. You know that, right? We care about you. I want you to stay alive, not only for Audrey, but for us too. For me."

She moved the phone away from her ear, a hand pressed to her mouth. Two deep breaths and she was back, reassuring him, sounding calm. "It was just a strange turn of events that I can't really discuss right now."

"I don't understand why you were even there. You don't work for the Savannah PD anymore. Thank God."

"About that . . ." The conversation about her return to Homicide was coming earlier than she'd anticipated.

"Elise?" He'd picked up on the hesitation in her voice.

"David and I were just sworn back in. We're working the case."

"My God. What the hell are you thinking? I'd hoped getting Audrey out of Savannah would make you come to your senses. We all care about you. We just think you've fallen in with the wrong people."

David. He'd never liked David.

"You could move out here. To Seattle. Get a job as a private investigator for an insurance company. Or for a divorce lawyer. Something safe. You know what the temperature is right now? Seventy degrees and sunny. I don't know why I stayed in Savannah as long as I did. Audrey loves it here. You'd love it too."

She'd been to Seattle a couple of times. "When I was last in Seattle, it rained the whole time."

"We get rain, but that's not a bad price to pay for less crime. Less *weird* crime." He always thought he knew what was best for her. Always. There would never be any convincing him otherwise.

"I've gotta go." Thank God her daughter was headstrong. "Put Audrey back on the line. I want to tell her good-bye."

Despite his growl of frustration, he passed the phone to Audrey.

"I tried to call Grandpa, and he didn't pick up," she said. "Is he okay?"

Elise would have liked to know the answer to that question herself. "He was fine last time I saw him."

"You should get Strata Luna to make you a protection spell. I'd make you one, but I don't have the right ingredients. And if Dad found out . . ."

"Don't let him walk all over you." Elise didn't like to say anything negative about Thomas to Audrey, but this called for it. "He'll try."

"Don't worry. He finally gave up on trying to make me wear pastel clothes."

They both laughed.

"And it might be nice today, but it rains here. A lot. It's like *Blade Runner* without the flying cars."

Elise laughed again. God, she missed her daughter. "Be careful."

"Right. Like you would know all about careful."

They said their good-byes and disconnected.

"The mortician who handled the Remy account is retired but still alive," David said when Elise caught up with him in the foyer of the funeral parlor. "Living at an assisted-living center on Abercorn."

* * *

This time around they didn't have to pull out their badges. The regal black woman at the assisted-living-center reception desk recognized them immediately and led them down a hall smelling faintly of urine and strongly of cooked cabbage.

"Mr. Winslow is in the early stages of dementia," the receptionist explained. "He has good days and bad days. I haven't seen him yet today, so I don't know how he's doing, but I can tell you this is the best time to visit. Evening is the worst, when confusion is the most pronounced. It's called sundowning, and many dementia patients suffer from it, bless their hearts."

In the TV room, she introduced them to Abraham Winslow, who sat off by himself, staring at small yellow birds hopping from branch to branch in the indoor aviary, the caged birds themselves seeming a condensed echo of the human story going on within the walls of the care center.

The man was painfully skinny, knee bones sharp below loose jeans. He wore wide red suspenders and a T-shirt that had turned a sad shade of yellow.

"I think he'll be glad to have the company," the woman whispered, meaning even if they were cops.

Once she was gone, Elise and David grabbed chairs and sat a few feet from the man. Elise dug in her bag, pulled out a tablet and pen, prepared to take notes.

Without much pause or consideration or question, Winslow said, "Good to see you," as if he knew them. Elise's neighbor had developed Alzheimer's, and Elise knew early-stage patients were notorious for faking name and facial recognition. Still concerned and embarrassed by their memory loss, they pretended to know things that had slipped away. Given Winslow's reaction to meeting them, Elise was afraid they weren't dealing with a reliable source.

She asked him if he had any memory of a funeral-home client named Frank J. Remy.

"Sure I do." Winslow wore a faded cap that he removed and slapped back down on his head, as if preparing for some kind of job that might involve hard labor.

"How do you remember him?" David asked. "Was there something that stood out?"

"You could say that." The words that followed assured Elise of Winslow's reliability. "He was a murderer. We didn't get many murderers at the funeral home. I think I only embalmed a few in my career." The hat action was put into play again. "And there was the other thing." The words were spoken as if Elise and David knew exactly what that other thing was.

"What thing?" David asked.

"It was in all the papers. Didn't you read about it?"

Another sign of dementia, when thirty years ago seemed like yesterday. But dementia patients could also exhibit acute recall, the brain banishing the most recent to shine a bright light on the far distant. "I must have missed it," Elise said.

"That's not very good police work."

She smiled. "That's why we're here. So you can tell us what we don't know. We need your help, your memories. Can you give us any interesting details?"

He *did* seem happy to have company. Did he have family? If so, did any of them come to see him?

"The body was in the cooler and I pulled it out, like always." Winslow related the story as if he'd told it a million times. "I wheeled it into the embalming room, unzipped the bag. Next thing I know I'm waking up in the hospital."

Elise and David looked at each other. Winslow continued, seeming to relish having an audience. "That's right. You can read about that too. I almost died. Was in the hospital for two, maybe three weeks."

"What happened to Remy's body?"

"The guy who worked for me, name was Gerald Sanchez, did the embalming, far as I remember."

"We're going to need to talk to him," David said. "Do you know where we can reach him?"

"That's gonna be kinda hard." Winslow chuckled. "Sanchez died about a month after I took sick. They thought it was the air in the mortuary that brought us both down. I installed a new exhaust system, but it was too late. My business was ruined. Had to file for bankruptcy. Place sat empty for maybe fifteen years; then somebody bought it and started over. Don't remember the name."

"Hartzell, Tate, and Hartzell," David said.

"Huh?"

"Never mind."

"By the time it reopened, people forgot about what had happened to me."

Elise closed her notebook. "I'm sorry about your business, Mr. Winslow." The funeral home certainly had a dark history.

"What did they think was wrong with you and Sanchez?" David asked. "Did you ever have an official diagnosis?"

"Toxicity due to formaldehyde fumes. That's bad stuff, you know. Carcinogen. But some people said it was rootwork, a mojo. People were afraid. Didn't make any difference what caused it. Poison in the air, or some kind of spell. People quit bringing their dead to me."

"Do you think you'd remember what Frank J. Remy looked like?" David asked.

"Don't know. My memory's not what it used to be." He quickly went on to defend himself. "But it's not bad. Everybody forgets things now and then, 'specially when you get to my age."

Elise opened her phone app and scrolled to the image she'd downloaded of Remy. If Winslow identified the face correctly, they'd know the body switch took place at the funeral home. "Is this the face of the man who was in the body bag before you took ill?"

Winslow squinted at the screen. "Who's that? Some relative of yours?"

His inability to identify Remy correctly might mean the body had been switched before it reached the funeral home. Or it could mean Winslow just didn't remember what Remy looked like.

Elise tucked her phone away and dug out one of her old Savannah PD business cards with her cell number on it. It seemed pointless, but she handed it to the old man, hoping he didn't stumble across it in the middle of the night and call her just because it was a phone number that was somehow in his possession.

With the card in his hand, he turned his head to watch the birds again, a vacant half smile on his face. He seemed to prefer a yellow one that was more active than the rest. Did the birds like it in there? Elise wondered. Did they want to fly? Really fly? Or was it a relief to never have to worry about anything? Not that birds worried, but what about migration? Building a nest? All of those things birds did?

"Thanks so much for your time, Mr. Winslow," she told him. "Call me if you think of anything else."

"Was I any help?"

Elise smiled at him. "Yes. A lot."

"When will you be back?"

"I don't know."

Maybe she would come back. Just to visit him.

"That was unexpected," David said once they were outside melting in the sun once again. As they approached her car, Elise hit the unlock button on the key fob.

"Do you think he knew what he was talking about?" David asked. "Or was he just diving into some dream from his dementia vault?"

"I'm not sure what to think. He was convincing."

"I agree." David pulled out his phone. "I'm calling Research to see if they can corroborate his story." He moved to a spot of shade, dialed, and lifted the phone to his ear. "We'll need hospital records on Abraham Winslow," he said when the specialist answered. David provided the month and year. "Also any newspaper articles pertaining to the Winslow Funeral Home. See if Winslow filed for bankruptcy. See if any police investigation was ever launched."

A pause, a thanks, then he hung up.

"Over thirty-six years ago," Elise said, feeling skeptical. "Another long shot."

"So let's say it's all fairly factual," David said.

"Was Sanchez in on it?" she wondered aloud.

"That's what I'm thinking. Something is used to put Winslow out of commission while Remy is revived and replaced with a dead body. Maybe whatever knocked Winslow out was supposed to kill him, but he was young and healthy and he didn't die."

Elise picked up the thread. "Sanchez helps with the body switch, and then he's killed too so he'll never reveal what happened."

"Why did they even bother with a body? I don't get that. And we can't dismiss the fact that Winslow didn't recognize Remy."

"So they had a record of the process? So a body would be there if any other mortuary worker came across it? Maybe they wanted the casket to have the true feel of a body. Even if they'd added weight to the casket and sealed it for the burial, a dead body has a different heft than say, cement blocks."

"Or was our John Doe somehow connected to the case? Maybe not so randomly, and the casket simply was a handy way to get rid of him?"

"Maybe."

David adjusted his sunglasses and flexed his shoulders as if his body ached. “What an awful place.”

“That could be us one day,” Elise said.

“We should make a pact right now.”

“To do what?”

He raised his eyebrows. *You know.*

“A pillow?”

“A nice fluffy one.”

They opened car doors, slid inside, and lowered windows. Then it was back downtown to prepare for the press conference.

CHAPTER 13

David was pretty proud of the press-conference-in-the-cemetery idea. Avery had been skeptical, but he'd quickly come around after David explained the advantages of sticking with the cemetery theme. They needed the public's help, and with the possibility of Remy still being alive and having lived in more than one state, they also needed media coverage. Lots of media coverage. Lamont had called David a media whore, and maybe it was true. Not that David was proud of the title, but they were living in an age in which social media had an alarming and disturbing amount of power. He wanted to plug directly into that power.

A press conference in a Civil War cemetery, with its ancient, lichen-encrusted tombstones and curtains of Spanish moss, would guarantee good coverage. David hoped by tomorrow morning the story would be in thousands of Facebook feeds. The shooting of a mayor in a cemetery was news, but a press conference held in one made it bigger news.

They were almost ready to begin, the exact presentation location carefully chosen. Mics were in place near the area of the cemetery that butted up to the back of the three-story brick Savannah PD building. Cables snaked across grass, and people sat on altar stones chatting and drinking from to-go cups while waiting for events to get under way.

Cemeteries had once been used as gathering places. Years ago families packed picnics and spent entire days among the dead and buried, much like people went to parks or beaches today. So holding the event in Colonial Park Cemetery didn't seem a stretch, really.

David spotted Elise heading his way. Even from a distance he could see she wasn't happy.

"A press conference in a cemetery?" she asked. "Are you kidding me? Who ordered this circus? Avery? The mayor? I'll bet it was the mayor. It reeks of his media pandering."

"I'll give you one guess. Who was recently accused of being a media whore?"

She looked at him in surprise. "This was your idea?"

He nodded and rocked back on his heels.

"You should have run it past me."

"You might not have noticed, but you aren't in charge here anymore. But hey, do you wanna be in charge? I'm sure that could be arranged." The mayor would jump on that. "Maybe you could even take Coretta's job as head of the criminal-investigation department. I hear they haven't found a permanent replacement for her."

"I can't believe you're joking about Coretta."

"I'm not joking about Coretta. I would *never* joke about Coretta."

She blinked. It was actually more like a short, two-second nap; then she was staring at him again.

It seemed he was always struggling to keep their relationship in that safe place, that somewhat neutral place, but things were slipping; things were getting weird between them again. He was pretty sure he knew the cause. He'd tried to hide it, but he was glad to be back in Savannah and he was glad to be back with the Savannah PD. Surprised him too. And deep down, maybe in a place Elise hadn't yet acknowledged, she was pissed that he was glad to be back.

"I don't care about the press conference," she said. Such an obvious attempt to convince herself of her lack of interest.

"Of course not." It came out with a little more sarcasm than he'd intended.

Avery strode toward them—a welcome diversion. "Showtime." His hair was damp, and he was sweating through his light-gray jacket. They took their places in front of the brick wall embedded with tombstones. Above them the wind gently wafted Spanish moss almost as if a director had shouted "Action" and given a nod to turn on the fans. Avery tapped one of the mics, winced at the feedback, and announced they'd be starting soon. People gathered closer, growing quiet in anticipation.

Avery coughed into his hand, then began.

He did a good job filling in the basics, recounting the events of that morning, beginning with Lamont's death. "The mayor is going to be fine," he assured them. "One woman, a reporter with WTOC, was also hit. Her injury was less severe, and she'll be back to work in a week or so." Then he got to the good stuff. He told them about the body in the coffin and how it didn't belong to Frank J. Remy.

All hell broke loose with that information. Questions came fast and furious. Reporters began shouting at the same time.

Avery sweated harder and panicked more.

He had the same reply to almost every question. "I don't know the answer to that." He'd point, and three people would shout more questions at him. His replies were all variations on the same: "I don't know." Avery wasn't skilled at redirecting, giving them a little something no matter how vague. David felt sorry for him and wondered how long he should wait to jump in. He didn't like to see a friend sinking so fast and hard, but he also didn't want to undermine Avery's position by answering for him.

Now came the time for the more astute questions, the most intense from none other than Lucille Bancroft, Avery's girlfriend. "What's the consensus among you?" she asked. "Do you think Frank J. Remy is still alive?"

With no outward sign of recognition, Avery didn't hesitate to give her the same unhelpful reply he'd given the others. "At this point we don't know the answer to that."

She looked down at the tablet in her hand, read from her notes, then plunged ahead before other reporters could break in. "We're all aware of the situation in Florida. Of the bodies that were found in and around Ocala. Children, hidden in the walls of houses. That's a pretty sick mind and a unique and disturbing image. Would you say the recent discovery at the house here in Savannah matches the Florida MO?"

Avery gave her a long, wounded look. Poor guy. "It's close." He pressed his lips together and scanned the crowd for someone who might have an easier question, one he could answer.

But Lucille was tenacious, and David was getting a good idea of who the alpha was in the relationship. "Do you think it's the same person?" she asked bluntly.

Sweat ran down Avery's neck. "Possibly, but it could be a copycat."

"If it *is* the same person, can you tell us more about the abduction of Zane Novak? Doesn't it seem logical that the Florida killer has moved his killing field to Georgia?"

Other reporters jumped in, several talking at once. "What's the danger to residents? What's the police department doing to protect citizens?"

It was time to come to Avery's rescue. "This investigation is just unfolding, and we're still gathering information," David said, holding up his hands. "And in that light, we're asking for the public's support and help. If anyone knows anything, if anyone has seen anything, please call the local Crime Stoppers number."

Elise did her part in helping to cut through the chaos. "Also, within the next few hours we'll have a media file available online that we'll be updating as information comes in," she said. "By tomorrow morning we hope to have an aged composite of Frank J. Remy, and we'd appreciate your help in getting that photo to the public. If Remy is still alive, he might be someone's neighbor. He might be someone's father. He might be a regular patron at a bar or café. We need your eyes and ears in order to catch the perpetrators." She stepped away from the mic. Cool. In charge. Not a tremble to be seen, not even from David's close proximity.

Hands shot up. Avery pointed.

"This is for Detectives Sandburg and Gould." The question came from a young man who hardly looked out of high school. "Are you back?" he asked. "We know you were in the cemetery this morning when everything went down, and we understand it was Detective Sandburg's gunshot that hit the escape vehicle. But what I think most of us want to know is—are you back? Are you both working on this case? And if you *are* back, are you back for good?"

Knowing how much she hated their return to the department, David looked at Elise and gave her a half smile. He felt bad for her, but not as bad as he should.

In answer to the question, he reached into his pocket. When she saw what he was up to, she did the same. They both pulled out their leather cases and flipped them open.

David hadn't been going for praise or even approval. Not even drama. It just seemed a nice visual reply. But as soon as the badges were out, applause erupted.

Two minutes later the press conference was over. Crews appeared to dismantle mics and break down equipment while officers congratulated David and Elise on their return. Elise handled it well, all things considered. It was one thing to be congratulated on a job you wanted, another to be congratulated on one you didn't.

David spotted Lucille moving toward them through the crowd, and before he could silently warn Elise and give her the chance to vanish, the reporter caught up with them, giving Avery a smile of familiarity now that she was no longer firing questions at him.

Elise appeared ready to say something, probably thought better of it, and simply turned and walked away. As the remaining group stared at her back, Avery muttered something about Elise's recent bad experience with a reporter. Then, shrugging off the awkwardness of her departure, he let David know Lamont's belongings were being removed from the building behind them. "Your old office will be ready for you tomorrow."

Before he lost his ride, David excused himself and caught up with Elise, relaying Avery's news.

"Oh good. One of us will get a dead man's desk. I'm sure there's no bad mojo there."

Minutes later, in the car heading in the direction of his apartment, David said, "I know you aren't happy about this, but think of it as kind of a do-over." He raised his window and turned the air down a notch so he didn't have to talk so loudly. "This is our chance to do things differently. Retain some kind of life in the midst of all the chaos and horror."

"Is that possible?"

"Here's my plan, and it's simple. We don't go for full immersion. We try to have a life at the same time. Something completely separate from what's going on back there, at the department."

"I don't even have a life to get back to, not with Audrey gone."

"You make it. You *make* the life."

"When did you get so positive? Aren't you the one with the dark soul and I'm the one who's practical?"

It occurred to him that he was hungry. Was he the only one who ever thought about food? If he never suggested it, would Elise eat at all? Maybe. After a blood-sugar crash, once she realized the cause. She was one of those people who could probably live on nothing but food pills if they ever became a viable thing. "I think we should run the marathon."

Before Elise could come up with an argument, before she could point out that she could barely walk not all that long ago, he plunged on: "Just give it a try. Start out slow. Run a block, walk a block. You have old injuries you're worried about. I get that, but you'll know pretty quickly if it's too soon."

"When's the marathon?"

He pulled out his phone and searched the Internet. "Three weeks."

"Three weeks. Thirteen miles. That's ridiculous."

"If you aren't ready, just walk like Avery said. And if you can only do a few miles, do a few miles. These are fund-raisers. They don't have people who monitor and shame you." He adjusted his sunglasses. "Tell you what. I'll stop by your place tomorrow morning. Say, six o'clock. We'll walk-slash-run for thirty minutes, tops. No big deal. You've been saying you want to start something new, something that has nothing to do with crime."

"I was thinking more along the line of a baking class. Like sourdough or something."

"Really? Baking? You?"

"Yeah, I can bake."

"I'm the baker."

"Maybe I want to outdo you."

"I have nothing against challenging you to a bake-off. Bread? Cookies? Pie? How about pie?"

"I'd have to take the class first."

"Running is more fun."

"I seriously doubt that."

"Tomorrow morning. Six o'clock."

"That's ungodly."

"I usually hit the streets at five. I'm slacking for you."

She pulled into his apartment parking lot and left the car in gear, foot on the brake. "I like the idea of trying to create a life outside Homicide," she said. "It might even help my case with Audrey. But I'm feeling skeptical about the running."

He unlatched his seat belt. "It's a great time of day. Birds singing. Cafés setting up outdoor seating. The smell of coffee and that sweet stench of the paper mill."

He could see the second she caved.

"Six o'clock," she said.

He resisted the urge to high-five himself. Instead he opened the door and stepped out. Then, leaning down so he could peer inside the car, he said, "Go home. Get some rest. I'll see if I can track down your dad."

CHAPTER 14

Arriving home, Elise did a quick pass around the exterior of her house to make sure she'd had no unwelcome visitors. Inside, she set the alarm and checked doors and windows. House secure, she entered the first-floor guest room where her father had been staying. His bed had been stripped, and his clothes were no longer in the closet. When she'd passed his door that morning, his bed had been made, so this had to have happened after the cemetery incident. She called Sweet's cell. No answer, so she called Strata Luna.

"He's gone," Strata Luna said. "He dropped off some clothes and told me he was leaving." She sounded resentful, as if blaming Elise.

"Do you know where he was going? Did he say?"

"No. But he made it clear the two of you couldn't live in the same town."

"I'm sorry. But he's an adult. I didn't chase him away."

"Really? 'Cause I'd say that's exactly what you did."

Elise was tired of fighting with people. It seemed she was arguing with everybody nowadays. She told Strata Luna good-bye and disconnected.

In the kitchen, she opened the refrigerator and stared blindly for a full minute before pulling out a beer, digging an opener from a drawer, and popping the top off the bottle.

As a detective, she'd learned to work backward, follow the clues from the end to the beginning. Not for the first time she attempted the same technique with her life, trying to figure out where the wrong turns were located. It was hard, because there were so many. And one of those wrong turns had produced Audrey, so how could it ever be considered a wrong turn? Odd to think one of the biggest mistakes of her life, her disastrous marriage, had resulted in the most important person in her life.

In the living room, she drank the beer too quickly, hardly tasting it, mainly hoping for a buzz. Polishing it off, she leaned deeper into the couch and reached for the afghan. Going upstairs to bed seemed too much of a commitment to an old life. Like the previous night, she put her head down and feet up, fully dressed, and reran the events of the day.

Her focus was scattered, her thoughts jumping from Audrey to the raising of her hand to take an oath in the mayor's hospital room, David being pleased about being back, and those disturbing times during the day when various locations had brought up the past with jolting and disturbing clarity in a way she hadn't experienced before. All of the things she'd buried deep were resurfacing. It would take time to bury them again, but she *would* bury them. She'd get them under control.

Exhaustion prevailed, and she fell asleep, dropping into disturbing dreams of a house and the evil man who'd tortured her. Like a few nights ago, she was startled awake by the sound of someone on the porch. She jumped to her feet and peered through the peephole to see the same shrouded figure.

Not fully awake, still trying to shake off the dreams, she grabbed and raised her gun, jerked open the door, and froze, distantly aware of the alarm she'd set earlier counting down.

Beneath the hood, in the faint light cast from her house, was a face she hadn't seen in a long time, a face she'd hoped to never see again, belonging to a man who was supposed to be dead.

Atticus Tremain.

She wasn't a screamer, but she felt a scream deep in her guts, trying to escape, blocked by a smothering tightness in her throat.

"Is this the Elise Sandburg residence?" The words came out a stammer, spoken in the same white fear she felt.

She shifted her stance, the movement allowing more light to illuminate the porch. A kid. A young kid wearing a hooded sweatshirt.

Not Tremain. He looked *nothing* like Tremain.

She lowered the weapon. She found her voice. "What do you want?"

"I-I've got a delivery." He lifted a basket covered with plastic wrap and tied with a red bow. "It's from the mayor's office. I stopped by earlier, but nobody was home." Talking fast, words tripping from his mouth. "I was told not to leave it on the porch. That it would get stolen in this neighborhood."

Jesus.

She took the basket. "Wait here." She left him standing there while she punched in the alarm code, the room going silent. Then she dug a ten-dollar bill from her bag to give the poor kid. When she returned to the door, he was gone, his car speeding away. She would have done the same.

She closed the door and locked up, reset the alarm, sat down on the couch, and stared at the gift basket on her lap. Apples and oranges, cheese, local honey, crackers. A card tucked between two packets of tea.

She'd aimed a weapon at a kid. It made her wonder about what she'd seen a few nights ago. The cloaked figure in the street. Maybe she'd been wrong about that too. But no, on the table near the door where she always tossed her keys was the Ziploc bag. That really happened.

With shaking hands, she opened the small envelope and pulled out the card. *Welcome back.*

She carried the basket to the kitchen and dug through a metal tin full of odds and ends to finally find the scrap of paper she was looking for. It contained the name and website of a psychologist Major Coretta Hoffman had recommended a couple of months ago, before her death. Back in the living room, Elise pulled up the website and was able to schedule an appointment online. The first available opening was two months out. She chose a date and time and included a note explaining the reason for her visit, along with a request that she be called if they had an earlier cancellation.

CHAPTER 15

John Casper pulled into the morgue parking lot and cut the engine. Predawn, the sky in the east a lighter shade of black, the day already in the low seventies—a temperature that felt cool and pleasant after the heat of the past week.

He was sad, and he was hardly ever sad. He didn't like the feeling. He didn't know what to do with it. That's what love did to a guy. Made you sad, made you hurt.

Mara was angry with him.

What had happened between them wasn't really a fight, but she'd hardly spoken at dinner. He was inexperienced, and he didn't know how to fix it.

Mara was just as fascinated by dead bodies as he was. They'd clicked from day one. Of course she was sweet and kind and beautiful. That didn't hurt either, especially when it came to someone like him, a geek who'd never thought he'd find anybody because of the dead-body thing. Even though he was young for his profession, he'd resigned himself to remaining single the rest of his life. He'd given up.

And then Mara came along.

But now his occupation, the thing that had drawn her to him, was the thing she no longer liked about him. He knew her sudden shift was because of concern for him, that the danger of the job had taken her by surprise. Him too. He'd never really thought about danger. She'd said something about how they could move to Dallas and both get jobs where she'd been working when they met. A place that was cold and clinical and removed from the action. Something *safe*.

"We've been married a month, and you're already trying to change me," he'd told her, gathering up dinner dishes of uneaten food while she stood watching from the doorway, arms crossed. Then she'd turned and silently walked to the bedroom. He'd joined her a short time later, and they'd tried to talk, but it was awkward, mainly because John didn't know how to engage in a conversation that was unpleasant. He could joke around, he could riff, and he could tell her he loved her. Those things came easy. But not arguing. So he hardly said anything, and what he did say probably made little sense.

"I never thought you'd be in danger," she told him before turning her back and pulling the covers over her shoulder, upset with him for not saying more. Cold shoulders were real.

Preoccupied, arranging and rearranging the words he'd say to his young wife next time he saw her—beginning with how much he loved her—he unlocked the morgue door, stepped inside, and canceled the alarm. He was reaching for the light switch when he heard footsteps outside. Before he could turn, the unlocked door slammed against the wall. In the darkness someone crashed against him, propelling him to the floor. Air escaped his lungs, like a dead body expelling gas when cut open.

He reached for his pocket, intent on retrieving his cell phone to call 911. A boot stomped his wrist. Bones crunched. He wailed in pain and rolled to his side.

With his uninjured hand, he struggled to push himself to his feet, managed to get his knees under him. The boot connected with his side, his ribs, his kidney. He buckled again, blinking rapidly, trying to clear his vision. Two intruders. Probably male. Medium size. Hooded sweatshirts pulled down low, too dark to see a face.

"What do you want?" It hurt to talk, hurt to breathe. This wasn't a robbery. They weren't here for his billfold. He was pretty sure of that.

He thought about Mara's warning. He'd have to tell her she'd been right. He might even tell her he'd think about Dallas. Those were words he could say, words that might come easier next time.

The door slammed closed, the sound followed by a metal click as the lock fell into place. One of the thugs hit the wall switch. Fluorescent bulbs buzzed, illuminating in sequence down the long, narrow hallway. The two hoods were pulled back, and John got a look at the assailants towering over him. One guy's face was a mess, almost like part of his skull had been blown away, leaving a crater above his nose, between his eyes.

As a medical examiner, John had seen a lot of disturbing things, but this was up there near the top. Because the guy with the messed-up face was alive. More disturbing? Behind the deformities was a face that looked familiar.

The guy gave him a smile that couldn't really be called a smile. Crooked, the nerves most likely damaged or severed. The other man was older. White, in his sixties. A bit on the heavy side.

John's phone buzzed. Without thought, he went for it. The guy with the messed-up face placed a foot on his arm and shook his head. The gesture seemed almost friendly. John didn't check his phone.

He'd seen them, could ID them. They had no plans to let him live.

Should have carried a gun. No, that wouldn't have done any good. He'd never pull a gun on anybody. His love of dead bodies didn't extend to killing.

He heard the turn of a key in the lock.

Few people had access to the morgue, and he and Mara were the only ones who ever came so early. He let out a silent wail of despair as the door opened. Mara spoke his name the way she often did when arriving. Just a hello to let him know she was there.

He found the air he needed to warn her. "Mara! Run!"

That heavy boot again, this time kicking him in the head.

CHAPTER 16

"Those aren't running shoes."

Elise looked down at her black canvas sneakers. "They'll do."

"You have to get running shoes." David had arrived at her house at 6:00 a.m. on the dot, his very promptness exasperating.

"This is inhumane." She was often up this early, but she didn't participate in anything physical at such an ungodly hour unless making coffee and walking to her car counted. "I feel fortunate to have pulled this ensemble together."

It was already too hot for full-length sweatpants, so she'd cut off a pair just above the knee. A blue Savannah PD T-shirt completed the outfit. David was dressed in jogging attire—gray cotton shorts, white T-shirt, shoes that probably cost a fortune.

"Leave your phone," he said. "You don't have any place to put it, and I've got mine." He nodded at the band on his arm.

"I'll carry it."

"You want your hands free."

"I'm not concerned with technique. If I'd known you were going to be so anal on the very first day—"

"Okay, okay." He gave up. She locked the door and pocketed her keys, and they left her house, heading in the direction of Forsyth Park.

Three blocks in she was breathing hard, her bad leg aching. She slowed to a walk, hand to her side. Pathetic and embarrassing. David fell in beside her.

"Go on without me," she gasped. Her shortness of breath caused the words to sound more dramatic than she'd intended, almost as if they were dealing with a life-and-death situation and his remaining behind would be the end of them both.

"No."

"This is ridiculous. You won't get in a good run."

"I ran to your place. Once we're done, I'll run back to mine. No big deal. It'll get easier quickly," he promised. "You'll be surprised."

"I'm limping. Did you notice?" Her phone buzzed.

"Ignore it."

She wasn't sure if he was talking about her limp, her phone, or both. She checked the screen. "Avery."

"Call him when we're done. This is our new plan, remember?"

She answered, hitting "Speaker" so David could hear too.

"You need to come to the morgue." Avery sounded odd, and his voice held a tone she'd never heard in it before. Elise shot David a concerned look, and they both halted in the middle of the sidewalk.

"What's going on?" She thought about Mara's paranoia yesterday, and her heart began to slam. "Is John all right?"

"Just come. Now."

"Be right there."

She and David ran back to her house, Elise forgetting about the pain in her leg and stitch in her side. When they reached her car parked in the alley, David spoke her name. Calmly, firmly.

She sharpened her focus to see him standing beside the driver's door, hand out. It was a moment before she understood why he wanted to drive. She was shaking. Again. But this time it wasn't subtle. This time it was that extreme kind of shaking she'd witnessed in the field when interviewing someone who'd lost a friend or loved one. The kind of shaking that didn't even look real.

She curled her hands into fists and dug her nails into her palms in an attempt to get her body under control; then she tossed him the keys. Seconds later he was behind the wheel and she was in the passenger seat.

Racing to the morgue, they met an ambulance speeding in the direction of downtown. David pulled to the shoulder, waited for it to pass, then resumed his driving.

And they both wondered . . .

They heard the sirens and saw the black, billowing smoke long before reaching their destination. The street was clogged with vehicles, so many they were forced to park two blocks away. Hurrying the rest of the way on foot, they were stopped by firefighters. With no badges to flash, gaining access to the scene presented a challenge. Elise finally pulled out her phone and called Avery, who emerged from the crowd to act as escort.

His jeans and T-shirt were soaked, his hair saturated and dripping. It took Elise a moment to realize he'd been inside the building while the sprinkler system was running. "Fire's out," he said. "They're trying to get the water shut off." The words were spoken in that flat, meant-to-inform way that went along with death. Numb words, the brain locked into the events at hand and the need to communicate simple information. "I put extra patrols in this area right after the cemetery shooting. Officers were driving past every thirty minutes. One pass, everything looked fine. Next one, all hell had broken lose. Perpetrators long gone."

"Is it John?" Elise's voice shook as much as her body had earlier.

Avery nodded.

She stared at him, trying to read through the horror in his face, fearing the answer. "Dead?"

"No, but it doesn't look good. He's been taken to Saint Joseph's/Candler."

The ambulance they'd met on the way to the morgue. *Not dead.* Elise clung to those words. "Injuries?"

"Don't know."

Elise began moving toward the building. David and Avery ran after her. "Elise, wait," Avery said. "That's not all."

She stopped.

"It's Mara."

Elise was breathing hard, almost panting, peripherally aware of David standing beside her, waiting for Avery to continue, not wanting to hear what he had to share.

Avery swallowed, struggled to speak, finally said, "*She's* dead. Mara's dead." He broke down, buried his face in his hands, and began sobbing. Numbly, without realizing what she was doing, Elise touched his arm, rubbing up and down in an attempt at comfort while her mind denied what he'd just told them. *Not Mara.*

Her thoughts raced and jumped from one kind of awful to another, finally landing and settling on John. This would kill him. If he lived through his injuries, this would kill him.

The media had beaten them there. Elise was aware of their lurking, of cameras with telephoto lenses pressed to faces. She didn't care. This was bigger than their photos and the stories they would write that might or might not be true.

David was struggling too. She saw he was trying to figure out what had led to such an awful thing, while Elise found herself returning to the conversation she'd had with Mara not twenty-four hours earlier. She'd dismissed her fear. She'd been annoyed by it.

Avery uncovered his face, wiped his eyes with the back of one hand. "Looks like she was strangled. And John was beaten so badly I didn't even recognize him at first."

"Jesus," David said under his breath.

"Mara's body?" Elise asked.

"Still on-site."

They resumed their approach to the building. "It's bad," Avery warned. "Real bad."

The fire marshal stopped them. "Sprinklers are still running."

"Fuck the sprinklers." David pushed past him and strode inside. Officers tried to stop him. He shoved them out of the way with a look so fierce they dropped back. Avery and Elise followed close behind, Avery mumbling "Holy shit" over and over.

Emergency backup lighting was operating. Not much, but a few bulbs cut through the darkness of the windowless building. Beneath the odor of burnt wires and melted plastic was the unmistakable scent of gasoline. Water from the sprinklers pelted them, and within seconds David and Elise were as drenched as Avery, the deluge making it hard to see. It plastered hair to their heads and dripped off their chins.

They waded through water two inches deep, stepping over saturated acoustic tile that had fallen from the ceiling to reveal the dark bones of the building. The water sloshing around their shoes was tinged pink. Blood? If so, it would have taken a lot to give such a large amount of water that hue.

"First responders found John here, by the door." Avery pointed.

Elise turned her back to a sprinkler. "Was he conscious?" She blinked. Water ran in her mouth, muffling her voice as she spoke.

"They said one of his eyes was open, but it didn't look like he was registering anything. When I arrived, they were loading him into the ambulance."

Had the intent been to burn the place down, or trigger the sprinklers? Whatever the reason, the results were the same. Severe damage.

"The medical team was here," Avery said, continuing to fill them in on what had transpired before their arrival. "There was nothing I could do, so I pulled my gun and moved down the hall."

While the sprinklers continued to soak them, Avery paused at a door, fiddling with the knob. "I didn't see anybody, and I couldn't find a passkey to the evidence room. It locks automatically whenever anybody leaves. Through the glass you can see whoever attacked John has been in there."

David and Elise took turns looking through the window in the door. Evidence files were strewn around the room. Computers were smashed, data files probably destroyed, along with security footage.

Avery kept talking. "I figured it was the guys from the cemetery. That's probably what you're thinking, right? They wanted the body once, so they were probably here to finish what they started. So I went to the coolers."

He sloshed away, Elise and David following, the three of them moving deeper into the building, past the autopsy suite they'd been in just hours earlier, to the cooler room with its row of stainless-steel doors. Avery stood in the center of the room while the sprinklers continued to rain down on them. He shifted from one foot to the other and motioned toward the stainless-steel doors. "Open them." Like a dare.

David opened the first drawer, and Elise pulled back the sheet. Lamont, a hole in his chest and a sutured Y incision. In all that had happened, Elise had forgotten about Lamont, forgotten his body would still be there.

David opened a second drawer.

Elise had been focusing her thoughts on John Doe, half expected to find the body had been taken. But it was there, in the vault, doused with some type of acid, the face melted. Shifting her gaze, she noted that the hands had been doused too.

Somebody didn't want them to discover the identity of the body. "So that's what this is all about. Not money, not drugs. Whoever did this wanted to make sure the face was unrecognizable and no prints were left behind."

David shut the drawer. "All for nothing if John got the autopsy information entered into the database."

Which he might or might not have done, given how busy he'd been yesterday.

The odor of gasoline was stronger now, and the water sloshing around their ankles had an oily sheen. If someone were to strike a match, the surface would catch fire. But they continued on, numbly following where Avery led.

"I'm guessing they made her open the evidence room," Avery told them. "Then maybe when they didn't find what they were looking for, or even if they did, they came in here."

They were in the break room now, the place where Mara used to offer homemade ginger cookies when people stepped from the autopsy suite looking pale and ready to pass out. She claimed she'd gotten the recipe from a coroner she'd trained under in Dallas. "Secret formula," she'd always said with a smile.

The plate was still there, covered in clear wrap, a couple of cookies left. Elise didn't want to stop looking at the cookies, but she forced herself to take in the rest of the scene.

There was Mara, on the floor, her body crumpled like a doll's, legs askew, arms at odd angles, eyes open, the rain from the ceiling running across the porcelain of her skin. Elise thought about how much John adored her, how much they all adored her, how wonderful it had been for John to have finally found someone to share his life.

It was Elise's turn to let out a sob, her turn to press her hand to her mouth. Beside her, David looked stunned. She saw his grief and had to look away.

Had they made this happen? If they hadn't come back, if they'd gone on that vacation, the truck with the body would have gotten away, and the police would never have known that the coffin didn't contain the body of Frank J. Remy.

"We did this," she whispered.

David wiped water from his face and muttered some weak attempt at a protest, but he had to be thinking the same thing. And then she remembered her father's warning. He'd told her to let it go.

From beyond the break room came the sound of activity. Two members of the crime scene team appeared with cases, both men wearing plastic rain ponchos. Elise was glad to see Abe Chilton, the head investigator. He wouldn't miss anything. He gave them a grim nod, then shouted to anybody listening, "Somebody turn off this fucking water!" The scene was chaos.

"What's going on?" Avery spoke to no one but himself. "What *the hell* is going on?" He blinked, reached for a wall. "Think I'm gonna pass out."

David grabbed his arm. "Let's get out of here."

They left, moving three abreast.

Just like old times.

Elise distantly noted that the sprinklers were no longer raining down on them. She wished they were still on, still drenching their interior world, because the water had muted everything, made it seem less real.

From deep in the heart of the building, something kicked on, and a few emergency lights responded.

In the hallway, David pulled Avery out of foot traffic as the crime scene team moved back and forth. Avery leaned against a wall while David and Elise waited for his color to return. Once it did, she said, "I'm going to the hospital. Will you be okay here?"

He nodded. "Somebody needs to contact their parents." It was obvious he didn't want the job.

"When we have more information." Elise headed for the exit door.

David ran after her.

CHAPTER 17

They headed straight downtown, Elise driving this time, feeling the need to do something, grip something, focus on lights and streets. Her clothes, her stupid and inappropriate clothes, were soaking into the car seat, her wet hair plastered against her neck. Both she and David smelled like gasoline.

Her mind was clicking along, trying to make sense of everything, when she became aware of David fiddling with the dashboard dials. "What are you doing?"

"Turning on the heat."

She glanced at the outdoor-temperature gauge. "It's seventy-five degrees."

"I'm cold. You're probably cold too."

"It doesn't matter."

"We should change before going to the hospital. Take the next exit."

"No." Stopping at her house, then David's apartment, would take too much time. "We can't waste a moment." John could be dying.

David pulled out his phone, poked at the screen, muttered about it being wet and dead.

It was still early, but rush-hour traffic had begun. Four lanes, blasting toward downtown. Elise passed in the right lane, one wheel on the shoulder. Without comment, David grabbed the handle above the door as she swerved back into the fastest-moving lane.

"I can't quit thinking about the conversation with Mara yesterday," Elise said. "I dismissed her. I was annoyed by her worry. God, I can be such a bitch sometimes. If someone else had said the same thing, I would have given it more merit. But because it was Mara—"

"Bank that." David opened his phone and pulled out the battery. He dug a small pack of tissues from the glove compartment, pulled one free, and wiped off the phone and battery. "Put it wherever you have to put it, but put it away with that other stuff you put away and never look at."

His words felt like a slap. She'd expected some empathy, not an attack. "Go to hell."

"This is not the time to go soft."

"I think it's okay for me to feel something right now." Her voice was tense, and there was no way he could miss how mad she was. "Mara is dead. John might be dead."

He put his phone back together, tried to restart it, failed. "Which means we have work to do." He dropped his phone into the cup holder between the seats.

Elise wasn't sure she'd ever heard that formidable and deadly tone in his voice. Her anger faded. He was right. They had to focus. They'd both just witnessed Avery's mental state. Somebody had to keep it together.

If David's dressing-down and dismissal of her emotions was meant to get her back on track, it worked. This wasn't about her or how she felt. This was about Mara. John.

She pulled into the ER lot, tires squealing. Shooting into the first available slot, she braked, cut the engine, and dove out of the car. Side by side, she and David ran for the entry doors. They didn't have their badges. They were wet, wearing jogging clothing.

The nurse behind the counter recognized them instantly. Checking her computer screen, she said, "Mr. Casper's in surgery." She gave them directions to the waiting area. "I'll let the doctors know you're here."

"Can you tell us anything about his condition?" Elise asked.

"No." She shook her head. "I'm sorry."

They thanked her and headed down the maze of hallways.

"We're here so often we should just rent a room," David said.

Elise didn't laugh. She was still processing the news that John was lying on an operating table instead of dead downstairs in a stainless-steel cooler. "At least he's alive, but I was hoping we'd get here in time to see him, talk to him."

"I know you were."

She pictured the scene. "But he would have asked about Mara. You know she would have been his first thought. And I'm not that accomplished an actress. I'm afraid he would have read her death on my face. Maybe this is better. Not seeing him. I wouldn't have wanted him to head to surgery knowing Mara was dead."

In the waiting area, the receptionist brought them blankets. "They're warm," she said. "And you two look cold." Elise had to think about that. Yes, she was cold. Wet clothes and air-conditioning didn't go together.

Wrapping the blankets around their shoulders, she and David sat on a hard couch. At one point David found a coffee machine and returned with two cups, handing one to Elise. "Somebody needs to call Mara's parents before they hear about it on the news. Let me use your phone."

"I'll do it. You can call John's family."

He didn't argue, and she saw the relief in his eyes.

Elise pulled her phone from her pants pocket, wiped the damp screen, and was relieved to find that the device hadn't succumbed to water damage. She contacted the police department. Research was able to quickly locate the number of Mara's parents.

When her call was answered, Elise introduced herself and heard the catch in Mara's mother's voice.

They always knew.

She gave her the news, then asked, "You have my phone number, right?"

The woman hesitated, probably checked her screen, answered, "Yes."

Right now she was too numb to absorb much more than the awful news, but in an hour or so she'd begin to have questions. Elise explained about John, said they didn't know anything yet, then told her to call when she had questions or needed more information.

Done, she handed David her phone and listened as he gave John's parents a quick sketch of what was going on and where he and Elise were. He told them he'd have the surgeon call once John was out of surgery. From David's side of the conversation, it sounded as if they were planning to catch a flight to Savannah. Elise wasn't sure how John would feel about that. Neither he nor Mara had been particularly close to any of their relatives. Neither set of parents had been at the wedding, and Mara had often remarked that John was closer to Elise and David than he was to his own family.

Elise was a homicide detective. She dealt with death and the dark side of life on a regular basis. And although she'd dealt with an unusual kind of loss—the loss of her mother and father due to abandonment—she'd never lost anyone close to her, but she'd come close with Audrey. Now she'd lost Mara and might lose John. And suddenly the world was so much darker and so much more unbearable.

It was always a surprise to accidentally stumble upon the thoughts that broke you, that wrapped around your heart and squeezed it hard. She'd found them.

She tossed the blanket aside, put down her coffee, and walked deliberately to the nearest restroom. It was empty, so she locked herself in a stall and cried. At some point she heard the outer door open, caught her breath, got herself under control, flushed, pulled out toilet paper, blew her nose. Footsteps came close, and knuckles rapped lightly on her door.

"Someone in here!" she shouted.

"Elise."

Damn.

"Do you *mind*?" Had he come to tell her to get a grip? Pull herself together? That they had a case to solve?

Through the closed stall door, he said, "I'm sorry about what I said earlier in the car. That was shitty of me. I was freaking out, and I turned it on you." His voice tightened. "John's a good friend."

She pressed her forehead against the door, tried to catch her breath. John was David's *best* friend.

"Don't try to hide your emotions," David said. "You do too much hiding. Ignore what I said on the way here. That was bad advice. Really bad advice, and the last thing you should be doing. Hell, I'm the one who's always saying you need to talk about things more."

She opened the door.

He had a hand braced against the stall. Damp and wrinkled clothes, hair dried in clumps. She sniffled and wiped at her nose. "You look like hell."

"So do you."

How did David do it? *The loss of a child.* How did he face every single day with this pain? And not only pain, fear. She'd felt that fear when she thought Audrey might be dead, but it had lasted only *hours.*

The pain—it was a physical thing. Her head and heart felt as if they were being crushed. "How do you do it?" she found herself asking him. She immediately regretted the question. Why had she shined a light on him and his suffering?

Forget I said that.

He seemed to know she wanted to take back her question, but he answered anyway. "I don't. Not always."

How quickly the euphoria of Chicago had faded, and how quickly she was once again face-to-face with the dangers she brought into her own life, their life. Someone had to do it, but did it have to be her, them?

He put an arm around her. "Come on. The operation is over, and the doctor is going to talk to us soon."

Back in the waiting area, the surgeon finally made an appearance. Time had shifted, was hard to track, and Elise had no idea if a few minutes or a few hours had passed since they'd burst into the ER.

The doctor wore blue scrubs, a cotton cap over his head, a mask around his neck. She could tell it was bad. Someone needed to turn down the lights. They were so harsh. So blinding. So brittle.

"We were able to stop the bleeding in his brain," he said. "We're giving him medication to hopefully control the swelling. Unfortunately, he lapsed into a coma before surgery, and he's not rousing. Not a surprise considering the severity of his injuries. Right now all we can do is wait. His hand is a mess, bones crushed, and it will need pins. That will be dealt with once he's stable."

He might or might not wake up. Those were the unspoken words. And how awful to think that at least right now he didn't know about Mara.

"You should go," the doctor told them. "If there's any change, you'll be contacted." David handed him a scrap of paper with the number of John's parents, and the doctor promised to call immediately.

They both needed to change clothes before heading to the police station. Elise drove David to his apartment, pulling to a stop in the parking lot. He grabbed his dead phone, got out, but didn't shut the door.

Looking straight ahead, she said, "I'm not sure he can live without her."

"I'm not either." Bent at the waist, he peered inside, hand on the roof of the car. "Want to come in? I'll fix scrambled eggs. I'm not hungry, but we both should eat something."

"Thanks, no. I need to be alone for a little while. I'll meet you at the office."

"Okay." He slapped an open palm against the roof and closed the door.

On her way home, Avery phoned. "I tried to call David, but it went straight to voice mail."

She told him what was happening with John. He told her arrangements were being made to bring in a temporary medical examiner, Hollis Blake from Atlanta. Elise knew the name, knew the woman. Cold and hard-nosed, nothing like John. "The morgue will be closed down for a while, and someone else, maybe Blake, will be doing the autopsy on Mara." He paused. "I wanted to know if you'd like to be there. For the autopsy."

"No."

"That's what I figured, but thought I'd ask." He sounded sane, together. Probably shut off, doing his job.

Back home, Elise grabbed the portable phone from the counter, sat down on a stiff kitchen chair, and speed-dialed her ex-husband's number. When he answered, she told him about John and Mara.

"Audrey will want to come back to Savannah for the funeral," she said. "But I want you to make sure she stays in Seattle, do you understand?"

He did.

"And Thomas? I'm not going to fight for custody."

He made a small sound of protest, or maybe a sound of concern.

"You were right," she told him. "As long as I'm in Homicide, Audrey's in danger. She can't be here. She simply can't."

"I'm sorry, Elise. I'm sorry this is happening."

"I'm glad she has you and Vivian. You're a good father. Vivian is a good stepmother. Audrey is lucky."

A long pause, then Thomas said words she really didn't want to hear right now. Words of concern. "Are you okay?"

She pressed fingers to her lips. "No." Her voice cracked on the single word.

"I can come to Savannah. I can catch a plane tomorrow."

Thomas was good in a crisis. He would take control. He would do things like make sure she ate and slept. "No. Don't."

"Okay." He understood that he could do nothing for John.

"But thanks. Can I talk to Audrey now?"

A minute later Audrey was saying hello. Elise told her daughter about Mara and told her about John. Audrey began crying, and, as Elise expected, said she was coming back for the funeral.

"No." Elise's voice was firm. "You can't come home. If you try, I'll stick you right back on a plane. You need to stay in Seattle."

"I know you're worried about me, but you're there now. I'll be safe."

"No, you won't. You'll never be safe around me."

"So you don't want me to come home? Ever?"

"Not while I'm a homicide detective."

The silence on the other end of the line was a building of pressure. Elise braced herself for the explosion. When it came, a torrent of words poured into her ear, all cruel, all truthful. "You're always talking about how Grandpa left you. Well, you're just as bad. You're doing the same thing!"

"Don't say that. I'm looking out for you." Elise realized those were the same words Sweet had spoken to her not that long ago.

"I have to go," Audrey said.

"Don't hang up."

Elise heard a familiar click, followed by a dial tone. Her daughter's favorite form of good-bye.

CHAPTER 18

In the second-floor hallway of Strata Luna's pink mansion in the Victorian District of Savannah, Jackson Sweet paused long enough to risk a glance at the Gullah woman barreling down on him, her eyes flashing. They'd just spent two hours watching news reports about the morgue fire. At first, when they'd heard one person was dead, another severely injured, they'd feared the casualties might be Elise and David. Sweet's calls to both had gone straight to voice mail, and his fears had grown until he got through to Avery, who told him they were okay. The dead victim had been Mara, John Casper's wife. And Strata Luna was now channeling her earlier fear into rage, and that rage was directed at Jackson Sweet.

He had to get out of there before the storm hit full force.

He spun on his heel and ducked into her bedroom, where he began digging through his canvas backpack, hoping to make a hasty exit through the underground tunnels.

"You gonna tell me what's going on?" she said.

"I've gotta go." He kept his back to her, knowing if he turned around, she'd be standing there, hands on hips.

"Why'd you move out of Elise's? Why'd you tell me to lie when she called? Why are you slinking around, coming and going through the tunnels? Why you been hanging around here for days on end? I know you're hiding. And if you ain't gonna share with me, then I'm done with you. I'm not a girl anymore, Jackson, and your howling under my front porch don't do what it used to."

He heard her pacing, heard the rustle of her black dress.

"And even though I love you," she said, "that love is poison in my veins. It makes me stupid and weak, and I'm not stupid *or* weak. So to see you gone—it would hurt, but you damn well better understand that I'd just as soon see you gone as have you around here keeping secrets from me and dragging me into your lies. I won't put up with that. No, sir. Not anymore."

He zipped his backpack. Tested the weight, turned around.

Goddamn, she was formidable. She'd always been formidable, even when young, but now she was a force. She'd come into her full power or whatever a person might choose to call it. He understood why mere humans scurried away when confronted by her presence out there in the world. It wasn't just the rumors of what she could do and spells she could cast; it was her person, tall, intimidating, threatening.

He loved her.

Yes, it was the pathetic truth. Jackson Sweet, brought down by a raging Gullah woman. Maybe it was the cancer, maybe it was knowing it could return and his life might end sooner than later, maybe it was regret, because he sure as hell had a lot of that, but lately he'd come to realize how much Strata Luna meant to him.

He hefted the backpack straps over his shoulders. "I'm hiding to protect people." And then it hit him that she'd said *she* loved *him*. She'd never said that before. Neither of them had said it. Of course she'd also said love was poison.

True.

"Who you protecting?" she asked. "Let me guess. Jackson Sweet?"

"Elise, among others."

She snorted. "When you gonna learn Elise doesn't need protecting? At least not the kind of protecting you give her. Which isn't protecting at all, but running away." Could she look more disgusted with him?

"When you gonna learn running away never solved anything? Or *protected* anybody? That's just some fool excuse. You try to make yourself look all noble and stoic, but sometimes I think you ain't nuthin' but a coward."

"You say much more and I might have to slap some sense into you."

"You ever hit me, or Elise, or Audrey, and you'll never see another sunrise."

What did she want from him? He was here. He'd come back. Nothing he did was right.

"Mara is *dead*," she said. "John Casper might be dying. Is the man who did this the man you're hiding from?"

"Maybe."

"And did hiding here protect Mara?"

He didn't answer.

"Step up. Be a man."

"Don't make me mad. You don't want to see that." He'd always been a man. More man than most. "You know I'm a man. And you know I'm not afraid of anything."

"Really?" She lifted her chin and gave him a sideways look, then delivered the next words one at a time. "Everybody's afraid of somethin'."

He thought a moment, searched his brain, shook his head. "Not me."

"How about relationships? How 'bout love? You might not be afraid of monsters and murderers and evil. I don't even think you're afraid of dying. But you know what I think puts fear in the heart of Jackson Sweet?" She didn't wait for him to reply. She expected no reply. "Relationships. With me. With your own daughter."

"I've tried with Elise. It's never going to work between us. She's made that clear more than once."

"What about me? What about us?"

He let the backpack slip from his shoulders. It hit the floor with a thud. Then he grabbed her by both arms and pushed her backward, shoving her down on the bed. "Don't ever say I'm not a man." He fumbled with his jeans while she stared up at him, angry and defiant, but waiting for him. Once he'd freed himself, he lifted her skirt, not surprised to find she wasn't wearing underwear. In one thrust, he was deep inside her. "I'm here right now. I'm with you right now. Isn't that enough?"

"Are you here?" She stared at him with those dark, liquid eyes of hers. "Are you really?"

They made rough love—like two cats in heat, as she always said. But he didn't know if she'd ever want it tender. He wouldn't know what tender with Strata Luna would look or feel like.

Twenty minutes later he got up from her bed and reached for his clothes.

"Where you goin'?"

He tugged on his boots, bent to tie the laces. "None of your damn business, woman."

She laughed. The witch laughed. A deep, throaty sound that made him want to kick off his pants and plunge into her all over again. Instead he stood and watched her in silence as he fastened his belt. She was naked, lying on her back, making no movement to cover herself.

Her physical beauty always took him a little by surprise, covered as she usually was from chin to toe with her black dresses. Right now she looked like an oil painting, and he felt a little jealous of all the other men who'd made love to her over the years. And the ones who'd shared her bed more recently. Maybe even that very day.

"Stick close to home," he said. "And don't go anywhere alone." Not really a warning she needed, since he couldn't recall a time she'd ever ventured beyond her security gates without a driver.

"Don't tell me what to do. I'm not a dog to do your bidding."

"You did my bidding a moment ago."

She smiled slyly with her red lips and shook her head. "Honey, you did mine. You should know by now I never do anything I don't want to do."

She was in danger. Everybody he cared about was in danger. Didn't she understand? Their relationship had become fodder for local gossip. One of the reasons he hadn't left town was out of concern for her.

The moment he'd heard about the discovery of the Novak boy's body, Sweet had suspected Remy even though the killer was supposed to be dead. The very public attack at the exhumation, along with the subsequent discovery of the wrong body in the right casket, and Sweet's suspicions were confirmed. Remy was alive. And if Remy was alive, then he was coming for Sweet. Or worse and probably more in line with Remy's need for thorough and satisfying revenge: he was coming for the people Sweet cared about. But Remy might be less eager to put on a show if he thought Sweet was no longer in Savannah. And Sweet would do a better job protecting the people he cared about if nobody knew he was still in town.

"I mean it, Marie." He was the only person who called her by her given name. "Stick close to home or Black Tupelo. I can reach both through the tunnels."

"Does that mean you're coming back?"

"I'll be around."

Not what she wanted to hear. She picked up a ceramic figurine and heaved it at his head. He ducked and laughed. The statue hit the wall and shattered.

CHAPTER 19

Elise and David spent the rest of the day at the crime scene. They talked to the fire marshal, brought in specialists to catalog both the files and external drives that would then be taken to digital forensics, sifted through what was left of evidence, met with team leaders, delegated tasks in the hope that no crucial piece of evidence would be missed. Electricians were on site, and people in hazmat suits were suctioning up water. With the coolers down, the bodies awaiting autopsy and burial had been readied for transfer to the hospital morgue.

This time John Doe got a police escort just in case somebody tried to hijack the coroner van. Strict orders accompanied the body. Since there was no coroner on-site, the evidence label was signed and sealed by Elise, and just in case anybody downtown got in a hurry to free up more cooler space, David affixed a sticky note: *Do not process or bury.* He signed his name.

Throughout the day Elise checked her phone, hoping and fearing for any news from the hospital. At one point she called only to be told there had been no change in John's condition. The only thing to do was stay busy and focused.

The site was still a crime scene. After the crew dispersed and went home for the night, officers remained on guard. It might have been a cliché, but criminals often returned, so law enforcement would keep their eyes open for anybody suspicious, while also deterring the morbidly curious.

Elise and David wrapped up the day with another few hours at the police department, where they accessed the morgue database. As they'd both feared, John hadn't had time to upload photos, X-rays, or notes. They called it a night and headed for the parking lot. It was late, after eleven, but neither would get much sleep. Elise didn't like the thought of returning to an empty house where she wouldn't be able to stop thinking about the last conversation she'd had with Mara.

"My phone's working again." David held it up, lit screen facing her. "So you'll be able to reach me. I'm going to stop by the hospital on the way home."

"Let me know if there's any change."

He nodded, and they split up and moved toward their cars, their bodies casting long shadows. Once home, Elise lay down on the couch, gun within reach, fully dressed in case she got a call about John and needed to rush to the hospital. The couch and living room also put her in close proximity to front and back doors in case anyone decided to visit in the middle of the night, but so far she'd seen no indication that the person who'd left the cremains on her porch had returned.

She was conditioned to grab sleep where and when she could. Tonight that sleep was strange, filtered by the events of the day. At some point Elise woke up, unsure what had brought her to the surface but sensing it had been a sound not delivered by her dreams. Unmoving, holding her breath, she listened—and heard the alarm system begin its countdown.

Someone was in the house.

She heard the gentle click of the back door as it closed, followed by the soft scuff of a footfall against the wooden floor.

In the dark, her hand closed over her gun. She might not be exceptionally strong, but she was fast. Surprise had always been her best defense. In one motion, she erupted from the couch and pinned the intruder to the wall, her forearm pressed to a throat, Glock to a temple.

"That's the second time you've pulled a gun on me." The voice belonged to her father. He followed up with a critique. "Good reflexes. Glad you're being vigilant."

She lowered the weapon, released her hold, and stepped back. "You should have said something." She noted that she was cool and calm, her heart not even pounding. Not a natural reaction, but after the events of the day . . .

"You didn't give me a chance." In the white plastic box on the wall near the door, he entered the alarm code. The chiming stopped, and they both moved deeper into the living room, Sweet turning on a lamp.

Elise dropped down on the couch. "It's late. What are you doing here? Not to mention I was told you were no longer in town."

"I decided to stick around, but I'm keeping a low profile. I heard what happened and wanted to check on you." He settled himself in an overstuffed floral chair, booted foot to knee. "I'm sorry about Mara. And John Casper." He sounded like he meant it. He probably did.

She looked away, carefully placing her gun on the end table, refusing to let him see the pain in her eyes. "Maybe if you'd given us a little more information, what happened at the morgue could have been avoided."

With hardly enough time to process her words, his eyes flared. "Don't put that on me."

She couldn't argue with him right now. Elbows on her knees, she leaned forward and rested her forehead against the heels of her hands. "Shut off the light."

He ignored her. "I want to help. I'm ready to help, ready to tell you everything."

She uncovered her face and waited.

What he told her wasn't that much of a surprise. Things he'd alluded to earlier, recently, and months ago. About how he'd framed Remy to get him convicted.

"I couldn't catch him," Sweet said. "He was too good, too clever, too cunning. The evidence I had was circumstantial, no matter how damning. You have to remember we didn't have the resources you have today. I tried everything. Brought him in for questioning, but couldn't break him. Arrested him, but couldn't hold him. And I *knew* he was committing murder, that he had an insatiable appetite for children, and his crimes were escalating."

"Why didn't you just kill him?" Not that she approved of his taking the law into his own hands, but he'd once bragged about doing just that. Taking out people who needed to be taken out. Remy seemed a deserving subject. "You said you've killed people. It seems a child killer would have been about the most justification you could find in that book you live by."

"I should have. You don't know how much I regret *not* killing him, but people were watching me, suspecting my less-than-orthodox methods of justice. I was afraid I'd get caught, go to prison. Another murder came along at the right time, and I framed him."

"And the real killer got away." She didn't try to hide her disgust.

"He wasn't someone who preyed on innocent children. Sometimes you have to make choices that aren't easy."

"There are tough choices; then there are whatever rules you live by. Totally different things."

"Can we not argue about my code of ethics? That's not why I'm here."

She gave him a look that said, *Continue. I'll listen.*

"You pretty much know the rest. Remy was charged with first-degree murder and given the death sentence."

"And 'died' before it could be carried out."

"Right." He settled deeper into the story, heavy on the reminiscing. "The Remy I knew was extremely manipulative. He could talk people into things. It wouldn't have been that hard for him to find the followers he needed to carry out an escape. He's probably still puppeteering."

"I agree."

"When I heard about Zane Novak, I was already wondering about Remy," Sweet said. "And then I saw the bodies in the house, and I knew Remy was alive and had used the same place to stash the Novak kid. I figured he saw something about me on the news or the Internet and followed me here."

"To kill you?"

"That would have been too easy for him, too straightforward. I think he's looking for more satisfaction than a direct kill. That would be humane. He needs to get me back, make me suffer."

"Are you talking about getting to you through Audrey? Or Strata Luna?"

"Maybe." It seemed as if he wanted to say something else but changed his mind and went another direction. "I started thinking if I vanished again and if you stopped looking too closely, let Lamont handle it, maybe Remy's attention would be diverted. Instead everything was amplified. The way I see it, Remy is now dealing with two issues. Trying to keep you from tracking him down, and trying to stick with his original plan of revenge."

He leaned into his chair. "I don't know how the morgue fits into this, or if it's even connected. But let's assume it is. I wasn't good friends with Casper or Mara, but I did go to their wedding. Going by the Novak kidnapping timeline, Remy would have already been in Savannah at that point. He might have been tailing me, saw me at the wedding. Hell, I could see him face-to-face and not recognize him. He might have served me a tea or beer somewhere. It's been thirty-seven years. He'd look like a different person."

"I'm not sure he was after Mara and John because of you." Elise curled back into the couch, tugging the afghan free and covering her legs, sticking her arms underneath. She couldn't get warm. "The evidence room was ransacked. They must have forced Mara or John to open it. And then the fire, and the sprinkler system . . . It's going to be hard to determine what they were after, or what's gone and what was lost. Georgia Bureau of Investigation is sending specialists down from Atlanta. They'll begin processing the scene in depth first thing in the morning. Bottom line is, the perpetrators didn't want that body identified."

"Had John completed the autopsy? Was everything loaded into the database?"

"Basic information was entered during the autopsy. Height, weight, sex. But he hadn't yet uploaded anything beyond the basics. We might never know everything he found in the autopsy, but they were definitely trying to destroy evidence. And they succeeded."

"What kind of evidence does a body that's been buried decades contain?"

She told him about the face and hands. "They didn't want the John Doe identified."

He was silent, as if trying to make sense of it. She could see he wasn't fully convinced that covering up the corpse's identity was the main motive. "It might have been a smoke screen, something to divert your attention."

"From what?"

"I don't know. What about the Novak kid? Did John do that autopsy?"

"Yes, but John would have entered Novak into the database by then."

"What about evidence?"

"It depends. Physical evidence eventually ends up downtown, but the timeline for final processing and storing isn't that rigid. There might have been evidence at the morgue."

"The possibility he was looking for Novak evidence is something to keep in mind. Because when it comes to Remy, there's no direct line. No A leads to B leads to C."

"Thanks for the input." Nothing sarcastic about her reply.

"I'm sorry about Mara," he said. "She was a sweet kid. And John. Both of them."

The sympathy got to her. She wasn't ready to see sympathy in Sweet's eyes, on his face, in his voice. And damn, if she didn't begin crying. It had been bad enough to cry in front of David, but her father? It wasn't a window to her emotions she'd ever wanted him to see. He didn't deserve that much of her.

Unlike her breakdown in the restroom, she managed to get herself under control pretty quickly this time.

"Have you eaten anything?" he asked, seeming to understand that emotions were closer to the surface when a person was hungry and exhausted.

She pressed the back of her hand against her nose and sniffed. Had she? A food table with sandwiches, coffee, and water had appeared at the crime scene. But had she eaten anything? "I don't know."

"That's never a good sign."

He left the room, and she heard him rummaging around in the kitchen. He returned to place a plate in front of her. At that point she expected him to leave. Instead he watched her eat two slices of cheese and half an apple before slapping his knees and getting to his feet. "I'm off. Lock the door, and set the alarm behind me. And get some sleep." He eyed the couch. "Maybe in a bed."

CHAPTER 20

After Sweet left, Elise sat on the couch absorbing their conversation; then she decided to take his advice and sleep in her own bed, even if just for a couple of hours. But when she stood up, she was overcome by a strange and yet oddly familiar sensation.

Her legs and arms felt weighted. The room tilted. She reached blindly for the couch, steadied herself, then aimed for the front door and managed to lock it. But when she turned to punch in the alarm code, she couldn't make out the numbers on the box. She blinked, squinted, then collapsed to the floor. Rolling to her back, she patted herself down, searching for her phone to call 911. Couldn't find it.

Her skin was on fire.

Like a transforming werewolf, she ripped off clothes, tossing piece after piece aside until she was naked. Panting, she got her knees under her, pushed herself upright, lurched to the kitchen, and jerked the refrigerator door open, letting the cold air move across her hot skin. She was beyond thinking, beyond trying to analyze what was happening. She was just reacting, trying to make it stop.

The heat moved deeper, into her organs, through her veins, to her brain. The light in the refrigerator was too bright, like staring at the sun.

She turned away and lunged for the counter, feeling for the portable phone, touching it, knocking it to the floor, beyond her reach. Gripping the counter, she followed the granite to the sink, groped for the faucet, turned on the cold full blast. She ducked her head under the stream of frigid water, her only objective to stop the heat in her brain. At some point she inhaled, choked, straightened. Still burning up.

Without shutting off the water, she shuffled away from the sink, stiff legged. By pure instinct, she found the back door, opened it, and stood in the threshold. The cool relief she'd hoped for didn't come. Down the steps until she felt smooth live-oak leaves and the sharp edges of patio brick under her feet.

A patio John and Mara helped build.

She looked up at the swirling stars. From a far-off window, a violin played a sad song. With a hand pressed to her stomach, she rounded the house, moving fast across the shifting ground. She spotted a streetlight and headed for it.

CHAPTER 21

David's cell phone rang. In bed but not asleep, cat on his chest, he answered, hoping for but dreading news about John. It ended up being a direct call from a patrol officer who introduced himself as Ryan Freeman.

"We've got a bit of a situation here." The Freeman name didn't ring a bell, and the voice was young, hesitant. "Nine-one-one got a few calls about a naked woman wandering around town. Last report came from high school kids who spotted her in Laurel Grove Cemetery. I'm the responding officer."

"Did she kill somebody? Because I'm Homicide. I don't deal with meth heads."

"Well . . ." Freeman hesitated. "The reason I'm calling is 'cause I'm pretty sure this is something you'll want to keep from reporters, something you might not want on record. Because I'm pretty sure the woman in the cemetery is Detective Sandburg."

David dropped back against his pillow. Prank call, but who and why? "How'd you get this number?"

"This is no hoax." He rattled off his badge number.

David sat up, the abrupt movement causing Isobel to let out a protest and jump clear. A prank caller wouldn't have had the presence of mind to share a badge number.

"She's on the grave," the officer said. "*The* grave. The one where she was left as a baby. I'm from Savannah. My friends and I used to go there when we were in high school. Everybody knew that grave. And I know Detective Sandburg when I see her."

"Is she injured?" David asked, in high-alert mode now.

"Not that I could tell. I think she's just really high."

"Elise doesn't do drugs." David got out of bed. With the phone wedged between his shoulder and ear, he pulled on his jeans, released and caught the phone, and began moving for the door, grabbing a dress shirt from the back of a chair as he went. "Where are you?"

"I'm near the main entrance of Laurel Grove, north of Highway 204. I decided to park and walk in so I didn't scare her off."

"Be there in five minutes."

He made it in just under and located Freeman, who was standing near one of the pillars that marked the entry to the cemetery. Now David recognized him. Freeman was one of the department's newer hires. He didn't look much out of high school but was probably at least twenty-two.

David pulled up behind the patrol car, cut the engine, got out.

"I tried to engage her in conversation," Freeman said as they fell into step beside each other, "but she was unresponsive."

The only light source was the small Maglite the officer aimed at their feet as they walked the dirt path toward the grave site. It didn't take long to get there, probably because David was jogging, the young officer trying to keep up, weighted down by his forty-pound belt. Once they had a visual, that visual being the stone altar and a dark shape on top of it, the young officer trained the light on the ground, possibly out of respect for Elise's modesty. If it was indeed her. Too damn dark to tell.

Exasperated by the cop's prudish behavior, David grabbed the light and aimed it at the person lying on the altar stone like a human sacrifice, surrounded by unlit candles and the offerings people left behind.

It took only a moment to confirm that it really was a naked woman. And not much longer to confirm that the woman really *was* Elise. The light blinded her, and she flinched, raised an arm to her face, and turned away.

What. The. Hell?

David redirected the beam to the ground and passed the flashlight back to Freeman.

"Maybe it's some sort of ritual," the cop whispered.

"No," David said. That was the last thing Elise would be involved in.

"I always thought . . . always heard—"

David suddenly realized what was going on. "You're afraid of her."

"Who isn't?" No hesitation, no shame. "I know about her. And I know Jackson Sweet is her dad. She hangs around with Strata Luna." Shrug in his voice. "So yeah, I'm afraid of her."

David shook his head and approached the altar stone, the officer and flashlight trailing behind. How hard had Freeman tried to engage her? The situation would have been awkward as hell for anybody, especially a rookie.

David spoke calmly to Elise. When she didn't react, he picked up her wrist, felt her pulse. Her heart was beating fast. "Are you hurt?" he asked, unbuttoning his shirt. He repeated his question, louder, closer. This time he got a response.

"Hot." It seemed impossible, but that one simple syllable bordered on garbled. "I'm hot."

"I usually just crank up the AC when I'm hot, but okay."

The cop let out a snort, and David felt annoyed with himself. He hadn't been going for comic relief, but the wiseass in him couldn't shut up, not even now.

It took some coaxing, but he was able to cajole Elise off the altar stone. Once she was upright, he slipped his shirt on her and buttoned the buttons while she stood there, arms dangling. It was unnerving to see the normally volatile Elise so docile, and it made him feel better to think she'd probably kick his ass later.

The cop's shoulder radio squawked, and the dispatcher's voice reported a robbery nearby.

"I'll take it from here," David told him. "Thanks for calling me."

Once Freeman was gone, David pressed a palm to Elise's forehead. She felt warm, but not feverish. A high fever would have explained a lot. "Your hair is wet."

"Had to cool off my brain." Speech still slurred.

At his car, he tucked her into the passenger seat, closed the door, circled, and got behind the wheel. Under the dome light he noted that her eyes were glassy, her pupils huge.

"Did you take anything?" He made sure to speak clearly and directly. "Any drugs? Medication?"

Earlier on the phone he'd been adamant about Elise not using drugs, but now he wondered if the young cop had been right. At the hospital during John's surgery she'd been upset, more upset than he'd ever seen her. She'd cried. *Really* cried. He'd witnessed that kind of breakdown from her only one other time, and that had been Audrey's abduction.

If she'd taken something, then maybe she'd mixed that something with alcohol. Maybe what he was looking at was a bad reaction. "Did you take anything to help you sleep?" Prescription sleep aids were notorious for causing odd behavior the patient didn't even remember the next day.

If she could come up with a plausible explanation, then maybe he wouldn't have to take her to the hospital. Freeman was right. The fewer people who knew about this, the better.

She ignored him, or maybe she hadn't heard his question. Instead she hit him with one of her own. "I need to ask you something." She stared at him with curiosity combined with the sudden intensity of a sharpshooter.

"Ask away," he said.

She was visually examining his hair, his eyes, his mouth, and for a brief moment he wondered if he spotted some clarity of thought in her face. Maybe she was coming down. But then she hit him with her question.

"Who are you?"

Holy hell. He latched her seat belt, hit the door locks, and took off in the direction of the hospital.

CHAPTER 22

Less than twenty-four hours earlier David had mentioned renting a room in Candler because he was there so much. Now here he was again, this time waking up in a chair in Elise's room. His neck was stiff; the shirt he'd given Elise in the cemetery was wrinkled and back on his body.

He needed coffee and his beard itched.

Nearby Elise was lying in bed, covered by a print hospital gown, IV in her arm. They'd sedated her upon her arrival. She hadn't been out of control, but she'd been agitated and confused when David pulled up to the ER doors. Thankfully restraints hadn't been necessary, but just in case she got worse or woke up confused, David had slept in a hellishly uncomfortable chair, keeping one ear tuned for any sound of movement. At some point in the early-morning hours, she'd awakened briefly. And that time she recognized him.

"You've had an episode," he'd told her in response to her questions of how and why. Of course being Elise, she'd tried to get up and leave, only to fall back against the pillow.

Right now she was awake again, her pupils only slightly dilated. Tests had been run, but so far the doctors had nothing. Whatever was going on, she seemed on the mend.

David pushed himself out of his chair to perch on the edge of her bed. "You done with this?" He indicated the food tray someone had brought in at an ungodly hour. This wasn't boot camp. They shouldn't be waking patients at the buttcrack of dawn.

She nodded. He picked up a slice of toast and took a bite. "You up for questions?" The toast was cold and soggy. He finished it off and wished for coffee. "What about these eggs? You should eat these eggs."

She shook her head and looked away, unmistakably queasy. He covered the tray.

"I don't know much," she told him.

"Let's start with what you do know. Where did you go after you left headquarters?"

"I drove straight home. Fell asleep on the couch. And then Sweet came by."

"Sweet?"

"He didn't stay long. We talked a little; then he left. I don't remember anything else until waking up here."

Good and bad. Maybe she could be spared the embarrassment of last night. "You don't have a memory of being in Laurel Grove Cemetery?"

She concentrated, trying to dredge up something. "No."

"That's where you were found."

"The last thing I remember is Sweet leaving my place. He told me to lock the door, but I'm drawing a blank after that."

David and Officer Freeman were the only two people who knew the full story, the only people who knew the identity of the person lying bare-ass naked on a grave. He let out a sigh. This was good.

"Why are you looking at me like that?" she asked.

"Because I'm worried about you."

She put a hand to her head. "I feel hungover."

"Did you take anything last night?"

"You mean drugs?" She had enough energy to bristle.

"I'm not accusing you of Schedule 1 narcotic use. I'm talking about medication you might have reacted negatively to. I've had a few binges that resulted in my waking up in a puddle of my own piss, so I know things happen."

She looked at him in horror. Had he revealed too much?

"My God, David."

"What? I'm just sharing. And that was a long time ago."

"When you were a teenager?" she asked hopefully. "Or a two-year-old?"

He'd been trying to make a point. Embarrassing things happen when you're wasted. But no way was he going to tell her it was just a few years ago. Not now, when she was looking at him like that.

She gave his original question more thought. "I don't think I have anything like that in the house other than antidepressants I've never taken."

"How about drinking? Just drinking? Because after yesterday nobody would fault you. I have to confess to seriously fighting the urge myself when I got home."

"Maybe I had a stroke." She felt her face for signs of paralysis. "Or an aneurism. People my age have aneurisms."

"The tests they ran last night were negative for anything of that nature. We're waiting on bloodwork now."

"Care to take a guess?"

"I'd say you were drugged."

"Like roofied?"

He pulled out his phone and called Jackson Sweet. Somewhat of a surprise that he answered, but then he'd never dropped out of contact with David like he had Elise. At first David was evasive with his questions. "Just following up on some events from last night." When Jackson had no information to supply, David pressed him for more details, especially details about Sweet's visit to Elise's and what had transpired during that visit.

"I gave her something to eat."

Seemed harmless. "Elaborate."

"Nothing much. I suspected she hadn't eaten all day, so I cut up cheese and an apple."

"That it?"

"That's it."

David ended the call before Sweet could question him.

Elise stretched her hand toward the wheeled table just beyond her reach.

David pushed it closer, poured water from the pink plastic pitcher, and passed the cup to her. "Your dad says he gave you an apple and cheese. You didn't mention that."

She nodded, remembering now.

"Did you watch him handle the food?"

"I stayed in the living room while he was in the kitchen." She stared, and he could see an argument forming. "You suspect Sweet of drugging me?"

"It's fairly easy to inject fruit with drugs."

"As much as I'd like to think it was him, no, it wasn't Sweet."

"Three days ago I would have been thrilled to hear you say that."

"But not now."

"You were fine when he arrived. Not fine when he left. And the timeline. He didn't stick around. He gave you the food and got the hell out of there. I have to say, it looks suspicious."

She finished off the water. "It wasn't Sweet."

He refilled her cup, passed it back to her. "Where did the fruit come from?" he asked. "Where did you buy it?"

She paused, the cup halfway to her mouth. "I didn't. It was in a gift basket. From the mayor's office."

David called the mayor's office. A few redirects, followed by a brief conversation with the mayor's secretary.

"No one sent a basket," she said. "Not from this office, anyway."

"You sure?" David asked.

"Positive. I would have been the one to order it."

He ended the call and shared the information with Elise. "The delivery was from an unknown person."

"Candy from a stranger."

He raised his eyebrows in agreement.

She leaned deeper into the pillow. "I should have known the gift was a little too generous, considering the source." Her voice was weaker. She needed to rest.

David gave her a wry smile and slipped the half-finished water from her hand. "How about now? Have you started to remember anything else from last night?"

Despite her grogginess, she was still able to pin him with a hard gaze. "Why do you keep asking me that?"

"I'm just trying to put this together. The more information I have, the better."

Her eyes narrowed. "Did something happen?"

"No."

"You're lying."

"Nothing unusual."

Why didn't he just tell her? She'd catch him. She always caught him. "You were in the cemetery. Someone reported a woman high on meth wandering around. The cop on patrol called me. End of story."

"Okay."

"Okay."

Five minutes later David called Sweet back. "Meet me at Elise's house in fifteen minutes. I want you to walk me through the events of last night."

"I'm underground."

"This is important. Be there." He ended the call, then told Elise, "I'll be back later."

In the hallway near the elevator, he ran into Strata Luna.

When Strata Luna entered a building, the world took notice. You could feel the ripple of her presence as it hit one person after the other.

David always likened it to a sound wave, invisible, but you sensed it. The awe, the fear, the curiosity. She was larger than life, and the long black mourning dress that covered her from head to toe just added to the drama. Not for the first time, he wondered what she'd look like in a pair of jeans and a T-shirt. Would no one notice her, or would she still command attention? He was pretty sure the world would sit up, take notice, back away.

Her gaze swept past the mere mortals to land on David, one mortal she knew and recognized. "Jackson told me Elise was here."

David cocked his head, and they moved to the side of the corridor. Trying to ignore the carts, nurses in scrubs, and furtive, wide-eyed looks, David spoke in a low voice while filling her in on everything but the nudity. He could trust Strata Luna, but it was better to keep that information close.

"I'm not surprised by any of this." In fact, she seemed to have expected it. "It's a spell."

David had no patience for talk of spells right now. "This isn't the time."

"Someone left a spell on her doorstep the day you got back from Chicago. Did she tell you?"

"No." Damn Elise and her secrets. Of course the spell wasn't what concerned him. Someone lurking around her house? That did.

"A killing spell," Strata Luna said. "That's some dark and serious work. I told her to check the yard and foundation, look under the porch. She just laughed." She straightened, puffed out her chest. "She's lucky to be alive. I'm gonna make a purifying spell as soon as I get home. And speakin' of home, where's Elise going when she leaves here? She shouldn't be alone, and she shouldn't go back in that house until we know it's clean."

"I'm hoping the hospital will keep her a few days; then we can figure it out."

"I have room. A lot of room. And I've been in your apartment. Not big enough for you and that crazy cat of yours. But then, maybe you and Elise are together now . . ." Eyebrow raised.

"We're not together."

"That disappoints me. What kind of man are you? Want me to put together another love spell since you can't seem to make anything happen on your own?"

"I sure as hell don't want another love spell. The first one got me in too much trouble."

"Okay, but you two should be together."

He shook his head. "That's never going to happen, so let's not go there."

David was relieved by the appearance of Avery, who shot from the elevator, out of breath, frantic, most likely afraid he was losing someone else he cared about. David put him out of his misery. "She's going to be fine." Then he waited for a reaction or some follow-up comment on what had occurred last night. Avery seemed to know nothing. That was good. Freeman must have been keeping his mouth shut.

"I'm heading to get an update on John," Avery said. "Then I'll look in on Elise."

David gave the detective a pat on the shoulder and told Strata Luna to keep an eye on Elise while he was gone; then he left to meet Sweet.

***

He and Sweet arrived at Elise's house close to the same time. Sweet took in David's wrinkled clothes and unshaven jaw without comment. David noted Sweet wasn't looking so dapper himself. His jeans were dirty, and David doubted he'd been doing any gardening lately. Sweet was no longer living at Elise's place, but from the looks of his clothes it seemed he might not be living with Strata Luna either. When he said "underground," he must have meant it.

"Let's get inside," Sweet said. "I don't want anybody to spot me."

They circled the house to find the back door wide open. Inside, water was running in the sink. Sweet pulled a paper towel from the holder and turned the faucet off. "Do you know zombies, real-life zombies, not the fictional kind, are often created by the transdermal delivery of tetrodotoxin?"

"TTX? Yeah, had a little run-in with that a couple of years back."

"So you know it can be delivered in many ways. Ingestion, through the skin, and breathing the dust. And do you know the curse of Tutankhamen is thought to not be a curse at all, but the inhalation of poison deliberately left behind for any would-be tomb robbers?"

"Man, you and Elise sure are related."

"What I'm trying to say is, don't touch anything. I know you suspect food, but the drug, and I believe it will be found to be a drug or combination of drugs, might have been administered transdermally, which means it could have been left anywhere." He glanced around. "Door handles are a prime choice."

Hands at waist, David said, "Death will come on swift pinions to those who disturb the rest of the pharaoh."

Sweet glanced up in surprise.

"What?" David asked. "I know my history." Actually, he'd seen it in a documentary. "It was engraved above the door to the tomb."

They moved through the house, continuing to discuss the pharaoh's curse as they went. In the living room, Elise's gun and phone lay undisturbed near the couch. On the coffee table was a plate containing cheese and the remaining slices of an apple, now dark.

"So innocent looking," Sweet said.

David gave him a sharp glance to see if he was serious. "You're kidding, right?" He pointed. "It's an apple. A damn apple."

Sweet shrugged in disagreement. "Apples symbolize comfort. Home."

"Apples symbolize evil. Haven't you read any fairy tales?"

"If you were to plant an apple tree for your kids to climb, why would you plant it? Because it's evil? No, because it represents the promise of the life you want for your family."

"I'm not going to get into an argument with you about apples." Sweet was *just* like Elise. "We're both right." David pulled out his phone, called the department, and told the dispatcher to send a crime scene team to Elise's house. "We don't need sirens. And there's no body to process."

Upstairs they moved room to room. Like the rest of the house, it appeared undisturbed.

"So far you've talked about a scientific explanation for all this mojo stuff," David said. "And yet you were once known as a conjurer. I don't get it."

"I'll be the first to admit there are a lot of things that simply can't be explained by science, but I'm also not against milking a good thing. Scaring the crap out of people, especially when it comes to people who believe, can often bring about confessions. Who's to mess with that?"

"I have nothing against an opportunistic strategy." David headed for the stairs, thinking they'd seen enough. And he had more than one reason for asking Sweet to meet him at Elise's. "You going to tell me what's going on?"

It was hard for Sweet to part with anything, but once they were back downstairs he finally opened up, telling David about framing Remy, and about how he was sure the guy was back, and that he was after a sick kind of revenge.

"That's why I've gone into hiding. You probably think I'm doing it to protect myself, but that's not it."

"I get it. Can't have a show if nobody's watching."

"Thing you have to realize," Sweet said, "everybody's in danger. You, Elise, Strata Luna, John. John's in grave danger."

"Because he might be able to ID the perpetrator."

"Right."

"We've got eyes on him, but with extra guards also protecting the mayor, it's stretching us thin." David would pay from his own pocket if the department pulled John's guards due to funding. "Anybody else who might be in danger that you can think of?"

The older man gave it some thought, then shook his head. "I'll let you know if I come up with anybody."

Sweet left, and David waited for the crime scene team to arrive. When he told them what was going on, they ordered him out of the house and scurried to their van for hazmat suits.

CHAPTER 23

Savannah Carmelite Monastery

It wasn't unusual for days to pass without anybody seeing Loralie, the woman who lived in the cottage behind the monastery and took care of the flowers in exchange for room and board. But when the third day came and the flowers near the arched front doors were dying from lack of water, people began to wonder. And when a few of the sisters noticed an unpleasant odor coming from the backyard and the vicinity of the cottage where Loralie lived, young Sister Valentina was sent to check. When her knock went unanswered, she tested and opened the door.

A foul odor rolled over her. She gagged and pressed her wimple to her mouth and nose. After a brief hesitation, she forced herself to step inside. God didn't like cowards.

The one-bedroom cottage was dark, the shades pulled down tight, and it took Sister Valentina's eyes time to adjust after the brightness of the outdoors. As she waited, she became aware of a low hum. It was a sound that was both familiar and foreign, something she knew deep down she should recognize but had a hard time putting into context.

When the room finally lightened enough for her to make out the furniture and lamps, she froze. The sound was flies and bees. So many that the bloated face of the body on the floor seemed to move.

She forgot her vow of silence and screamed, loud and long. Then she turned and ran from the cottage, continuing to scream as she hurried to the big house, her black shoes flying across the grass, her skirt billowing behind her. A sister near the back door dropped a stack of books and stopped Sister Valentina, grasping her by both arms.

"It's horrible!" the young sister sobbed, her cry the loudest sound the monastery had heard in over one hundred years. "Loralie is dead!"

CHAPTER 24

Sure you're okay?" Avery asked.

For the second time in less than twenty-four hours Elise found herself trying to reassure Avery. "I'm fine."

"What the hell happened?" His eyes were bloodshot, his face unshaven, clothes rumpled. A lot of that going around.

An hour or so earlier David had left the hospital to inspect Elise's house, and Strata Luna was long gone, leaving in a swirl of black skirts as she announced she was going home to concoct a spell and prepare a room for Elise.

Elise hadn't agreed to either.

Avery had shown up in her room after checking upstairs on John Casper. No change. Now the detective was anxiously pacing and letting out heavy sighs. She was about to tell him he should leave when his phone rang.

He answered, moving away from her bed to hover near the door. Moments later he hung up and announced he was leaving. "Possible homicide at the Carmelite Monastery."

She pulled in a sharp breath. *Carmelite Monastery.*

Avery had delivered the news in a perfunctory manner. He didn't realize her connection to the religious haven, and why should he? She must have reacted in some way, because he went on to explain something that needed no explanation. "You know, the place out on Coffee Bluff."

"I've been there." She peeled off the IV tape, then slipped the needle from the back of her hand, pressing the entry site with her fingers to stop the bleeding. "Shut off that IV." She kicked the covers, got out of bed. With no free hand to hold her gown closed, she walked to the closet in the corner of the room. It was empty. "Where are my clothes? My belongings? There's nothing here. No phone, no bag, nothing."

She looked over her shoulder. Avery stood with his back to her, like an awkward child. She released the pressure on her hand so she could use it to clutch the back of her gown closed.

"Nurse?" Head out the door, Elise looked down the hallway. A middle-aged nurse paused in her rapid walk to somewhere else.

"Where are my clothes?"

"They should be in your room. We always give patients a labeled bag when they check in."

"There's nothing here."

"I'll look into it." She continued down the hall. She wouldn't be back soon. Elise was sure of that.

Avery attempted to slip from the room.

"Wait," Elise said. "I'm coming with you."

"You haven't been released." He glanced down. "And you're barefoot."

She grabbed him by the arm. "There's a gift shop downstairs where they sell clothing."

"Jesus, how does Gould deal with this?"

"He does what I say."

"I find that hard to believe."

Downstairs she grabbed a pair of black yoga pants and slipped them on, then tied the hem of her gown to one side so it draped across her hips instead of falling to her knees. A pair of black flip-flops completed the getup. At the counter she presented the bar code tags for scanning and told Avery to pay.

Then they were heading for the possible homicide.

The Carmelite Monastery was located several miles from the hospital, on a dirt road that ran from Back Street to Forest River. It was a place of seclusion, where the nuns had very little contact with the outside world. Some had even taken a vow of silence.

At the end of a flat dirt road flanked by trees and shrubs stood a two-story brick colonial Elise remembered from her previous visits. The scene wasn't as serene this time. Police cars were parked at odd angles, and men and women in uniform moved back and forth, each with their own task in mind. The county coroner's van was there, possibly driven by Hollis Blake, the ME who'd been shipped down from Atlanta to temporarily or not so temporarily take John Casper's place. Elise spotted David's black Honda.

With the vehicle still rolling, she unfastened her seat belt and grasped the door handle, jumping out as soon as the car stopped. Avery quickly followed.

She knew the way and took a path around the building to the back. The sun beat down on top of her head, and she caught a whiff of the purple petunias languishing in a cement urn.

The house was tiny. "Darling," a word Elise wouldn't use aloud, seemed to apply to just this kind of abode. Small cabin with a red door, white windowpanes, green planters that had been overflowing with lush red petunias last time Elise had visited. Today the containers held withered brown leaves and spindly sticks.

It was Loralie's job to care for the flowers.

Elise had been to the cabin only twice. On both visits it had been clear she wasn't welcome. But over the past couple of years she'd sent the occasional gift, never knowing if it had reached Loralie, or if she'd enjoyed it or thrown it away, unopened. Elise wasn't sure why she tried.

In truth, she doubted she had the capacity it would have taken to forgive or have even a slight relationship with her mother.

"What's she doing here?" David directed his question at Avery, ignoring Elise, seeming unsurprised to see her standing there, straight from her hospital bed. Even more unsurprised that she still wore the cotton gown.

He must have come directly from her house, because he was dressed in the same rumpled shirt, had bedhead, and still needed to shave. On his hands were black latex crime scene gloves.

"This wasn't my idea," Avery said. "I tried to stop her."

Elise pushed past Avery, intent on getting inside.

David took a wide stance and blocked the door with one arm. "You aren't going in."

"Yes, I am."

"Elise." He was calm, direct. "Stop and listen to me. You don't want to go in there." His voice dropped. "It's your mother. I'm sorry, but she's dead."

"I know."

"Think about how hot it's been lately."

They stared at each other. "It's okay," she said. "Don't try to shield me from this."

"It will do no good for you to see her."

"It might."

"You'll never be able to forget it. I know. I've been there."

"This is different. She's not a loved one."

"She's your mother."

"She gave birth to me. That's a totally different thing."

He considered her for a long minute, then dropped his arm and stepped aside.

It must have already gotten around that the body on the floor was Elise's birth mother, the woman responsible for leaving her on a grave all those years ago. As soon as the crime scene techs spotted her, they silently backed away, someone pausing long enough to shove a pair of latex gloves in her hand.

Elise heard David say something about leaving her alone. Avery's phone rang, and he answered it, moving away from the tiny house as he talked. Footsteps and voices faded, and then everyone was gone, the only sound in the room the buzzing of hundreds of blowflies, along with a few bees.

Odd the way bees, a pollen insect, were drawn to death. What was it about the horrible scent that confused them? Made them think it was something sweet, something good?

Elise snapped on the gloves.

The cottage was hot, unbearable really. Elise did a mental calculation, factoring in the highs of the past few days, knowing a small room in southern Georgia could reach temperatures of 120 during the day. The body was so severely bloated that an ID would have been hard if not for the tangle of long gray hair. The lips and eyelids were turned almost inside out, legs and arms double in size. Most of the crime scene team had been wearing hazmat suits. Understandable. It was going to be a challenge to move and transport the body without gas escaping. A small explosion could occur, splattering guts on anyone within a few feet or even yards.

Even though the body was grossly deformed, there was no way to miss the ligature marks around the throat, the pool of dried blood under the head.

Murder.

Two days gone, she'd guess. Which meant it had happened before the incident at the morgue. And if the same people were behind it, it meant they—*or he*—had been very busy.

This was a message. Clearer than the others, since Loralie was directly connected to both Elise and Sweet. And who was next? That was the big question. Because at this rapid rate there had to be a next coming very soon.

Minutes earlier, in Avery's car, Elise had been thinking about how she'd never be able to forgive her mother, alive or dead. But looking at her now, knowing what a harsh life she'd led . . . Elise's throat tightened.

She was too hard on people. She was known as the cop who treated criminals with compassion, but where was her compassion when it had come to Loralie? And even to her father?

She turned from the body and moved slowly around the room, looking for anything that might give up evidence. Just as she remembered, the space was sparse and fittingly monastic. The only real sign of life was the overflowing ashtrays—evidence of Loralie's chain-smoking.

Nothing seemed out of place. There was no sign of struggle, so at least that was something. Loralie had been taken by surprise. Death had come quickly. She hadn't suffered long.

Elise looked through kitchen cupboards, pausing when she came upon a stash of unopened cigarette cartons and boxes of pralines. It took her a moment to realize the cigarettes and candy were the gifts she'd sent.

Why hadn't Loralie smoked or eaten them?

Elise heard footsteps and looked over her shoulder to see David approaching. "Avery had to leave, and the crew needs to get back in here."

She closed the cupboard door. "She didn't smoke the cigarettes I sent her. Or eat the candy. It's all here. I wonder why."

"Saving the reminders of you."

She smiled and shook her head. "I seriously doubt that. Your lack of cynicism is frightening sometimes."

"Oh, I can be cynical."

"I should have sent a book," Elise said. "Or something that wasn't for consumption. But she said she wanted cigarettes and pralines."

The crime scene team was filing back inside. David nodded toward the door. "Let's go."

Outside they both snapped off their gloves and tossed them in a nearby biohazard bin. The day was already hot, and wordlessly they moved to a small patch of shade, away from the police and forensic team, upwind from the cottage. From somewhere that couldn't be seen, Elise caught a whiff of damp marsh. It almost covered up the stench of death.

She looked toward the brick colonial, at the cluster of nuns standing near the back door. Loralie had lived there over twenty years. The nuns had protected her, given her a place to hide from the world. But the world had come to them.

"If this is Remy," David said, "and I think it is, then this *is* revenge. He's coming after people connected to Sweet. Your father listed the people to warn, but Loralie wasn't one of them. Not that it would have helped. She's been dead awhile."

"I'm guessing two days."

He nodded.

Elise crossed her arms, hugging her stomach, feeling uneasy. "How far is Remy's reach?" She was thinking about people beyond Savannah. She was thinking about Audrey, who was possibly the person Sweet cared for most in the world, Strata Luna being the second.

"Right now Savannah seems to be his focus. But I think we should contact friends and loved ones as far away as, yes, Seattle. Tell Audrey and Thomas to keep their eyes and ears open. If nothing else, I wouldn't put it past him to try to at least contact Audrey with a call or e-mail, just to shake her up. And shake us up even more."

David's phone rang, and he did a screen check. "Avery." He answered, listened, told him he was on his way. Once he disconnected, he said, "Our office is ready. But that's not the real news. The composite artist has come up with an image of an aged Remy, and Avery is calling a press conference so we can get the drawing into circulation as quickly as possible. He wants me there."

Without further discussion, they circled the big house and moved in the direction of his car. "I'll drop you by Strata Luna's on the way."

"I'm coming downtown too."

"Sit this one out. Go to Strata Luna's. Get some rest. Come back tomorrow."

"There's no way I'm going to be able to lie around at Strata Luna's while she plies me with food and mojos. You know that."

They got in the car. David lowered the windows, turned the ignition key, and guided the vehicle across grass and past milling people until they were riding over the dirt road that would eventually turn to blacktop and return them to town. "Okay. I give up," David said. "Let's grab some food and swing by my place. You can chill with Isobel while I take a shower and get into some clean clothes."

They stopped at Parker's Market on Drayton Street. Five minutes later they were in David's apartment. He put the carryout on the counter. "Make yourself at home. I'm heading for the shower. Eat without me. I'll either eat on the way or once we get to headquarters."

The thought of food made her stomach churn, but she knew she needed to eat something. She sat down on the couch. Isobel immediately appeared, circling Elise's ankles. Instead of opening the paper bag, Elise leaned back and closed her eyes. She was so exhausted she could hardly process the past hour, let alone the past twenty-four. Just the idea of trying to pull food out of the bag, unwrap a sandwich, and bring it to her mouth, *chew*, seemed impossible.

"Sure you don't want to stay here?"

Elise woke with a jolt.

David stood in the living room, dressed in clean clothes, hair damp, face freshly shaved. He belted his gun and reached for his jacket. "It's not as safe as Strata Luna's, but it's the next best thing."

At some point Isobel had gotten on her lap. Elise lifted her aside and stood up, careful not to let David see how weak she was feeling. "I'm coming."

"You didn't eat?"

"Fell asleep."

"I noticed."

He grabbed the bag of uneaten carryout and gave a quick pet to Isobel, and they were out the door, heading for Savannah PD. On the way, David's phone buzzed. He read the message aloud: Avery, reminding him that the meeting would be starting in an hour.

At the police station David parked in his old spot. They took the wide sidewalk to the front door, said hello to the woman at the desk, and passed through the metal detector. Elise had nothing to leave in the container or gather on the other side. David grabbed his belongings, and they shot straight for the elevators before anybody could catch their eye.

Stepping into their old office on the third floor was equal parts sad and soothing. "Never expected to see this place again." Elise looked out the window at Colonial Park Cemetery.

"Which desk do you think Lamont used?"

"I'll bet mine," Elise said. "It has a view."

"I think he would have found more satisfaction using my desk, even if it faces a brick wall."

"Maybe he alternated."

She needed to find some proper clothes before the press conference. Maybe she could borrow a jacket from someone, or dash around the corner to one of the nearby shops. "It makes me uncomfortable to even talk about him," Elise said. "Because there's nothing nice to say."

David plopped down in his old chair, testing the bounce, grabbed the bag of food, and began unpacking it. "Just because a guy's dead doesn't mean he wasn't an asshole."

CHAPTER 25

The press conference was supposed to be brief, so it was held without any fanfare in a police-department room used for such things. Low ceiling, bright lights, podium, Georgia state flag. Flanked by Elise and Avery, David looked out at the audience settling into metal folding chairs. Most wore press and media passes around their necks or clipped to pockets. David glanced at Elise's pale face and once again thought she should be in his apartment or at Strata Luna's. He'd thought so before Loralie's murder, but now . . .

From lost-and-found she'd dug up a floral top with a round collar, along with a yellow cardigan. If their current circumstances weren't so dark and dire, he would have joked that she looked like she was dressed for a sixties sitcom.

Avery started the conference before everybody was seated. That's how anxious he was to get it over with. He dove in and held up a copy of the composite drawing. Said a few sentences, adding, "You'll be able to download it from our website." Gave them the website. "We'll be circulating it nationally too, with a strong focus on Florida."

They'd all three looked over the sketch from a reputable artist. And they'd all discussed the unfortunate generic quality of the piece and talked about how it was going to generate false leads. White dude in his early sixties, average weight, salt-and-pepper hair.

Hands in the crowd went up, some held high, like in grade school, others demonstrating a polite half raise. David preferred the half. It wasn't aggressive, and it was a lot more likely to get a go-ahead from him.

True to her earlier performance, without waiting to be chosen, Lucille shot to her feet. Cradling a clipboard and iPhone, she asked if they'd yet assigned anyone to the chief-of-police position, vacated over a month ago.

"That's not a position we assign from within," Avery told her. "The mayor's office is working on it."

He'd barely finished when she hit him with something else, her questions taking on the tone of an interrogation. David's feelings about Lucille were quickly mimicking Elise's. "What about the body found at the monastery?" Lucille asked. "Any connection to the Novak homicide or the incident at the morgue?"

Avery tried to hold his ground. David had to give him points for that. "This conference is about the composite drawing, nothing else," Avery said.

But the questions kept coming. About John Casper and Mara, about the yet-to-be-disclosed identity of the monastery homicide victim.

David took pity and jumped in. "As Detective Avery said, this meeting is for the sole purpose of sharing the composite sketch of what the man named Frank Remy might look like today," he said. "He's our focus right now, and with your help we're hoping we can wrap this up fairly quickly."

Lucille actually appeared to pout a little before plopping down heavily.

Another cluster of hands. More questions. "Who's he targeting? Who's in danger?"

Elise finally spoke. "At the moment we don't think the general public is at risk, but his focus could always change. There's no way to sugarcoat this. He's killed children, so parents need to be especially cautious."

Avery gripped the podium and shifted his weight. "That will be all for now. Thanks for coming." That was one way to shut down a conference. Blunt, with no transition.

Disregarding Avery's statement—or reacting to it—Lucille stood again. "I want to discuss what happened to Detective Sandburg last night," she said. "I'm talking about the cemetery incident."

David tensed at the word "cemetery."

"Is it wise for her to be here today?" Lucille asked. "To have someone who's obviously mentally unbalanced working such a high-profile and serious case?"

A collective gasp. Heads turned.

Avery frowned. "I don't know what you're talking about."

"Really?" She was looking at her boyfriend with hostile eyes. Nope, David didn't like her. Not at all. He leaned in, speaking into the mics. "Detective Avery is done fielding questions."

"I think you're trying to cover something up," Lucille said. "But you didn't take into account the power of social media."

"Back off." Those surprising words came from Avery. "This conference is over. You have our contact information. Keep an eye on our website." He pushed mics aside with an abrupt and frustrated movement. David didn't know if Avery was mad at his girlfriend or outraged for Elise.

Lucille—God, what tenacity the woman had—stepped closer to the podium and began jabbing her finger around, pointing at Avery, then Elise, then at the phone still resting on top of her clipboard. "I'm talking about YouTube."

She planted her feet on the floor and fixed her gaze on poor Avery, who had a look of bafflement on his sweating face. "I'm talking about the video that was posted an hour ago, featuring none other than the acclaimed Detective Sandburg."

David wanted to be somewhere else, anywhere else.

"Who, I happen to know, you have a crush on," Lucille told Avery. "Which is why I'm guessing she's still here rather than being committed."

Smartphones were whipped out. Heads dipped. Fingers poked at screens as every reporter in the room searched YouTube to find out what the hell Lucille was talking about.

"Better look fast," she told them. "It'll be pulled due to nudity."

David touched Elise's arm. "Let's get out of here." He steered her toward the door. She took a few stumbling steps, then slammed on the brakes.

Avery was checking his phone along with everyone else. David knew the detective hit pay dirt when his mouth dropped open.

Elise twisted away from David, strode to Avery, and put out her hand for his phone, all the while cameras snapping. "Let me see."

Avery pivoted away, his back to her. She reached around and managed to grab the phone, tilting the device to landscape mode in order to view it in all its glory while David watched from over her shoulder.

The video was reminiscent of the day the mayor had flattened her with a finely aimed punch. That had gone viral too. But this was worse. Much worse.

In silence she watched the whole thing. All two minutes of it. When she was done, she shoved the phone back at Avery, turned, and launched herself at David. Now she was the one doing the pushing. Moments later they stood in the hallway, alone except for a camera high on the wall.

Her face had been pale earlier, but now her cheeks were bright red. "So this is why you were asking if I remembered anything. Why didn't you tell me? How did you think I wouldn't find out?"

"I like your shirt. It's . . . uh, homey."

"Oh Jesus."

"Okay, okay." His voice held a pleading tone he wasn't at all proud of. "You weren't supposed to know. Nobody was supposed to know. I had no idea there was a video."

"I can't believe you kept it from me."

"I was trying to protect you."

"That's not protecting me! That's withholding information. That's a lie of omission."

"If it makes you feel any better, the video is dark. You can hardly make anything out and can't really even tell it's you. I thought it would be better if you didn't know. Do we always have to fight?"

"Yes, we do!"

Behind them, reporters filed from the room, everyone discussing the video. One guy advised a colleague to grab it using a special app "before it's removed."

That thing was never going away.

David's phone rang. Relieved to have an escape, any escape, he answered, listened, ended the call, and scrolled through recent text messages to stop on the one referenced in the phone call. "I think you'll find this interesting," he told Elise. "Preliminary results of your blood test." He turned the screen so she could read it. "Tetrodotoxin and something else they haven't yet identified. Good news, right?"

"How's that good news?"

"Avery's girlfriend—or maybe ex-girlfriend now—is going to try to discredit you and get you pulled from Homicide. This is all we need to prove you aren't dealing with a mental issue." And the tetrodotoxin . . . Sweet had been on the right track. David needed to call and tell him about Loralie, but he had something else to take care of first.

CHAPTER 26

David tracked down and found the cop from the cemetery in the break room. Without speaking, he strode across the room. In front of everybody, he grabbed Officer Freeman by the shirt and shoved him against the nearest wall, aware of chairs scraping behind him, aware of Freeman's bulletproof vest beneath his shirt, aware of the surprise on the young officer's face.

"Did you post that video?" David demanded.

The cop made no attempt to fight back. "I had nothing to do with it," Freeman said. "Nothing. I wouldn't do anything like that. It must have been the kid who made the 911 call. I'm going to look into it."

"Damage is already done." David released him. "Sorry for jumping to conclusions."

"It's okay, man. I understand getting mad. Your partner and all. We tried."

David left the room while officers on either side fell away. He returned to the office to find Elise gone. He started to send her a text, then remembered she didn't have her phone. It was at her house, next to the couch, or possibly collected as evidence. In any case, if she was avoiding him, he knew it was best to let her cool off.

He went online, got the contact number for YouTube, and called the company. A brief intro and he was passed to someone in charge. Five minutes later the video was gone.

For now.

Sweet picked up when David called, but somehow he'd already heard the news. His voice was emotionless as he asked how Elise was handling the death of her birth mother and the cemetery video.

"I'm on her shit list right now," David said.

"Join the club."

"I've got another call. Gotta go." They disconnected, and David checked his screen. Odd. It was his mother. Maybe she'd been following the news. Hell, she might have seen the YouTube video. He answered.

She didn't mention the video or Elise, and she didn't mention what had happened at the morgue. "I'm at the airport," she told him in a cheerful voice. "Can you get away long enough to pick me up and have lunch?"

He drew a blank. "Airport?"

"The Savannah / Hilton Head International Airport, silly." Her voice lost some of its cheerfulness, and he tried to recall if she'd told him she was coming. Had they made plans? Had he forgotten?

"I'll take a cab if you can't pick me up."

"No." He needed to step away from Elise and the department anyway. Even an hour would help. "I'll be there in fifteen minutes."

"Same car?"

"Yep."

He picked her up, and even though he didn't have time, he took her to the Crab Shack near Tybee Island, and they ate outside. Halfway through the meal he pulled off his tie and rolled up his sleeves. A fan blasted air at them and he gulped down ice tea, but it wasn't enough to keep him from sweating through the back of his shirt.

Throughout the meal his mother acted as if she'd been expected, and he was afraid to ask, because he didn't want her to know he'd forgotten. But she finally admitted she'd wanted to surprise him.

He couldn't decide between being pissed or relieved.

People always wanted to see the Atlantic when they visited, so when they were done eating David drove to the beach, where they got out of the air-conditioned car and walked to the ocean, stopping in the area where waves had packed the sand cool and firm. No need to mention that this had been a crime scene a few months ago.

They stood in silence and watched a cargo ship in the far distance, David with his hands in the front pockets of his pants, his mother dressed in clothes from the foreign land of Ohio. Dark knit slacks and one of those loose, draped tops that seemed to be so popular among women over fifty. Her hair, which at the moment was whipping about her head, was still a medium brown, but she'd been dyeing it for years, so it was hard to say what her color would really be today.

"How do you stand the heat?" she asked. The wind blowing off the water plastered their clothes to them, the strong breeze not quite enough to make the ninety-eight degrees tolerable.

"I kinda like the way it makes my legs feel heavy and my brain feel sluggish. Like a natural sedative."

She didn't respond, and he glanced over to find her staring at him without a flicker of appreciation on her face. He obviously hadn't gotten his sense of humor from her.

He shrugged. "Once the Ohio gets out of your blood, you get used to it."

"I don't think I could ever get used to it. I wouldn't *want* to get used to it."

David considered himself a patient man. Only a few people in his life had caused him to take steps he should never have taken and do things he should never have done. But his mother . . . She pushed buttons only a mother could push. He loved her, but good God. And he was glad to see her, but what worried him was the agenda behind her surprise visit, which she still hadn't gotten around to sharing.

He'd mentally reviewed a list of possibilities, starting with a serious illness she wanted to reveal in person and ending with a plan to revamp his life. He suspected the last one but feared the first.

He bent down and picked up a small pink shell, brushed it off, and handed it to her. "Everything okay?"

"Yes, and no. I'm worried about you."

"You could have called to ask how I'm doing. And you could have let me know you were coming. Not that I'm not glad to see you."

"I was afraid if you knew I was coming . . ." Her words trailed off.

"I'd have a chance to sober up and hide the drugs?"

"David."

"Come on, admit it."

She shrugged—a sign of admission. "This way I'll know for sure that you're okay. That you haven't just hidden the empty bottles and told your prostitutes and pimp friends to stay away for a few days." In answer to his expression, she added, "Yes, I knew about that. I've been around people with drinking and pill problems. I can read the signs."

"I'm clean. I've been clean for a while now. Look at me." He spread his arms wide. "Picture of health."

"You look tired."

"I haven't gotten a lot of sleep lately."

"I know it's unfair of me to say I wish you were in another line of work, but I do. And ever since Christian—" The sudden change in his expression caused her to stop abruptly and downgrade her choice of words. "Well, I worry all the time." Then the blunt honesty came. He didn't like her blunt honesty. "I feel like I'm losing you. I lost Christian, and now I'm losing you."

He had to admit he'd distanced himself from her after Christian's death. He'd been so messed up. He could fool a lot of people, most people, but he couldn't fool his mother, so he'd pulled away. "You aren't losing me."

"Murders in our city have increased twenty percent over the past five years," she told him. "The mayor and his team have decided to hire someone seasoned to run the homicide department. And the chief of police contacted me to ask if you were available. This was before the mayor was shot. They'd heard you'd been fired. You're number one on their list, David. And you wouldn't be in the field or on the street. You wouldn't even have to carry a gun if you didn't want to."

His mother, who'd been a stay-at-home mom years ago, was the mayor's secretary and assistant . . . and had been more than that at one time. She didn't know he knew, but he was a detective, for Chrissake. And he'd experienced adultery firsthand. Not as the one who dealt it, but as the victim. David had never cheated on his wife, never even thought about it, and he'd never cheated on a girlfriend. That kind of thing wasn't in him. He saw it as a character weakness, and it bothered him that his mother had been involved in such behavior.

Sometimes he found himself wanting her to explain it to him, the reasoning and self-deception that went along with people who had affairs or even short flings. He wanted to know. But most of the time he just tried not to think about it. Now, when she was telling him the mayor wanted to give him a job, he couldn't help but wonder if the two of them were still a thing.

"You want me to take a desk job," David said.

"A *safe* job. Come back with me. Talk to the mayor and chief of police. Just talk to them."

"It would be a waste of all our time. I'm not leaving Savannah."

"Why not? What do you have here? You left Ohio because you were in pain, because you needed to get far away from everything that had happened there, all the reminders. I understand that. But you're better now. Savannah has been good for you, up to a point, but I think it's time to think about leaving. You aren't appreciated here. You don't belong here, in this strange place. You were fired, for Pete's sake. Why stay? And think about being safe. A safe job. Don't you want a safe job?"

"Please drop this."

"Is it because of Elise? Are you two finally a couple?"

"No."

"But you like her. You've liked her for a long time."

"Yes."

"Don't wait too long. Don't waste your life here waiting for her. You're still young. You could remarry. You could have more children."

"I don't want any other children." His voice cracked a little.

"It's cruel of her to lead you on." Her voice rose. "You could have anybody. *Anybody.*"

"She's not leading me on."

"I don't know what else you'd call it. I don't think she's good for you, David. I really don't. She and the city of Savannah and that Strata Luna person have cast a spell over you. Not that I believe in that nonsense, but you know what I mean. Elise attracts bad things, dangerous things. That's probably why you find her so fascinating, but I'm afraid she's going to get you killed."

"Elise saved my life." He wouldn't explain that she'd saved it in more ways than one.

"A life she put in danger to begin with."

"Oh my God." He put a hand to his head and turned away, then back again. "I can't have this conversation with you."

Then she hit him with the big stuff. Oh, she was smart. She knew how to get to him. "If you came home, you'd be closer to Christian."

He'd been doing pretty well until that point. But her words hit him like a punch in the gut. She was talking about Christian's grave, talking about the flowers he never left there and the visits he never made. To help alleviate the guilt he felt over his avoidance, he'd always reassured himself that Christian had his grandmother, had her.

And the child was dead. The dead knew nothing. Dead was dead. And yet he felt ashamed. He was a horrible father.

"He doesn't know that I don't visit his grave."

"No, of course not." She pulled in a deep, stabilizing breath and straightened her shoulders. "It never stops hurting, does it?" Her question was delivered with pain and fear.

He knew that fear. That fear had been the driving force behind his descent into drug abuse as he'd attempted to drive away the acute and unrelenting pain of absence and loss. He'd seen the same fear in the faces of victims' parents. He knew that fear inside and out.

"I don't think so," he said.

Above their heads seabirds swooped and called and dropped to the sand, heavy and straight. The sound always reminded him of the bird cries in a song he couldn't fully recall. "Pretty sure it never stops."

It wasn't something he told people when they were faced with the loss of a loved one. Because it wasn't what they needed to hear at the time. They had to have hope and something to reach for; otherwise life would be too cruel and brutal to face. And damn it. This . . . *this* was why he didn't go out of his way to retain a stronger relationship with his mother. She brought the pain with her. And she brought him to the surface, and he didn't like it there. He'd fought long and hard to stay fathoms deep. And he'd been doing it, drug-free and mostly alcohol-free.

She was right. She was losing him. She'd started losing him the day Christian died and David blocked out everybody. The breach had widened the day he found out about her affair. Their only common ground was his dead son. How screwed up was that?

"It feels so foreign here." She was looking to the horizon, and her clothes were billowing, and with a start he realized she was getting older but also getting more beautiful. "Like another country," she said. "Does it still feel that way to you?"

"I wanted different. Needed it. As far as foreign . . . I think it will always feel foreign to me, but at the same time it feels like home." But would it feel like home if Elise didn't live there? He had to be honest with himself. Probably not. No, definitely not. Without her, he would still feel untethered and deeply wounded.

"It's so hot. Too hot to breathe. And the beach . . . Why do people like the beach?" she asked. "It's nice, but once I look at it a minute or two, I've seen enough."

Should he try to explain the draw of the ocean? How it was hypnotic and soothing and scary and powerful? How it was like staring at the majesty and wonder of stars, only the ocean was something you could actually touch? And underneath that water . . . There was no telling what was underneath that water. Marvels and mountains. "Being near a body of water has been scientifically proven to reduce stress." He didn't mention that she was compounding his stress at this very moment.

"Think about the job offer," she said. "I'll be in town for a couple of days. I'm staying at a darling place on one of the squares. Better yet, come back with me to Ohio. Just talk to the mayor. That's all I'm asking. And wouldn't it be nice to come home for a few days? You can visit Christian."

He hadn't thought about his favorite prescription cocktail, washed down with vodka, in a long time. But now, listening to his mother, he ran a tongue across his lips and imagined digging into his stash when he got back to his apartment. Just a fantasy, because he refused to allow her to send him over the edge.

His phone rang.

Thank God.

But his heart sank when he saw it was Elise. He answered.

"I would have sent a text, but I don't have my phone. I don't know where you are or what you're doing, but I'm leaving the office. I'll be back in an hour." She didn't even wait for a reply before disconnecting.

Still mad.

"I gotta get back to work," he told his mother.

"Elise?"

"Yeah."

Her eyebrows lifted, but for once she didn't say what she was thinking. She didn't have to. And no matter how much she was annoying him right now, he had to admit that she'd made some valid points about his relationship with Elise.

In the back of his mind he'd always imagined himself eventually "with" Elise. Maybe not married. Marriage didn't matter to him, but living together, sleeping together, sharing a life. Was he out of his mind? Delusional? Was he clinging to the idea because Elise had been the first thing he'd seen when he'd come out of his self-medicated fog? But if a real relationship was never going to happen . . . What if things didn't change? What if everything was just the same five years from now?

He didn't want that. All along he'd had this idea that if he waited long enough things *would* change. And maybe that was because all his life he'd been able to have any woman he wanted. And that set up the next question. Did he want Elise only because he might never be able to have her?

No.

That wasn't it.

He loved her. Love. That really wasn't the right word. She was his best friend, the person he thought of most of the damn time. Like now. And now. And now.

"This isn't your world, sweetheart," his mother said. "And Elise isn't your girlfriend or wife."

They strolled toward the boardwalk, their pace slow in the loose sand. He took her arm and helped her over a small dune and up the wooden stairs.

Minutes later they were in his car heading back to Savannah on the Islands Expressway. He thought about the case. Thought about how everybody close to him and Elise was in danger, and he made a decision. He drove straight through downtown and took Interstate 16 west toward Garden City.

"Where are we going? This isn't the way to the bed-and-breakfast." His mother looked at her watch. "I can check in now."

"I'm doing something you aren't going to like, but just remember it's because I love you."

She eyed the highway signs. "Is this the way to the airport?"

"Yes."

"What's going on, David?"

"I'm putting you on the next flight back to Ohio."

"Are you insane? And I don't have a ticket."

"We'll get you one. And if we can't get one to Ohio, we'll get you one heading anywhere but Savannah."

"I'm not boarding a plane. Not now. Not today. And I'm certainly not getting on some random plane going who knows where."

"Be adventurous."

"I like to plan. Why are you doing this? I came to see you. Do you hate me so much?"

Traffic was heavy. As he drove she kept up with her questions, hurt in her voice. He finally exited the interstate and stopped at a red light. Arm on the steering wheel, he turned to look at her. "Mom, I love you. Never doubt that. And that's why you have to leave."

"This has something to do with your job, doesn't it?"

"Yes."

"Those murders. Of children. The fire at the morgue and the death of that young woman."

"Yes."

"Oh my God." Hand to throat. "Do you think I might be in danger?"

"Yes."

The light turned. He accelerated.

"Leave with me. If I'm in danger, then you're in more danger."

He let out a sound of marvel at the wildness of her idea. "I can't leave."

"Just come. Like you said. Be adventurous."

"That would be an adventure for you, but it would be running away for me."

"So *run*. I'd rather have a live coward for a son than a dead hero."

"I can't leave. You know that."

"Because of her."

"Not just because of her. We'll have this wrapped up soon, and then you can come and visit. Stay a week. Stay two weeks. And I'll think about what you said. It makes sense. I know it does. You're right about Elise, about my hopes and my pathetic hanging on."

"I'm sorry." She squeezed his arm. "There's nothing more painful than loving someone who doesn't love you back."

"You talking about Dad?" If so, that was surprising news. His father had always seemed devoted.

"I've been in love more than once in my life." He heard the smile in her voice. "So, does this mean you'll think about coming home?"

Home. Was it home? He'd come to Savannah to run away. Maybe it was time to face life, face reality, no matter how painful or bleak.

He pulled the car into the parking ramp. He'd go inside. Buy her a ticket. Stay until she actually boarded. "I will."

CHAPTER 27

From her desk at the Savannah PD, Elise called a cab. Then, in order to avoid eye contact with coworkers, she took the emergency stairs to exit the building. The tetrodotoxin and whatever else had been in her system seemed to have worn off. She was understandably tired, and she had a headache that was on its way out thanks to ibuprofen. All things considered, she didn't feel too bad. Not physically.

There were three things she still needed to mentally deal with. Getting drugged in her own home, the cemetery incident, and her mother's death. Four things if she counted David's deception. She wanted to go home and crawl into bed. Instead she was heading there to try to talk the crime scene crew into releasing some of her belongings.

"This the place?" the cab driver asked as he pulled up in front of her house. From her viewpoint in the backseat, Elise spotted a crime van and something official taped to her door.

"Wait here and I'll come back with cash."

No surprise to find that the notice on the front door was an official "Uninhabitable, Do Not Enter" warning.

She entered.

Inside, she found a small crew of people in hazmat suits and carbon-filter masks wiping down surfaces with swabs and sticking the swabs into sample tubes.

One of the crew spotted her and broke away. "You can't be in here." He didn't look familiar, but he seemed to be in charge and seemed to know who she was.

She introduced herself anyway. "I have to get some things," she said, rattling off a list.

"Not until we give the all clear."

"I understand, but it's hard for me to do my job without those items."

He stared at her. Something other than the color of his skin reminded her of Strata Luna. He walked away, huddled with the crew, then returned with her laptop and a Ziploc bag that contained her phone, keys, billfold, and badge. "I shouldn't do this, but they've been tested and dusted for prints."

"Thanks. When do you expect to be done here?"

"Collecting samples? In a few hours, but we won't be able to give you the all clear for a few days."

"And if I don't get an all clear?"

"This goes on record as contaminated property. More tests will be conducted to determine what steps need to be taken by the homeowner in order to pass inspection."

Elise pulled a business card from her billfold and handed it to him. "Text or call me when you have any information."

Outside she paid the cab driver, then circled the house to the alley. Thankfully her car wasn't under restriction. Or at least didn't appear to be. Before anybody could stop her, and without glancing in anyone's direction in case someone tried to flag her down, she hopped in her blue Camry and blasted down the alley. Two blocks later she pulled over to check the messages that had arrived when she'd been without her phone.

Nothing too surprising other than a voice mail left not long ago from the psychologist's office. There'd been a cancellation, and they could get her in on short notice, short notice being in an hour rather than the scheduled appointment two months out. Elise's initial reaction was to turn it down or ignore the message, but the idea of waiting two months made her uneasy.

She called and accepted the last-minute appointment, then took Highway 26 in the direction of Thunderbolt and Whitemarsh Island. The address she'd been given led her to one of those gated communities where people moved to feel safe. The neighborhoods weren't as diverse, although they usually had good schools and hopefully not as many drugs. But the insulated and segregated nature of all closed communities made Elise uncomfortable, and it wasn't beyond the realm of possibility for a neighbor inside such a compound to be a mass murderer. Where better to plant yourself than a place that gave the impression of safety?

At the gate she displayed her driver's license rather than her badge. The guard gave her a nod, slipped back into his box, and did whatever he did in there to lift the wooden arm.

She entered the "safe zone."

The psychologist's office was located in a ranch-style home with a single palm tree in the front yard that screamed low maintenance. Even before Elise pulled into a driveway, she felt out of place, felt this wasn't going to be a good fit. How could someone who lived in a gated community understand anything she'd gone through? But then Elise reminded herself that the woman had come highly recommended by Major Hoffman.

"I've sent a lot of officers to her," Hoffman had told her.

At the door Elise didn't know if she should ring the bell or simply enter. She rang the bell.

A small, tan, blond-haired woman of about fifty answered. Some kind of perfume wafted Elise's way. It smelled like church.

"I'm Dr. Lundy." She held out her hand. "My assistant had an emergency and took the afternoon off, so it's just us."

Elise shook her hand, and the woman closed the door.

"Are you armed?" the doctor asked. "If so, I always request patients not bring weapons past this point."

"Of course." Elise pulled out her gun. With a clatter, she placed it on the reception desk.

The doctor picked it up with the ease that came with frequency but not experience. She circled the desk, opened a wall safe, and tucked the weapon inside. Turning with a smile, she said, "Just my own personal policy."

"Not a problem." Elise wanted to leave. Not walk out, but run. She supposed anybody visiting a psychologist would feel the same. Would she have felt more comfortable talking to a man? That was sexist, but this petite, smiling woman with the pale suit and styled hair and cloying perfume wasn't at all the type of person Elise would feel inclined to confide in.

But she'd at least try.

"This is awkward for me," Dr. Lundy said. "My assistant usually takes care of finances, but we ask that you pay up front."

"I have health insurance."

"I'm sorry, but often insurance won't pay for my services. If it does, you'll receive a refund."

"What's the charge?"

"Four hundred dollars."

Elise tried not to gasp. Four hundred dollars for one hour? "Do you take credit cards?"

The woman sat down at the desk and with a few key clicks and a finger-drawn signature from Elise, she processed the card.

Four hundred dollars. Elise wanted to murder Major Hoffman even though the woman was already dead.

They headed down a carpeted hallway to a room with the requisite couch—two couches, actually. Those were flanked by a couple of comfortable-looking chairs. The walls had been painted a soft blue. There were equally soft paintings with dreamy, floral landscapes. Everything was meant to soothe.

It was too obvious. Too staged. Even down to the orchid on the coffee table, along with the strategically placed tissue box. Nearby was a pitcher of ice water with slices of cucumber floating on the top. That water was costing Elise big bucks.

They sat down, Elise on the couch, Dr. Lundy in one of the overstuffed chairs. The woman picked up a timer from the middle of the table, set it, and they began.

"First of all," she said, "let me start by telling you a little about myself. I want you to know that I specialize in cases like yours, and my primary focus is on PTSD. I also like to begin by sharing my own philosophy." She poured two glasses of water from the pitcher, and placed one near Elise with an ease that said she'd done so a million times.

"What you have to realize is that trauma changes us," Dr. Lundy said. "Forever. We no longer react to people and situations the way we used to."

Elise supposed she appreciated hearing the woman's background and philosophy, but not on her dime. That information should have been provided beforehand on a website or in a strategically placed brochure in the entry area. To add to the unpleasantness, Elise was acutely aware of the timer ticking away. And yet the cop in her couldn't help but ask, "Have you been victimized?" After all, she'd said "we."

"No, but I've worked with a lot of police officers who've experienced trauma on the job." She took a sip of water, put the glass aside on a coaster. "I want you to know it's okay to not get over it. And it's okay to not share what happened with people closest to you. Some might consider that behavior denial, but keeping your personal experience close is a coping mechanism. And when you're ready to share, with family, with friends, with a lover, I can help." She adjusted her tablet. She readied her pen. "That's what I'm here for."

Reluctant though she was, Elise was also determined to get her money's worth. She dove in and told the doctor why she was there. She told her how she'd been held hostage for three days. Then she told her things she'd never told anybody. About the level of torture she'd endured. About everything Tremain had done to her.

Thirty minutes in, while the doctor was buried in her table, face hidden, Elise got to her feet and paced while she talked. At one point she stopped to stare at one of the soothing paintings, then let her eyes go blank as she spoke. She felt removed, as if she were relating something that had happened to someone else, not her. That seemed the only logical way to get through it, because there was no way she was putting herself back there. Instead she watched the events unfold as if through a window, as if observing someone else. She didn't hold back, speaking words and sentences she'd never spoken aloud, at times losing track of where she was and forgetting anyone else was in the room.

She was a cop, and one of her strengths was her observational skill and ability to replay a scene with accuracy and detail. She used that talent now, and she didn't stop talking until she'd covered everything, until she'd gotten it all out, every shocking detail.

It wasn't until she finished that she realized she hadn't given the doctor a chance to speak. There had been none of the questions like "How did that make you feel?" Even now, when it was time for the doctor's response, the room was silent.

Until the sobs hit.

They were the choking kind of sobs. The kind of sobs where you couldn't catch your breath, the kind that tore from deep inside and just kept going.

They were coming from the doctor.

Arms crossed at her waist, Elise turned to see the poor woman groping blindly for the box of tissues she'd pushed across the table earlier. Elise jumped forward and shoved it closer. Dr. Lundy grabbed several tissues, tried to blow her nose, but the sobs kept coming, getting in the way of progress. Elise patted the woman awkwardly on the shoulder in a *There, there* motion.

After a few minutes, when it didn't seem as though Dr. Lundy was going to stop crying, Elise said, "I'll just let myself out." She motioned toward the door and the hallway. "But I'll need my gun before I leave."

The floor around the woman's tiny feet was littered with soaked tissues. The doctor nodded. Without looking at Elise, she gathered up the box of tissues, hugged it to her chest, and left the room, Elise following close behind.

Lundy turned the dial and unlocked the safe. And still wouldn't look up. Elise wasn't certain if it was due to her shame at being so bad at her job, or if it was horror at the thought of making eye contact with a freak.

"I'll give you a full refund." Head down, Dr. Lundy slid the gun across the desk. "All of it, even the processing fee. I'm sorry, but don't come back. I can't see you again. I can't help you."

Elise slipped her weapon into the holster. "That's kind of harsh."

"I'm honestly not sure who to recommend to you. I don't know anybody who could sit through what I just sat through."

Funny how it was all about her now. After today Dr. Lundy was probably going to be in need of her own services. Secondhand trauma. Was that a thing? If not, it should be.

Still, Elise felt the continued need to reassure her. "That's okay."

Actually, Elise felt better. Not enough to tell Lundy to keep her money, but it seemed to have helped to tell a total stranger what had happened to her. A stranger she'd never see again. It also served as a warning. The information she'd shared today must be locked away and never dragged into the light again.

Dr. Lundy was still blowing her nose and still not looking up.

Elise said, "I'm going to go now."

Always trust your gut. It was a lesson she wasn't sure she'd ever fully learn. But she felt stronger, taller, more fearless. And to hell with everybody who'd seen her naked on YouTube. That was nothing compared to what she'd been through with Tremain.

Outside in her car her phone buzzed. She checked the screen, saw David's name, considered not answering, forgave him for not telling her the truth about the cemetery, answered.

"John is showing signs of consciousness. Avery and I are heading for the hospital right now."

"I'll meet you there."

CHAPTER 28

The doctor explained that John might not remain "conscious" long. He used air quotes around "conscious." "We expect a coma patient to slip in and out," he told them. He wore scrubs and one of those colorful caps surgeons sometimes chose over traditional green. "Don't worry if he doesn't wake back up for a day or two. Everybody's different. Each case is different. Also, be careful what you say. Try not to upset him. I realize you need to question him about the attack, but don't push, and avoid the topic of his wife. He asked about her, but so far we've managed to evade his questions. It could be detrimental if he knows what happened to her right now. Also, keep in mind that many coma patients are able to hear the conversations in the room even if they can't respond. So if, and more likely when, he slips away again, continue to watch what you say even to each other."

Elise was surprised they were the only ones there. "What about his parents?"

"They're arriving later today." He excused himself, saying he had an ER patient to look in on.

In the entry point to the ICU, Elise, David, and Avery took turns washing and disinfecting their hands, following the instructions posted on the wall above the sink. Normally only two people would have been allowed in, but considering the circumstances and the small window of time they might have, all three were given access to the bay where John was attached to machines and IVs, his head shaved and stapled, all of his beautiful curly hair gone, oxygen tubes in his nostrils, his repaired hand wrapped and resting on a pillow.

His eyes were open slightly. When the trio approached his bed, one side of his mouth trembled in what appeared to be a faint smile. They said hello, trying to take turns, talking over one another in their relief at seeing him awake.

When they fell silent, John spoke. "*Wizard . . . of . . . Oz.*" His words were faint and weak.

Elise frowned and shot a worried glance at David. Oddly enough, he smiled. "That would make you Dorothy," he told John. Ah, they were riffing on *The Wizard of Oz.* John was communicating. Understanding. Even joking.

His gaze moved beyond them, his eyes searching the room for the one person who wasn't there. "Mara?" he croaked.

Elise's throat tightened. From behind she heard Avery make a small sound of distress. He mumbled something about his phone and left the room.

"Mara stepped out for a little bit," David said, not missing a beat, the lie coming as easily as his earlier comment about Dorothy.

John crooked a finger ever so slightly at Elise. *Come here.* She stepped nearer and gently touched the back of his uninjured hand. He surprised her by latching on. His grip was weak, but it was a grip all the same.

She thought about the doctor's comments and got straight to the crucial question. "Who did this to you? Can you tell us?"

His mouth moved, but he struggled to form words. She leaned closer, straining to hear over the sound of the oxygen machine. He made a second attempt, failed, pulled his hand away, then gestured in a circular motion at his face.

She tried her question again. "John, who did this to you? Can you tell me?"

His eyes fluttered, then rolled back in his head, awareness gone. She would have been alarmed if not for the doctor's earlier warning.

The ICU nurse appeared and checked his vitals, giving them a nod of reassurance. Relieved that their friend wasn't in any new danger, Elise and David left the ICU. In the hallway they stepped aside. No sign of Avery. When he bailed, he bailed. "What do you think that was about?" David mimicked John's hand motion in front of his face.

"Maybe he was trying to tell us the perpetrator was wearing a mask."

"But then again, we're talking as if he was thinking clearly."

"He referenced *The Wizard of Oz*," Elise said, trying to convince herself that John would be okay, eventually. "And he knew he was Dorothy in that scenario. He was cognizant enough to make a joke you'd get. I'd say that's pretty remarkable."

"Yeah." But she saw the flicker of doubt in David's eyes before he turned to push the down button on the elevator.

Once the elevator door closed and they were alone, Elise said, "We need to follow the TTX lead." She realized she'd been holding out too much hope of John's being able to tell them who'd broken into the morgue. That had been foolish of her, but maybe part of that foolishness was simply the desire for her friend to recover. But they had to move forward now, without any help from him. He was on the mend. That was the main thing. And while he was getting better, she and David had a job to do.

"The obvious place to start is with James LaRue, our favorite TTX pusher," David said. "I'll see if he still lives on Tybee."

Officers had canvassed Elise's immediate neighborhood, and Meg Cook had followed up on the gift basket, both dead ends. "I don't understand the motive," she said. "The report stated that the entire apple most likely didn't contain enough TTX to kill me."

"I've wondered about that too."

"It doesn't seem to be Remy's MO, unless his goal was to immobilize me for capture and torture."

"I'm beginning to wonder if it's related to Remy at all. It could have been meant for your dad."

"The card said 'Welcome back.' It was for me."

"Then it almost seems like the goal was to publicly humiliate you."

"If so, it worked for about five minutes. Now I don't even care."

The elevator shuddered to a stop, and they both fell silent, waiting for the doors to open while Elise grimly wondered how long it would be before the next kill took place.

CHAPTER 29

That evening, after turning down Strata Luna's offer of hospitality and checking herself into a hotel on River Street, Elise met with John's parents in the ICU waiting room. They were a conservative-looking pair. Not a surprise. Elise could see where John got his curly hair, which was almost identical to his mother's. If she recalled correctly, Mr. Casper was a chemist.

She filled them in on the assault as best she could, but, given her awareness of the strained parent-and-son relationship, she was also deliberately discreet. She had no idea how much information John would want them to have. "An investigation is under way" were her lame wrap-up words.

She was getting ready to leave when Mara's parents joined them, their eyes red-rimmed. "We came to make arrangements to collect her body and take her home to Texas," Mara's mother said. "But we can't get permission to have her released. I don't understand. Maybe you can help us. I was told the autopsy was finished, so why can't we take her home?"

"The decision on what to do with Mara's body rests with her husband," Elise said gently.

"But he's not able to make that decision." The poor woman was heartbreakingly upset. "We have a family plot. We have space for her. We want to bring her home for a funeral. We can't wait around for Mark or Mike or whatever his name is to wake up long enough to make a decision."

Elise straightened. "John." The woman was in pain, she understood that, but John deserved recognition. And John's mother was standing right there. *Right there.* It was no secret that Mara's parents hadn't been happy with her chosen field, and Mara had alluded to a rift because of it, but Elise hadn't realized they'd never met John.

Mara's mother pulled out a tissue and wiped her nose. "If she hadn't gone into forensics, if she hadn't met a medical examiner who deals with homicide cases, this never would have happened. We wanted her to go into a medical field, but not forensics, not something that deals with death."

Her husband was a little more forgiving. "Even as a kid she was fascinated by dead things, always bringing them into the house."

Mara's mother added to the memory, but she wasn't as generous. "Pretty girl like that, hanging around dead animals, then dead people. I don't know where she got that. There's nothing in our family. Nobody in the funeral business or whatnot. And meeting that boy. It was his fault. He's alive and she's dead. Why didn't he protect her? What kind of man doesn't protect his wife?"

John's mother began to cry softly. Her husband blustered forward in a protest that appeared to be more for the sake of his wife than in defense of John. All of them were dealing with various degrees of shock. "You're talking about our son."

"Yes, I am. Your son who's alive."

Elise excused herself and stepped away from the toxic situation. With exhaustion washing over her, she left the hospital and made a quick stop at a downtown clothing store to stock up on everything she might need for the next several days. Done shopping, she grabbed some takeout before heading to the hotel. In her room she ate, then showered.

Back to living in a hotel. After the month in Chicago she'd begun to understand why people in bands lost creativity after too long on the road. On the surface, hotels seemed harmless enough. Everything clean, with nothing in the space that needed attending to. No laundry to wash or floors to vacuum. No repairs to feel guilty about not doing.

But hotels sucked something out of you, and they did it while you were unaware, relaxing on clean sheets or showering under water that hit your back like a gentle rain. In a hotel you became less. If you were in a band, you might start writing about watching TV. If you were a detective, you might start flicking through channels, looking for one of those reality shows about crime instead of thinking about your own case. Because the room became the real world.

She pulled herself away from reality TV to click over to the local news in time to catch a rundown of the day's events. She also caught Avery's girlfriend or ex-girlfriend, whatever the case might be, standing in front of the monastery, a mic in her hand. Apparently Avery had released the victim's name. Best to get it over with. And of course Lucille Bancroft hadn't missed the opportunity to attach it to Elise, ending the piece with a censored clip of the YouTube video, certain body parts pixelated for the evening news.

Elise surprised herself by laughing, shut off the TV, tossed the remote aside, and grabbed her phone. It was three hours earlier on the West Coast, so she sent a FaceTime request to Audrey. Now that the news about the cemetery and Loralie was out, she needed to talk to her daughter.

Elise downplayed the cemetery situation. Audrey was upset about Loralie even though they'd never met. Odd to think the woman both of them hardly knew was Audrey's grandmother. Shortly after telling Audrey good night, Elise received a text from David, asking where she was staying and if she'd seen the news.

Yes. She gave him the name of the hotel and her room number.

See you in the morning.

She expected to be awake all night, but she fell into a deep sleep and didn't know another thing until her phone rang early the next morning.

It was David, asking her if she wanted to go for a jog.

"You're kidding, right? I know we talked about maintaining our own lives from now on, but that was before Mara was killed and John was brutally attacked. That's an attack on family. That *is* my life right now."

"I feel the same way, but I have to run more than ever now. To keep my head in the game. So I'm going, regardless. I'll be in front of the hotel in fifteen minutes. Come if you want."

Outside, the riverfront was deserted except for a few delivery trucks, but the early morning already held the promise of oppressive heat. As they alternated between jogging and walking, David said nothing about her improper footwear. They didn't talk about the cemetery or the YouTube video. And by some unspoken agreement, they didn't talk about last night's news or John Casper. They talked about the case, they discussed theories, they made plans for the day.

Once their exercise was over, Elise didn't feel better physically, but David had been right. The exercise had reset her brain and lifted some of the fog brought on by the hotel room. And they'd actually gotten a surprising amount sorted out.

At the lobby door, David told her good-bye and took off, running in the direction of his apartment, moving faster now that she was no longer slowing him down. Back in her room, Elise showered, dressed, and ate the leftovers from the previous evening. She was heading for her car when her phone buzzed. It was David. Moving to a spot of shade, she answered.

"Just got to the office. Forensics has a print result from the monastery."

She heard the rustle of paper as he read the faxed report. "Remy?" she asked.

"Yep. No real surprise." David elaborated on his reaction. "I think the prints were left for us to find. In obvious places. On doorknobs, doorframes, countertops, refrigerator, even a full handprint lifted from the window glass."

"I agree." She moved toward her car, unlocked the door, and slipped behind the wheel, dropping the windows as she started the engine. "I think we need to call a meeting."

"We just had a meeting."

"Now that we have solid confirmation, we need to have a *private* meeting of potential targets. You, me, Avery, Strata Luna. I'd really like to get Sweet in on this too."

"He's around, but he's lying low. He might come if you have the meeting at Strata Luna's or Black Tupelo."

"Tupelo's an idea. It's neutral, they have food, and nobody will bug us." And she wasn't sure how Strata Luna would feel about Avery coming to her home.

"So, have we gotten past the cemetery thing?" he asked.

"I've got more important issues to deal with than worrying about the world seeing me naked."

"And it was dark."

"Not that dark."

"But dark enough. It's not like you were strolling down the middle of the street in broad daylight. Not like you were having sex on a tombstone." She could almost hear the shrug in his voice. "In some circles the video would have been considered performance art. The way you were posing on that cement slab. This could even lead to a new calling. Forget the coffee shop. I'm imagining a coffee-table book and tours of the grave where you were left as a baby. But if I remember correctly, the tours already exist. Scratch that."

"David?"

"Huh?"

"Shut up." She disconnected.

At the police department, they further organized the game plan for the day. First on their list was a visit to the Remy house site, where the crime scene status had been lifted, prematurely in Elise's opinion. She and David wanted to talk with the crew preparing the teardown of the building. The second was a visit to James LaRue's confirmed location on Tybee Island.

At the construction site, they passed out flyers of the composite drawing to men in hard hats. The real reason behind the visit was to warn them that Remy might show up, since perpetrators were known to return to the scene of the crime and Remy had already made that return once. "Keep your eyes open." She pulled out business cards and passed them to dusty hands. "Call if you see anything suspicious."

After that they headed to Tybee, David behind the wheel of the unmarked car.

"He might not even be home," Elise said. "Middle of the day."

"I can't imagine a mess like LaRue having a nine-to-five job."

Elise looked out the window at the marshland rolling past. "I feel sorry for him."

"That seems undeserving, all things considered."

LaRue did seem undeserving of sympathy, especially since he'd drugged her shortly after David had moved to Savannah. One day she'd dropped in to question him and he'd given her a glass of water tinged with TTX. Even so, Elise felt bad about the turn LaRue's life had taken. He wasn't an evil man. He was weak and had allowed himself to become misguided by disappointment and failure. She suspected he was a genius, and the motives behind his initial studies of tetrodotoxin had been altruistic, at least on the surface. But she suspected he'd also been driven by a desire for fame and fortune.

LaRue had hoped to come up with a formula that would allow TTX to slow the disease process. He'd even imagined the drug being used to induce a state of suspended animation that would aid in deep-space travel. Instead, after funding was pulled, he began using the drug to get high and succeeded in slowing his own body down enough to nearly kill himself more than once.

They found him where Elise had found him years ago. In a shack at the end of a dirt lane lined with cabbage palmetto and Spanish bayonet, the lane itself so dark that a few fireflies could be seen in some of the dense areas.

LaRue was home, and even though it was afternoon it looked as if they might have woken him. He didn't appear much different. He was still mesmerizing with his golden skin and brilliant blue eyes. But he seemed to be doing better in the hygiene department. Instead of the tangled mass of hair, his head was covered in tight braids. He wore gray jogging shorts and a red plaid shirt, unbuttoned, with ragged edging where the sleeves had been cut off many washes ago. She did some mental calculations and figured he had to be in his mid to late thirties, but he already gave off an air of despair. She missed the old cockiness.

He stared at them and scratched his head, the movement displaying wet armpit hair. Behind and above him, fan blades slowly stirred the oppressive air. He invited them inside.

"Can I get you a drink?" he offered.

Loud and in unison, Elise and David said, "No!"

He dropped down in a chair and smirked, most likely recalling what had happened to Elise in that very room.

The detectives sat on a couch, both of them sinking deep. Elise scrambled to position herself on the frame, away from broken springs. David just let himself go.

The heat was unbearable, and she got straight to the point. "TTX has shown up in Savannah."

That got his attention. Like someone with a gun pointed at him, LaRue put both hands in the air and shook his head. "That's nothing to do with me."

"You sure?" David asked.

LaRue unconsciously licked his lips. "I haven't touched that stuff since I got out of prison."

He still craved it, though. Elise could see that. "Do you have any idea where it might be coming from?" she asked.

"Anybody can get it. Anybody can make it. Of course a lot of those people end up testing the product and killing themselves." Probably why he hadn't been able to get any backing for his studies. Pure TTX could be lethal in even the smallest doses. She'd survived, but that was probably due to LaRue's superior knowledge of the drug.

"We know that," David said, "but we're looking for someone who might be selling it for recreational use."

"And you naturally thought of me."

"Yep."

LaRue pointed to Elise. "So that's what was going on with you in the cemetery." He put a fist to his mouth, trying to hide a smile.

Elise rolled her eyes. David showed him the drawing of the aged Remy, but he didn't seem to know anything. She pulled out another card and handed it to him. "If something comes to you," she said, "give us a call."

Easy to see LaRue was thinking they were the last people he'd ever call. She decided to appeal to the decency she suspected was in him. "We're not looking to bust anybody. We're looking for leads. This might or might not be tied to the child who was murdered recently."

LaRue nodded and stuck the card in the breast pocket of his plaid shirt, giving it a pat. "I'll even snoop around," he said, serious now. "No obvious stuff," he added, seeing her and David exchange a look of alarm. "I can be subtle. And who better to look for TTX than the guy who used to be addicted to it?"

Outside, after the shack door closed behind them, David slipped on his sunglasses and said, "Strange guy."

"He's an attractive and fascinating man."

"He drugged you."

"I've forgiven him."

"Oh my God. Listen to yourself. That from somebody who can't forgive her own father? Or me."

"This is different."

"How?"

"He's not family. He's not my partner, someone I should be able to trust."

"So you can forgive someone you hardly know, but you have a hard time when it comes to someone close to you?"

"Pretty much."

"That makes no fucking sense."

CHAPTER 30

A block from the Savannah River, in an area surrounded by brick warehouses, Elise pulled to the curb and turned off the engine. On foot she traversed a cobblestone alley to reach a narrow metal door that gave off the appearance of a back service entrance. In the center was a discreet Black Tupelo logo. There was no handle on the door, only a keyhole, a doorbell, and a tiny window covered with a heavy screen. Elise rang the doorbell.

Like a confessional, an inner window slid open. "Yeah?" came a male voice. Elise introduced herself. The confessional closed, and the actual door swung open. Inside, the darkness was a welcome escape from the heat. She paused and blinked, waiting for her pupils to adjust. The place smelled like fermented beer, cigarette smoke, and incense. A sound system played some kind of electronic dance music.

The young man who'd answered the doorbell glided closer. "Strata Luna is expecting you. She's set up a room for a private party."

Like all the people who worked for the Gullah woman, the young man was attractive and exotic looking. He might or might not have been Strata Luna's new toy. Yes, she was "with" Sweet, but Elise wasn't sure how much weight that carried, or if their relationship was exclusive. Strata Luna seemed to have a strong sexual appetite, an appetite a man recovering from cancer might not be able to satisfy.

Elise followed the young man deeper into the building, down a narrow hall, past restrooms. He leaned against a red door, knocked, and pushed it open. Strata Luna, Sweet, and David were already inside the private room.

"Get you anything?" the young man asked as Elise sat down.

"Sweet tea."

"Got the best in town."

"I remember that."

A few moments later Avery appeared with a tray of drinks. "I was heading this way anyway," he said, explaining his role as waiter as he placed the tray in the center of the round table and grabbed a beer. He gave Strata Luna and Sweet a wide berth, choosing to sit next to Elise. Shifting uncomfortably, he spoke in a low voice meant for her alone: "I'd planned to say this at the hospital, but sorry about that stuff at the press conference." Words out, he took a quick swig of beer, then another, relieved that he'd gotten through his apology and could move on with his life.

Strata Luna didn't even try to pretend she hadn't overheard. "You looked wonderful, baby," she told Elise. "Beautiful. You should pose. I should have one of my artist friends paint a nude of you. Have you seen the one of me in my home?"

"I don't think I have."

"It's gorgeous. Isn't that right, Jackson?"

Chin down, Sweet smiled at Elise.

The smile confused her. It was friendly, two people sharing amusement at the way Strata Luna applied her own standards to the somewhat uptight morals of the detective sitting across from her. A secret smile was something Elise would have expected from David, not Sweet.

"Could we not talk about that?" Elise asked. "It makes me uncomfortable."

"You white people have so many hang-ups. About sex. About nudity. A body ain't nuthin' to be ashamed of."

"I'm not *ashamed.* But I am a detective."

"Oh, do detectives not have sex?"

Two servers appeared with overflowing trays held high. Steaming bowls of shrimp 'n' grits were placed in front of the people seated at the table. Lima beans, okra, and candied yams went in the center, family-style. Plates and silverware were passed. Casual, but somehow elegant.

One of the servers, a young Hispanic woman, handed David a note, not even trying to be discreet. He looked at it, gave her a wink, and tucked it into his breast pocket. The servers vanished as silently as they'd come.

"We weren't expecting this," Elise said.

"I wanted to feed everybody," Strata Luna told her. "You've all been busy. All had a hard day."

David waited until they were well into the meal before telling them about the fingerprints and the confirmation of Remy as the prime suspect in the murder.

Elise brought up Loralie. Sweet grew very still and put down his fork. Then he got that look on his face Elise had seen at the airport. Cold, murderous, resolute.

"I never once thought to contact Loralie," Elise said. Would it have done any good? she wondered. Could a warning have saved her?

David handed her a bowl of candied yams. "Don't beat yourself up. I didn't think of Loralie either."

"This is what I was talking about," Sweet said. "I tried to warn you. I told you to look the other way and mind your own business."

Elise stared. "Looking away is not an option."

"It should be. You have to weigh everything. You can't just think of yourself."

Strata Luna put a hand on Sweet's in a silent attempt to shush him. Elise leaned heavily against the back of her chair, her stare turning into a glare. "I'm not just thinking of myself."

"You sure about that?"

"What about your aunt?" Avery asked, trying to defuse the situation. "She still in prison?"

Elise continued to stare at Sweet but answered Avery's question. "Yes."

"We should all be so lucky." Avery got to his feet and left the room, rejoining the group a couple of minutes later, another beer in hand. Elise glanced at the tray he'd carried in earlier and realized he'd finished most of the bottles himself. He seemed to be running hot tonight, and he didn't handle alcohol well under the best of circumstances.

"Let's face the obvious." He settled back down in his chair and used the bottle to point around the table, his voice rising in agitation. "We've been dealt the death card, and the killer is moving fast, with hardly a lull between incidents." He glanced at Strata Luna. "And no mojos are going to help."

"Calm down," Sweet said. "You're hysterical."

"Damn right. Know why? Because we're all screwed, but you're the one he's performing for. When it doesn't have anything to do with the rest of us." He took a dramatic swig of beer. "We should all move to some high-security commune somewhere. Every one of us here. To a place with a guard tower and a razor-wire fence, because I don't think we can stop him. This is like some damn horror movie. We know the enemy, but we have no idea where he is, what he looks like, or who'll be next. And he just keeps coming."

"I agree that you might be the only person here who isn't in danger," David said, addressing Sweet. "He's torturing you. Getting back at you. He's after the people *associated* with you. He knows you aren't scared. Not of him. But he's figured out your Achilles' heel. The people you care about, and the people they care about. This is his form of torture. Taking us out one at a time."

"Then I need to meet him face-to-face," Sweet said. "Kill him, and if I fail, let him kill me. One or the other and this will stop."

Strata Luna slammed down her glass. "Absolutely not."

"I don't think he'd be tempted by you," Elise said. "That would spoil his fun. If he killed you, his game would be over. He doesn't want it to end."

"I like the idea of a commune," David said, returning to Avery's idea. "Just in general. Think of all the brainstorming we could do."

Strata Luna sat back in her chair and considered him. "You're just lonely in that tiny apartment."

"I've got a cat."

"You need a woman." She glanced toward the door, in the direction the server had gone. "Even for just a night or two."

He shrugged. "Maybe."

Strata Luna and her fixation on sex. She wanted everybody to be doing it several times a day. And if they weren't, she felt it her duty to make it happen. Elise now saw that Strata Luna had probably encouraged the girl to approach David. She shouldn't care, but her brain kept flashing to an image of the two of them together. He hadn't seemed at all interested in staving off her advances. And why should he?

Elise took a swallow of tea. "Sex isn't everything."

Heads swiveled. Four pairs of eyes stared at her in horror.

"Well, it isn't."

Sweet finally cleared his throat and said, "There's an upside to all this."

"Really?" Avery was speaking in his beer voice, with his beer attitude. "I'd like to hear how there can be an upside to being a psychopath's target."

"While he's concentrating on us he's not harming and killing children."

Another swallow, some thought: "It's a stretch, but I guess that's something," Avery admitted. "Didn't expect you to go all Pollyanna on us and start looking for the bright side in something that has no bright side."

Sweet fixed him with a hard stare. "It's just fact."

"Whatever." Avery shifted in his seat, seemed to struggle with something new he'd only just remembered, and finally blurted it out, the confession explaining the need for him to down beers very quickly. "You guys don't need to worry about Lucille anymore. We broke up." He shook his head. "I don't know what I was thinking, dating a reporter. Out of my mind, that's what I was."

Elise shot him a look of sympathy. "I'm sorry."

He shrugged. "And now of course I suspect she was just using me to get the inside scoop."

"I doubt it." Elise wouldn't admit she'd had the same thought. She gave his arm an awkward pat. "You'll meet somebody someday."

"That's what I used to tell Casper, and look how that turned out."

That ended in a round of grim silence.

Phones vibrated and buzzed. Elise, David, and Avery checked their screens.

"Speaking of John," David said.

Avery filled in Sweet and Strata Luna. "He's opened his eyes again."

All three of them excused themselves, thanking Strata Luna for the meal.

Outside Black Tupelo, David borrowed Avery's phone, tapped at the screen, passed the phone back. Elise didn't understand until a car pulled to the curb in front of them. The passenger window dropped, and the driver asked if someone had called an Uber.

David stuffed Avery in the backseat. "Go home. Get some sleep. I'll text you if we have any new information." Before Avery could protest, David slammed the door and the car shot away.

Elise crossed her arms, admiring how smoothly David had executed his friend's exit. "That's one way to get a drunk Avery out of the picture."

CHAPTER 31

At the hospital David and Elise learned that John had been downgraded to stable condition and moved from intensive care to a private room.

"A second rousing so close to the first is an excellent sign," a young female intern told them as they stood near the nurses' station. "Chances of his lapsing into a coma again are remote."

"What about recovery?" Elise asked.

"His prognosis is guarded, but hopeful. It's possible he'll be fully functional in a year or so, with the proper therapy. But he has a long way to go, and he won't be back to work anytime soon. He's most likely going to need home health care or a nursing home. I was told his parents are talking about taking him to California to keep an eye on him."

Nursing home. David didn't like the sound of that. California. He didn't like the sound of that either.

"He's asking about his wife," the intern added, her voice dropping. "Getting agitated, threatening to go looking for her. We thought it might be best if one of you broke the news."

"I'll tell him," David said once he and Elise were alone outside John's door. He could see she was struggling. They shared a moment of compassionate silence while David steeled himself before leaving Elise in the corridor, door shut behind him.

He made small talk. Told John about his hard-nosed replacement at the morgue. "We can't wait to have you back."

John smiled, but it wasn't a real smile. It didn't reach his eyes, didn't light him up. "Did you see these staples?" He felt his bald head, gingerly touching the metal surrounded by healing red tissue. Beside him on the bed were semitransparent oxygen tubes he'd pulled from his nose to more easily converse. The oxygen machine was silent, too silent.

John knew. He had to know. Mara was gone. His love was no longer on the planet. That hole, that absence, had to be felt. She was his phantom limb.

David's throat tightened. He turned away so John wouldn't see the anguish in his face, feigning interest in what was going on outside, staring at the Savannah River and the freighter in the distance. He'd told his mother water soothed, but that wasn't always the case. God, no.

He took a deep breath, got his face under control, turned around, fake coughed into his fist. "I've got something I need to tell you."

John reached for the bed control, hit a button, raised his head several inches. Waited.

He knows.

"You're a good friend." John's words came slow and thick, his speech and thought processes not back to 100 percent. "I know what you're going to say. It's Mara."

David made an involuntary choking sound—someone trying to swallow his own despair. He was the wrong man for this job. John needed someone cool and collected. Someone removed from the situation. Maybe a priest or chaplain. "I'm sorry, John. I'm so sorry." What else was there to say? Tears burned his eyes, but he couldn't turn coward now. Instead he used the technique that had served him well over the years. *Just say it.* "Mara's gone."

At first David wondered if his friend had heard, or if he'd tapped out. But John finally turned his head toward the window even though he was too low to see anything but a sliver of sky. His lip trembled as he pulled in a shaky breath and said, "Well then."

Minutes passed, and finally John spoke again, his eyes still focused on the sky. "Nothing else really matters, does it?"

"We'll catch him," David promised. "Whoever did this. I know it won't bring Mara back, but it will bring you some closure."

John looked back at him with flat eyes. "How will closure change anything?"

"I know it doesn't seem important right now. Mara is gone. That's all that's real. But one day, if he's not caught, the idea of his still being out there will eat you alive."

David's words, as odd as they sounded, seemed to help John a little. "Tell me everything," he said. "Don't leave any of it out. Not matter how awful, how brutal."

David suddenly wished Elise had come into the room with him. He needed her there, had to have her there. "I'm going to leave you alone for a minute. I'll be right back."

He found Elise waiting in an alcove down the hall. He must have looked like hell, because she pressed a plastic cup of water into his hand.

He tossed back the water like a shot of whiskey.

"What happened?"

"I told him, and he wants to know everything."

"That doesn't surprise me."

"Oh man." He paced. He threw the cup in the trash and looked up at the acoustic-tile ceiling. "I've delivered a lot of bad news to people, but it's almost always been to someone I didn't know."

"You broke the news. I'll tell him the rest."

"We'll both do it. Now. I don't want to leave him alone too long."

"One thing I want to make clear," Elise said. "There's no way I'm going to allow John to be taken to some town over two thousand miles away to live with people who don't understand him. Who, I even suspect, might have mistreated him as a child and as an adult."

"He can't go back to the house he shared with Mara. Even if he could take care of himself, his life will still be in danger."

"Maybe we can use that as leverage to keep him in Savannah. I have the feeling his parents won't want him around if his presence poses a threat to them. We just highlight the danger issue, letting them know that in addition to care he's also going to need someone looking out for his safety."

"That should work." John's life *was* still in danger. Not only from Remy, but maybe from himself. "I'm not sure he can get through this," David said.

"Me either."

Inside the hospital room, David hung back and Elise worked her magic. She smiled just the right amount and in the right way as she approached the bed and took John's uninjured hand. "I'm so sorry," she told him. "We know how much you loved her. And how much she loved you."

He blinked, tried to pull himself together. "I need to know everything."

They told him. All of it. Everything that happened that night, at least everything they'd pieced together so far.

"I think I knew," John said. "Even when I was unconscious. I kept feeling like there was no reason to wake up, you know?"

David did know. It was a pain that never went away. Never. The next year, the next several years, were going to be hard as hell.

"What do you remember?" Elise asked. She narrowed down the following question. "What were you trying to tell me last time we were here?"

He frowned. "Were you here before?"

Not a surprise that he didn't remember their last visit even though it had been less than twelve hours ago.

"That's okay," Elise said. "Let's just start over. Do you remember anything about the man or men who did this to you?"

He thought about it, shook his head. “No.”

“Don’t worry,” David said. “It might come to you eventually. Let’s go back to before your assault and injury. We want to know how your attacker got inside. That could give us some insight. Do you recall what happened?”

“Someone was waiting for me. Like waiting for me to unlock the building. The door was forced open behind me. I’m not sure, but I think that’s when I was hit over the head.”

“I hate to ask you this,” David went on to say, “but I wonder if you’d mind talking about Mara. Her car was in the parking lot, so you must have driven separately. Was she already there?”

“I think I was there first. I remember her opening the door, calling my name.” His voice cracked.

“That’s enough for now,” Elise said.

She was right.

“Where’s Mara’s body?” John’s question took David by surprise. He hadn’t prepared for it. Apparently Elise hadn’t either.

“Still in the morgue,” she said. There was not much else to say other than explaining about Mara’s parents, and how they’d been unable to take the body back to Texas.

“She’s not in *my* morgue, though.” The words were a statement. John knew his morgue would be out of commission after the fire even though part of the building was now up and running.

“No.”

John raised the head of his bed more. He untangled the IV line from the safety rail. He was getting up, and David was afraid it wasn’t to take a stroll to the restroom. “Bring me a wheelchair,” John said.

“Not a good idea.” David tried to buy time. John shouldn’t be standing, and he certainly shouldn’t visit the morgue, not now, not in his present condition.

“If she’s not at my morgue, that means she’s here. Her body is in the basement.”

"Give it a day or so," Elise said. "Please. Lie back down."

"Get the wheelchair. If you don't take me, I'll do it by myself. I know the way." No use trying to stop him. And it would be better for him to go downstairs with them.

David stepped from the room and returned with a wheelchair. He positioned it next to the bed, locked it, and folded the metal footrests out of the way. Then he took one of John's arms, Elise the other, careful of his injured hand. Once John was settled, David lowered the footrests and placed John's nonskid socks on them while Elise attached the IV rack to the chair. Then, like a pack of criminals, they left the room and headed in the direction of the elevator.

At the nurses' station David announced they were taking the patient for a lap around the floor and they'd be right back. Heads behind the counter nodded their okay and returned to computer screens and charts.

Like most hospitals, Candler had its own morgue. Overflow, questionable death, and homicides went to what they still called the new place, or what John called his place, on the edge of town. The rest went to Saint Joseph's/Candler.

Downstairs the staff knew John, and Elise explained that they needed to view the body.

The young morgue assistant nodded. "She's in number four." He didn't have to check the computer. "If I'd had some notice, I could have set the body up in a viewing area. Would you like me to do that? It'll take a few minutes."

"That's okay." John's voice was emotionless. David wasn't sure if he was feeling weak or removed.

With Elise beside him, David pushed John into the large room with stainless-steel refrigeration units lining one wall. Motion-sensitive lights followed their progress. Mara had been there awhile already. Even in a cooler, a dead body's decomposition was inevitable.

They stopped in front of number four. Elise grabbed the handle. "Are you sure about this?"

John nodded and Elise opened the drawer.

David wheeled John closer, set the brake on the chair, and helped him to his feet while Elise unsnagged the IV line.

Ordinarily they'd leave the griever alone, but John was so fragile he could hardly stand. David stood beside him while Elise grasped the sheet and pulled it down, stopping just below Mara's shoulders and the top of the Y incision made by the medical examiner.

She didn't look bad. That almost made it worse. Her lips were an expected shade of blue, but someone had carefully arranged her shiny hair on each side of her face, parted in the center the way it should be.

She looked peaceful. She looked asleep.

Beneath his hands, David felt John shaking, the anguish building. They should have saved him from this, sheltered him. But how? As soon as they left the building he would have been down there on his own.

As David and Elise looked on, helpless, John collapsed over Mara's body, sobbing uncontrollably. At a loss about what to do for his friend, David looked to Elise for help. She was crying too, silently, a hand pressed to her mouth. Her eyes pleaded with him, begging him to make it stop, fix it, help John.

John pulled back slightly, enough to hold his uninjured hand just above Mara's nose. It took David a moment to realize what he was doing. Feeling for a breath. Because the dead didn't always stay dead.

"I keep thinking about the time I was doing that autopsy and the body woke up," John said. "Remember that?"

David and Elise nodded.

"So, I was thinking . . . maybe she's not really dead, you know? But she is, isn't she?" He examined her with his eyes and a brush of his fingertips. "I can see signs of decomposition. Maybe you can't, but I can. Some skin slippage, some mottling, some sinking of the sockets. She's been gone awhile. Mara, I mean. The person who inhabited this body. But I needed to be sure."

David held him by the shoulders, gently tugging him away. "Come on."

Upright, John continued to stare at his dead wife. "She liked dead bodies." He cast a glance around, his gaze going from David to Elise, looking for the slightest bit of comfort. "Right?"

Elise sniffled. "She sure did."

John completed his thought. "And now she is one."

More nodding.

"She looks good," John said. "She would have been happy about that."

"She does," Elise agreed. "Beautiful." Her voice cracked on that last word, and she turned away.

Without taking his eyes off Mara's face, John said, "I want to see the autopsy report."

"I'll make sure you get it." David attempted to guide his friend back to the chair. "John."

Blindly, John looked over, spotted David, registered his presence, and began sobbing all over again.

David pulled him into his arms and held him while Elise got control of herself. She gave Mara one final look, one final good-bye, pulled the sheet over her face, and closed the drawer, the sound of the latch echoing in the room.

As David arranged John in the chair, he felt Elise's hand on his shoulder. He wasn't sure what that touch meant. Maybe she just wanted to make contact with another living person, or maybe she was trying to reassure him, reassure herself.

They filed out, leaving Mara alone in the drawer as the lights clicked off behind them.

* * *

Back in the hospital room, John wanted to be alone. The trip downstairs had exhausted him.

"Try to get some rest." Elise smoothed his covers and made sure the bed control was within reach. She put a pillow under his injured hand while John pushed the button to lower his head. "Call if you need anything," she told him. "I'll check back first thing in the morning."

John nodded and closed his eyes.

It was a little after nine when David and Elise left the room.

"What do we do with him?" Elise asked while they waited for the elevator.

"It could be a long time before he can live alone." They had to face the reality of it.

"There's my place," Elise said. "I have the space, especially now that Sweet is gone. Main-floor bedroom and bathroom. He wouldn't have to deal with stairs. But until we catch Remy my home isn't safe."

"We made a decent amount on that Chicago job." David knew money couldn't solve every problem, but it might help with this one. "He can stay at my place. I'll pay for a caregiver if it comes down to that."

"I'll go half."

"Deal."

In the elevator, David surprised himself by reaching for her hand, taking it, rubbing his thumb across her knuckles. She didn't pull away, so he lifted her hand to his lips, kissed a few fingers, then let her go.

"What was that for?"

He wasn't exactly sure. "I'm just glad you aren't dead."

The minute he said the words, he cringed inwardly. Would she take it to mean he'd be as devastated as John if anything happened to her?

But she laughed. She thought he was joking around, trying to lighten the mood, as if that were possible.

"And I'm glad you aren't mad at me anymore," he added.

"I never stay mad at you for long."

"While I appreciate the sentiment of your revision, that's not really the truth."

"Something for me to work on, then. I'm sorry I got mad about the naked thing."

"I shouldn't have tried to keep it from you."

She glanced at the changing numbers above the elevator door. Without looking at him, she said, "I went to see a shrink."

"Wow. That's a big step." He was surprised. "Did it help?"

"Yeah." She gave it more thought. "I think it did." She smiled a secret kind of smile that made him feel excluded.

As they walked through the parking garage, and since they were confessing, he said, "My mother stopped by yesterday."

"Stopped by? How does somebody stop by Savannah? Doesn't she live in Ohio?"

"She flew." He spotted their cars, parked side by side, and pointed. They shifted directions. "I took her out to eat on Tybee Island, then put her right back on a plane. This is the last place any relative of mine should be right now."

"She just came to visit you? Out of the blue?"

"That, and she was trying to get me to move back to Ohio. Apparently there's a job opening."

Elise stopped and looked at him. "Are you thinking about it?"

He nodded. "I am." Until that moment, he hadn't realized it.

"And when were you going to tell me?"

He hit the unlock button. "Right now."

"Is this like an ultimatum or something?"

His initial reaction was to say of course not. But maybe it *was* an ultimatum. Maybe he was trying to force her hand.

Everything his mother said was true. About Savannah being his running away, about his unrequited relationship with Elise, about Christian's grave.

Why had he brought up the job, now? When they were experiencing one of those brief moments of camaraderie?

Because she should know.

And his waiting for her *was* a sickness. His mother had been right about that. He could be married; he could have children. Life wasn't over for him. But here? Here it was. Kind of. As long as he loved Elise from a distance, this would never feel like a real life.

And yet if she were to die, he would break. He would be just like John. Instead he was like Avery, moping around, making a fool out of himself.

Hands jammed in the pocket of his slacks, he felt the piece of paper the girl at Black Tupelo had given him. He'd call her. It would be good for him.

Even though it was a hundred degrees in the parking garage, he was aware of the chill coming off Elise.

"If you need a reference, put me down." She broke eye contact and got in her car.

CHAPTER 32

Elise didn't want to go back to the hotel. Not yet. Her mind should have been focusing on the case. Instead she was thinking about the blow David had just dealt her. A few days ago they were partners with their own business. The *Chicago Tribune* had called them a "homicide power couple," and now he was talking about leaving. His mother's visit seemed to have triggered it, but she suspected his response was compounded by the loss of Mara and the injury to John.

She couldn't blame him. It was true that most of the time she and David kept their heads down, focusing on the task of catching killers, but what happened to Mara and John had them once again questioning what they were doing and where they were going. No amount of jogging or trying to have a life outside work would fix the loss of a friend and team member. The old Elise would have felt betrayed by today's announcement, but David deserved a full life.

She didn't go to the hotel. Without calling to announce her visit, she drove to Strata Luna's. At the entrance to the property, Elise entered the code into the box, and the giant iron gates swung open, then closed behind her.

Her arrival must have alerted Javier, possibly by video or a silent alarm system. He opened the door before she could knock.

"Strata Luna told me you might be coming to stay," he said.

"Not today. I just want to talk to her."

"Sure?" Javier looked like a model and was another someone Strata Luna might or might not be having sex with. He'd been around awhile, so she must have a particular fondness for him. "I have a guest room prepared," he said. "You'll be safe here."

"Maybe another night."

"Strata Luna's in the courtyard near the fountain."

"I know the way."

She followed a hallway to a large room with a slowly turning ceiling fan. She was surprised to see her father sitting at a long polished table, a pistol in his hand, a box of ammunition near his elbow.

"You'll probably find this hard to believe, but I rarely carried a weapon when I was a cop." He gave her a quick glance as he tucked bullets into a magazine. "Looks like it's time to arm myself again." Finished loading the clip, he clicked it into a Smith & Wesson with the heel of his hand. "I heard what Javier said." Sweet stood up. "You really should think about staying here."

"I will."

"How was John?"

"Doctors hope he'll have close to a full recovery."

With a clatter, he buckled the holster around his waist, slipped the gun inside, adjusted it, and tested the weight. "That's good."

"He knows about Mara." She bit her lip, feeling weepy again. "He . . . ah, went to the morgue to see her." She stopped talking. Enough talking.

Sweet approached her. Without looking her direction, he paused, gave her shoulder a squeeze, then left the room.

Elise found Strata Luna where Javier said she'd be. Sitting on the edge of the fountain, trailing a hand through the water, causing the reflection of the moon to fracture.

Elise sat down on the fountain wall several feet away. "Why do you keep pushing your girls at David?"

Strata Luna let out a snort. "To keep him out of trouble."

"Are you sure it's not to make me jealous?"

Strata Luna's hand stopped moving, and she looked up. "What if it is?"

"You should stay out of it. That's all I'm saying."

"Doubt that'll ever happen."

They both laughed. Elise was surprised she was capable of laughing after the past hour.

"How's our boy?"

Elise told her about the visit to see Mara's body. And even expanded on it, delving into her own feelings about relationships. "I feel such grief for him, and I know it's selfish, but at the same time it brought home the fact that I'll never have what they have."

"Honey, you already have that. Or you could have that. With David, if you want it with David."

"No." Elise shook her head. "I can't."

"That's crazy talk. You're young. You're pretty. Like me, you can be a little aggressive and forward, but the right man will have no problem with that. He'll want his woman strong."

Then Elise told her the thing she hadn't even gotten around to telling the psychologist. Maybe the thing that was the real reason for her visit to Strata Luna's. "I can't let a man see my body."

"It's a little late for that."

"Are you talking about the video?"

"You looked fine, girl. Better than fine."

Everyone thought she'd been upset about the nudity. Of course she had, but her concern had gone much deeper than that. "It was dark, too dark to see the things I'm worried about."

"David won't care how you look, hon. That man wouldn't care if you had two vaginas." It was something only Strata Luna would come up with.

"I've got scars left by Tremain," Elise said. "So bad they're bordering on deformities. I don't want anybody to see them, especially someone I care about."

Strata Luna got to her feet. "Let me see those scars, those deformities." With one hand, she gestured up and down Elise's body. "Show me."

Elise let out a breath. Maybe it was a good idea. Let her see them. She looked around. "Here?" She glanced toward the house. There were cameras all around the property. "The last thing I need is to be caught on video again."

"You're such a prude. Okay, let's go inside. To my room. There are no cameras there."

Elise surprised herself by agreeing.

Inside the house, with the bedroom door closed, Strata Luna turned to Elise with hands on her hips. "Take off your clothes. I'll look you over, give you some advice, maybe put together some rootwork that can erase scars, even deep ones."

Elise stripped, her clothes dropping on top of her belt and gun and badge.

"All of it."

Once Elise was naked, Strata Luna made a twirling motion with one finger.

Elise turned without looking at the woman's face.

"Show me," Strata Luna said.

Show her? Weren't the scars obvious?

She pointed them out, one after the other, the disfigurements on her breasts, stomach, and pelvis obvious and impossible to miss, the ones on her back harder to spot because of the tattoo, also courtesy of Atticus Tremain. When she was done, she quickly dressed, head down, relieved to once again feel the weight of the gun on her hip and the clothing on her body.

Through it all, Strata Luna had said nothing. Strata Luna, the woman who had a strong opinion on everything.

When Elise finally looked up, she saw an expression on Strata Luna's face she'd never seen before, an expression Elise read as revulsion mixed with pity. And then the Gullah woman finally spoke, her voice reflecting what Elise had read in her expression. "Oh, child. You poor child."

That was it. That was the look. The look she didn't want to see on any man's face, especially David's. Strata Luna had seen a lot of ugly in her life, which was why Elise suspected she surrounded herself with beauty and beautiful people. And now she knew Elise wasn't even close to being one of those chosen few.

"I have to go," Elise said.

"Wait. Honey."

Elise moved toward the door, heard the rustle of Strata Luna's gown, knew the woman was following her. Elise increased her pace. "I'll talk to you later."

Before returning to the dreaded hotel, she swung by the police department to see if any substantial leads had come in on the Remy composite.

She liked the police station at night. Not that she disliked it during the day, but the night crew was a different bunch, and the building had a hushed and soothing quality that didn't exist during the day.

She checked the room set aside for the Remy case and was glad to see the young and capable Meg Cook, along with another officer, manning the phone lines, a cup of coffee and a half-eaten sandwich nearby. Meg smiled when she saw Elise.

"Anything new?" Elise asked.

"A lot of tips and possible sightings to wade through." She handed Elise a legal tablet. "I haven't entered these into the database yet. Also, no luck with the missing-persons search. Nobody in the county was reported missing around the time of the Remy burial. Also, I looked into prison records dealing with Remy's death. Didn't turn up anything unusual. I tracked down a guard who was working there at the time. His story was solid."

"Either people are afraid to talk, or everybody thought Remy was a dead man."

"I agree."

Elise looked through Meg's notes and spotted a couple of men worth checking out. She handed the tablet back. "Could you put together a long and short list of the most likely leads?"

"I'll get right on that," the young woman said. "Also, I just want to say I'm glad you and Detective Gould are back. Oh, a fax just came in you might want to see. I debated calling you tonight or saving it for tomorrow." She shuffled through papers and handed Elise a cover sheet and document.

"Never wait to call or text no matter how trivial something might appear." The document was a fingerprint report. She'd have to call David and let him know nothing had turned up from the prints lifted at her house.

Back in her office, Elise logged into LIMS, the Laboratory Information Management System. Looked like her blood tests had been updated, the outstanding toxins identified. She was doing online research on them when her phone rang.

The mayor. She wasn't the only one working overtime.

He didn't apologize for the late call, but he did surprise her by saying he was sorry to hear about her mother. And then he jumped into a demand for results. Some things never changed. "I want you and Gould to catch this guy. Not today, not tomorrow, but yesterday."

"I'll get right on that." Sarcasm was more fun when it was delivered to someone who was oblivious to it. Mean, but not mean. She hung up and went back to her research.

CHAPTER 33

As soon as David got home he called the girl from Black Tupelo. Before he could change his mind, he gave her his address, and she arrived fifteen minutes later. Things continued to move fast. She stepped in the door of his apartment and attacked him. In a good way. They started going at it, as if both had been starved for a long time, even though David figured he was the only one starving and she was just a really good actress.

They did it on the couch. They did it on the floor. They did it in the shower. And for a while he forgot about Elise.

Until his phone rang.

Lying naked across his bed, while the woman with the long dark hair straddled his thighs, he checked his phone.

Elise. "Gotta get this," he told the girl.

She pouted and moved down his body.

"David?" Elise asked. "Are you busy?"

The woman touched him, stroked him.

"Little bit." Did he gasp? He was afraid he gasped.

"I'm coming over. I have some things I want to talk about. Too much to discuss over the phone. Is it a bad time? You sound preoccupied."

He pushed the young woman away, gently but firmly. "No, this is fine."

"I'm actually outside your apartment building. I'll be right up."

He scrambled from the bed, slipped into a pair of jeans, pulled on a T-shirt, and walked the naked girl into the shower, pressing a finger to his lips. She smiled conspiratorially and made a zipping motion over her mouth. He supposed she was used to this kind of thing.

He started to close the door, paused, grabbed a large towel, tossed it at her. "In case you get cold." Then he shut the shower door, followed by the bedroom door. In the living room, he scurried around, kicking the girl's clothes under the couch, plumping and straightening cushions.

He heard footsteps outside his apartment. Before Elise could knock, he opened the door, ran his fingers through his hair. "Hey. Hi." He was suspiciously out of breath.

She shot him a puzzled look, stepped inside, and dropped her bag on the kitchen counter. "Do you have company?"

The two wineglasses. "No." He grabbed the glasses, put them in the sink. "One's from yesterday." He spun back around. "Would you like some wine?"

"No, but water would be nice."

He filled a glass and handed it to her. She was picking up on his odd behavior. Why had he shoved the girl in the shower? Why was he hiding her? Why did he feel like he was cheating on Elise? It had just happened so fast. He hadn't had enough time to figure out a game plan.

She walked to the couch and sat down. Took a long drink. "We've got some potential leads on the Remy composite. I want to follow up on those first thing in the morning. And I got a call from the mayor, who's demanding results."

"What's new."

"Also, the lab was able to lift a variety of prints from the cellophane on the fruit basket."

"None were Remy's," he stated.

"So far, no match at all."

"That's a bit of a surprise."

“I agree. I logged on to the LIMS, and a new lab report popped up. Two other substances were identified in the apple from my house. Barbasco vine and quinine branch. It makes sense that I was out of my mind.”

“I think I remember something about those ingredients making a Savannah museum worker gravely ill.” It had gotten a lot of press, and criminals were known for lifting ideas straight from the headlines.

“The substance leached through the skin and entered the worker’s bloodstream, resulting in odd and uncharacteristic behavior.”

“It could have killed you.”

“I doubt that was the goal, but yes. I think the idea was to do exactly what it did. Well, maybe the goal wasn’t for me to stroll around town naked, but to make people doubt my sanity and pull me from the case. And make me doubt my own sanity.”

“That’s it? What you came to tell me?”

“Isn’t that enough?”

“You could have called.”

“I wasn’t ready to go back to the hotel.”

“You should stay at Strata Luna’s.” He would have also suggested his place, but he didn’t want her to suddenly decide to stay tonight.

She wandered around the apartment, seeming to make a point of avoiding eye contact. “That’s not all. About that job offer you have in Ohio. I’d understand if you took it. I would.” She turned back around, held up her hand. “Let me talk. Honestly, I don’t know if I’ll ever be ready for a relationship. Seeing the psychologist the other day drove that home.”

“I thought you said she helped you.”

“She helped me see things more clearly. And made me realize this is the new me. And I don’t know if the new me will ever be ready for a relationship. And I don’t want you to wait for me. I want you to have a life.” And then she said almost exactly what his mother had said. “You could get married. You could have more children. I know you loved

Christian. I know you'll never forget him, but you could have another child. Two children. Three. You could find love again." She looked at him. "So please don't stick around here because of me. I don't want you to do that." She put the glass down on the counter and moved toward the door. "That's really what I came to tell you. I care about you. I think you know that, but don't wait for me."

David walked her to her car, ignoring her protest, watching until she drove off and her taillights disappeared. Back in his apartment, he jumped at a sound coming from the bedroom, then remembered the girl.

"Is she gone?" The Black Tupelo girl stood in the bedroom door wearing nothing but one of his unbuttoned white shirts.

"Get dressed, sweetheart. You're going to have to leave."

"I thought you said I could stay the night."

"I changed my mind." He retrieved her clothes from under the couch, made a useless attempt to brush off the cat hair.

"You're sad," she said. "Why are you sad?"

"Just get dressed." He pressed the clothes into her hand. "Get dressed and go."

Shortly after she left, his phone rang. Half expecting Elise, he was surprised to see Strata Luna's name on the screen.

"Elise was here earlier," she told him. "We were talking the way women do, and the conversation turned to sex. You probably know that she has some intimacy issues ever since her encounter with Tremain."

"We've never talked about it, but I suspected as much. And I don't know if you should be telling me this." Especially in light of what Elise had just told him.

"I'm not one to share private conversations," the Gullah woman said. "I keep secrets. That's what I do. But something happened tonight that might be a sign of a problem. A deeper problem."

"I'm listening."

"She'd just come from the hospital and was upset about seeing John Casper. And she started talking about how she'd never have what John and Mara had. And I said, 'Why, honey? I kinda think you might already have that and not even know it.' And she says, 'Nobody can see my body. Ever.' And I say, 'We've all seen your body.' And she says, 'It was dark.' Well anyway, she ends up stripping in front of me. To show me all the scars left by Tremain. I knew about the tattoo, and the scar on her hip where the Black Tupelo mojo had been. But she starts pointing out all these other areas. Deep scars. Deformities, she called them. Maybe twenty or more. Everywhere."

David sat down heavily on the couch.

"Thing is, I saw some small scars. Just a few thin lines that were nicely healed. Hard to see unless you're looking closely. Otherwise? The areas she pointed to that she called deformities? Those things she doesn't want any man to see, especially you? Honey, there was nothing there. And I mean *nothing*. Elise is scarred, but those scars aren't on her body."

CHAPTER 34

After leaving David's apartment, Elise adjusted her rearview mirror and made sure her doors were locked. A few minutes into the drive, she spotted a dark-green sedan behind her. She took some test turns. The car mimicked her.

She made a series of rights, increasing her speed, hoping to circle the block and come up behind the vehicle, but she couldn't shake it.

She called in a report, giving her location and a description of the car, then headed for the police station, hoping it continued to follow.

"Patrol unit is on the way," the dispatcher said.

Maybe the tail saw the light from her phone, because Elise barely finished disconnecting when the car dropped away and vanished. She was tempted to turn around and chase it, but that would be foolish.

Instead she parked in the hotel garage, under a bright light near the elevator and stairwell. At the door to her room, she swiped her card, pulled her gun, and stepped inside, making a quick sweep of the space. No sign that anyone had been there. Confident of her safety, she locked up and typed the day's report into the department's secure database.

Early the next morning, before the sun was completely up, she headed back to the parking ramp and her car. On the way, she got a call from the investigator in charge of processing her house.

"Ban has been lifted," he said. "Contents of the Ziploc bag matched the toxins in the apple. We also found some suspicious items around the foundation of the house, but nothing dangerous. Small cloth bundles containing ingredients wrapped in paper with your name written on it. Looked like spells." His voice held derision he either couldn't hide or didn't want to. A nonbeliever. She understood.

The new information told her the Ziploc bag and the toxic apple had come from the same person. The spells around her house? Most likely for protection, courtesy of Strata Luna, probably put in place by Javier.

She thanked him, disconnected, and was almost to her blue Camry when she spotted a flat back tire. Upon closer inspection, she saw that the tire had been slashed. Her friend from last night? Both front and back tires on the side facing her were damaged, and she guessed she'd find the same if she were to circle the vehicle.

She pulled her weapon. At the same time a man in a ski mask and bulky coat burst from behind a pillar. From the corner of her eye, she caught a flash of movement, ducked, and felt the breeze of a tire iron just missing her head. The man swung again. Her arm shot high in defense. The iron struck, knocking the gun from her hand with a clatter. He kicked her legs out from under her, and she hit the cement, momentarily stunned.

Tires squealed. A dark-green sedan came to a sharp halt a few yards away. The back door flew open. Another man in a mask. Both men reached for her.

She lunged across the floor, grabbed her gun, rolled to her back, pushing with her heels at the same time, putting distance between herself and the men as she pulled the trigger, firing a series of shots.

Glass exploded. The men dove into the car, doors slammed, and the vehicle sped away.

The entire encounter hadn't lasted over a minute.

A call followed by a short wait. Cops arrived to take her statement. Another thirty minutes and she was at the Savannah PD and arrangements were being made for her car to be repaired.

"That's gonna be sore for a while." David handed her an ice pack, and she placed it on her swollen and bruised forearm as she went over the description of the car again while David and Avery leaned against desks, ankles crossed, faces serious.

"Green," she said. "Dark green. Four-door. No plates. I don't know the make or model."

Avery unfurled his arms and gripped the desk behind him. "They've probably already hidden it."

She went into a description of the men. The heavy coat that seemed designed to hide body type. Then she told them about the car that had been following her the previous night. "I'm pretty sure it was the same vehicle."

"We're hoping the hotel security cameras picked up something," Avery said. "They're going over footage now. I told them to pull up the attack, which should be easy to find with the time stamp."

"You know what this means, don't you?" David asked.

"I'm the next target?" Elise said.

"Other than that."

She watched him a moment, then got it. "I'll call Strata Luna later today and let her know I'll be staying there."

That was the answer he wanted to hear.

With the restricted access lifted from her house, she and David stopped by that evening. Inside, she filled her suitcase with clothes and toiletries, wishing she could stay home, sleep in her own bed, knowing that would be stupid beyond stupid.

The move to Strata Luna's felt like the prison Elise suspected it would be. To make matters worse, Sweet hovered even more than David, announcing that he was coming out of hiding and would be driving her to work. She'd never be alone. She could walk to the market from the police station, but that was all.

The plan was a recipe for insanity, but she was the next target. None of them doubted that. As if she weren't even in the room, David and

Avery talked about taking her off the case, removing her from the PD completely. Ordinarily she would have been thrilled at the suggestion, but not now. Not until the case was solved.

And maybe that was the big secret, the things that kept cops on the job. Maybe a lot of them, Elise included, were addicted to the chase, to solving the puzzle.

"I'm going to go crazy here," she told David.

"At least you'll be alive."

"I'm hiding. I don't like hiding." But she'd learned her lesson about being stubborn. She'd tolerate the living situation. She'd tolerate and accept Sweet's escort to the office, and she'd try not to be a brat about it.

They received a simultaneous text. A message from Research. Abraham Winslow's story about the closure of his funeral home held up. He'd filed for bankruptcy, and an investigation had been launched. Pretty open-and-shut case, the message read. You'll find an extensive report in your e-mail.

David pocketed his phone. "I'm going to make the assumption everything else he told us was true."

Elise agreed. "We might never know what happened in the funeral home, but this helps establish a stronger timeline. Tomorrow we start on Meg's short list of possible Remy sightings."

CHAPTER 35

It was like having her dad drop her off at school, only decades late. All Elise needed was a lunch box and kneesocks. To make it even more ridiculous, Sweet was driving Strata Luna's big black boat of a car. Before Elise realized what he was up to, he docked it at the curb in front of the police department.

"Keep going, keep going!" Elise slid down in the passenger seat, trying to hide from the swarming media squatting near the entrance to the Savannah PD, cameras and mics in hand.

Too late. She and Sweet had been spotted.

Like a kid dreading the first day of class, Elise opened the door and swung her foot to the ground as cameras clicked. "I should have worn a dress and no underwear," she muttered.

Sweet pulled away, and she imagined him smiling that weird, secret smile.

Questions were shouted; mics were shoved in her face. She pushed the more intrusive ones away. Most of the reporters were local, but she spotted a couple from national outlets. Elise didn't speak to anyone and certainly didn't respond to any of the questions shouted at her, like "What can you tell us about the cemetery incident?" And "Have you been fired again?"

She remained focused on the door, got herself inside and through security to finally gain access to the safe zone. Upstairs David was already at his desk. He swiveled around at her entrance.

"Quite a circus out there, right?" He had a coffee in his hand, and his eyes were bloodshot. Nobody would be getting much sleep until this case was solved.

She put her laptop on her desk, next to another carryout coffee. "You should have warned me," she said, picking up the hot drink. "About the mob."

"I thought about it, but figured you'd come in the back like I did."

She took a sip from the cup. "Right up to the front door. In Strata Luna's car."

He laughed, and she didn't even resent him for it.

They got down to business.

First was a meeting downstairs with patrol officers. Then a check with the tip line to see if anything new had rolled in. Meg Cook was already at her desk and had a short list of leads for them.

Then it was back through the crowd of cameras and microphones to an unmarked car, David behind the wheel, air conditioner blasting away as they headed for the first address, a bakery located in a more industrial area, off Martin Luther King Jr. Boulevard. A few times David seemed on the verge of saying something. Then he'd sigh and squirm and make some comment about the road or the weather or the traffic.

"You're acting weird," she said.

"Am I?"

"If it's about what I said the other night . . ." Elise didn't regret what she'd told him. She'd meant every word. Even though it might have come across as melodramatic, it was something he needed to hear.

"I'm glad you let me know where you stand, where we stand."

"So are you thinking about Ohio? Does that explain the heavy sighs?"

"Actually I got a call after you stopped by my place the other night. Nothing about the current case. Just a friend sharing some rather disturbing news. If I seem preoccupied, that might be why."

"I'm sorry."

"No big deal."

"Want to talk about it?"

"Can't. Confidential. Still trying to figure out how to handle it."

Meg Cook's short list was made up of five white men in their sixties who'd moved to Savannah in the past year. Not unusual. People retired and moved to Savannah. Not quite the retirement destination Florida was, but a destination all the same.

The street-level bakery located in a brick warehouse was one of those places that felt like a throwback to the sixties, either intentionally or through apathy. Parking area of cracked cement, weeds, oil stains, and the crushing sun. Inside, no Wi-Fi, no espresso machine. Just bakery items and straight-up coffee served in white ceramic mugs.

They spotted their guy immediately. Name: Marshall Hughes. In his sixties, a little on the heavy side, white. Check, check, check. He wore a chef's apron, tied high over his belly. A cigarette dangling from one corner of his mouth would have been a nice touch.

At the cash register the detectives pulled out their badges and asked to talk to him privately. He gave them a concerned nod, slid the register drawer closed, and motioned for them to follow him to the back room.

Ovens, vats of oil, racks of cooling doughnuts, long tables with white boxes waiting for product. The place wasn't air-conditioned, and giant industrial fans blasted hot air in their faces. Elise could feel the sweat forming on her scalp and back.

"Coffee?" The guy grabbed a couple of cups from the drying rack near the sink and placed them on a round break table littered with dirty plates that he swept aside with his forearm.

Elise sat down. "I'm fine."

David eyed the cup in front of him. "Me too."

"Sweet tea?" The guy hovered. "Some people drink coffee all the time, but maybe something with ice?"

Again they both declined. Elise pulled out a small tablet, mentally noting that he was being a little too nice.

He joined them at the table. "So what can I help you with?" He seemed worried, but he wasn't acting nervous.

"Have you been following the local news?" David asked.

Elise produced a copy of the eight-by-ten composite. "If so, you've probably seen this."

"Sure."

David was sweating too, his hair hanging damp over his forehead. "Some good citizens called our tip line to tell us you bear a resemblance to our suspect." He pushed the image closer.

The guy examined it. "That doesn't look anything like me."

David leaned back in his chair. "I don't think it does either." He was playing good cop.

"How long have you worked here?" Elise asked.

He shrugged. "Six months, maybe."

"How long have you lived in Savannah?"

"Moved here shortly before that."

The questions continued. Elise asked where he'd lived before (Indiana), what had brought him to Savannah (warmer weather and the recent death of his wife).

"There aren't many jobs for guys my age," he told them. "It was either here or McDonald's."

David asked him where he'd been the night of the morgue fire and during the period of time they suspected Loralie had been murdered.

Elise documented his reply, then leaned forward, elbows on the table. "Have you ever been to Florida?"

"Coupla times."

"Within the last year?"

"Not for maybe fifteen years. Went to Disney World." He seemed to remember something. Elise was hoping for information, but in the end he was just playing host again. "How about a doughnut?" He got to his feet and gestured toward the cooling racks. "These are so fresh they should be slapped."

He laughed at his own corny joke, snapped on a pair of kitchen gloves, and pulled out a stainless-steel tray, grabbed two doughnuts with orange icing, and placed them and a heavy plate in the center of the table.

"We're trying this new line that we're going to launch on Johnny Mercer Day." Hands at his waist, legs wide, Hughes said, "This particular one is called 'Tangerine.'"

David picked it up and took a bite. "Not half-bad."

Hughes looked pleased. "We've got another one called 'Moon River.' It's chocolate with a blue river and yellow moon. Dough is rising for those right now."

"You should do one of Johnny Mercer's more obscure songs, like 'Loralie.'" David kept eating the doughnut, acting casual, but he was really watching Hughes for a tell, a reaction to the name of a woman he might have killed.

Hughes frowned. "I'm not familiar with that song."

"No?" David finished the doughnut. "Maybe I'm thinking of another one."

Hughes handed him a napkin. "'Lorna'? He wrote a song called 'Lorna.'"

David wiped his hands on the napkin, then squeezed it into a ball and dropped it on the table. "That must be the one. Anyway, you've got a great product here. And a great idea."

Elise broke in. "Would you be willing to stop by the police department and have your fingerprints taken?"

"So I'm a suspect?"

"No," Elise said. "We're just ruling people out who fit the demographic. That's how we do it. Fingerprints, sometimes DNA."

He thought about it a moment, then shrugged. "Sure, if it'll help. I've got nothing to hide."

From the front of the store, a counter bell rang angrily.

"Gotta go." Before leaving, he grabbed a cardboard box, filled it with doughnuts, passed the box to David. "On the house."

"What do you think?" David asked once they were back outside in the glaring sun. He hit the unlock button, and they got in the car.

"I think it's actually cooler out here than it was in there. But as far as he goes . . . I don't know. I wasn't picking up on anything. Didn't seem nervous, didn't seem like he was trying to hide anything. And there was not a hint of a tell when you mentioned 'Loralie.'"

"Remy isn't going to respond to situations the way most criminals respond. He kills children. He kills women. Let's give this a day or two, but I'm betting that guy doesn't come in for prints. If not, I'm making a trip back here."

"I think you're wrong."

He shrugged and passed her the box of doughnuts.

Elise called Meg Cook to tell her their first lead claimed to have never lived in Florida. "Can you verify that? And once it is verified, dig a little deeper to make sure his story holds up."

"Will do."

More stops, more white guys in their sixties. One panhandled for a living and said he'd made fifty dollars so far that day. He lived in a shelter. Elise wrote down the name and address of the place. David gave him a twenty and the box of doughnuts. The third person was a married man who worked part-time at a sporting-goods store at the mall. Nervous, wouldn't look at them, but agreed to be fingerprinted downtown.

Suspicious, but it could be he just had poor social skills. Or cops scared him. Regardless, Elise moved him to the top of their list. On paper, the fourth guy seemed the most promising. "Piano teacher," Elise said. "Private lessons in his home."

"A little too obvious," David said as they headed for the address. "But you never know. What about the fifth guy?"

"Professional clown."

"Oh man."

"Too obvious again, I know."

"What's Meg doing? Pulling up anybody who shares characteristics with past serial killers? Keep this up and we can have a serial-killer version of the Village People, complete with a clown."

CHAPTER 36

Lucille wasn't taking the breakup with Avery well. Not the type to chase a man, she'd nonetheless gotten up the nerve to invite him to a yoga class. And then, when it didn't seem he'd ever take the hint, she asked him out for coffee, then jogging—and quickly found that he talked way too much about Elise.

Lucille had never liked Elise, mainly due to her dismissive attitude toward reporters, but she'd begun to loathe her once she and Avery began dating. And now she blamed Elise for the breakup. Damn her. Beautiful. Tragic, with this trail of mopey men behind her, the biggest being her own partner. She was like that one girl in school every single guy wanted. And once they realized it would never happen, they moved on to the second- or even third-tier girls. Lucille was a third tier. She'd accepted that long ago, but it didn't mean she didn't want all first-tier women to die. Not really die, but just step out of the damn spotlight for a while.

Third tiers dated and married third tiers. That was the way it worked. Avery was third tier too. He just didn't know it. Most guys didn't know their own tier.

With a start, she realized she'd drifted off again, and looked up from her cubicle. She hadn't been able to write a damn thing for the past twenty-four hours, and she was beginning to worry. She wanted to go to a bar and get drunk. Meet a new guy. Feel attractive again, wipe

Avery from her mind. But going to a dive and getting blind drunk was foolish. She should do yoga instead. Or jog. Eat a healthy meal. Drink plenty of water. Get a good night's sleep. In other words, love herself, not beat herself up.

Still immersed in her pity party, she opened her e-mail and sifted through the most recent messages, hoping for a hook or lead, something easy, something she could throw together in less than an hour with very little thinking.

Days ago she'd gotten the bright idea to circumvent the cops and do her own investigating. On her website, she'd put out a request for info, along with the composite image of Remy. So far she'd received several e-mails with tips and possible sightings, but she'd been too depressed to follow up on anything. One e-mail now got her attention because the subject line contained the name of someone she considered her nemesis, Elise Sandburg. Sent from a Gmail address. No attachment.

She opened it.

It turned out to be from a man who'd witnessed the press-conference fiasco, someone who claimed to have dirt on Detective Sandburg. And he wanted money for that exclusive dirt.

Paying for a story was unethical behavior for a reporter, but she'd been desperate enough to do it a couple of times. And this was dirt on Sandburg . . .

She replied to the e-mail, waited, and within five minutes had a reply and a plan. She closed the browser, grabbed her bag, and left the building. "Checking a lead," she told a couple of curious faces.

Outside, she broke down and sent a text to Avery, asking if he wanted to get together to talk, just talk. He didn't reply, but that wasn't unusual. Even when they were dating he often didn't reply for a few hours.

She swung by the bank for cash, then drove to meet the informant in a location that wasn't a high-traffic, public spot, but wasn't something she'd consider remote or dangerous either. That didn't mean she wasn't careful. She jogged by herself at night. She knew how to watch her back.

Pulling into the park off Skidaway Road, she made sure her phone was in her bag. As an added precaution, she turned on the voice-memo app. Then she felt for her little handgun. It was pink. Ridiculous, but somehow it seemed a less threatening thing to carry.

Dusk was hours off, and the park wasn't empty. She met a jogger and a couple of walkers. Their presence reassured her, and she turned where she'd been instructed to turn, to a pretty area shaded by live oaks and Spanish moss. A couple of minutes more and she came upon a man standing in the middle of the trail, his back to her.

The hair on her arms moved, and her scalp tingled. Call it a sixth sense, but she immediately worried that she'd made a mistake. She felt for her gun, taking little comfort in the weight and feel and shape of it. Maybe this wasn't her contact. She'd just leave. Quietly, so the man wouldn't even hear her.

He turned around.

Her brain struggled to make sense of what she was seeing. She tried to find a face in the mess in front of her. There was a mouth and two eyes, but between those eyes was a crater where his nose should have been.

The eyes watched her without blinking.

She heard someone on the trail behind her. Before she could look, something slammed into her back. At the same time, bark exploded from the tree in front of her while hot pain ripped through her center. She looked down to see blood blooming on the front of her T-shirt.

The man with half a face hadn't moved. He was still standing there staring at her. It was hard to say if he was expressionless, but his eyes didn't register any kind of response, certainly no surprise. But as she began a slow fall to the ground, she saw one side of his mouth twitch in what might have been a smile.

CHAPTER 37

Abe Chilton, head of the local crime scene team, was on-site when David and Elise arrived. Even though they didn't hang out, David had always liked Chilton. The forty-five-ish Chilton had a wife, kids, seemed to love his job. In other words, he was surprisingly well adjusted for someone in his field.

Ten minutes earlier, data had scrolled across the dashboard monitor of David and Elise's unmarked car. *Unidentified female body*, location included. A moment later David's phone had rung. Avery.

"Shit just got even more real." He'd sounded out of breath. "Lucille is dead."

And now here they were, the situation, the body count, the targets themselves feeling more unreal by the hour, and it seemed even breaking up with an acquaintance of Sweet's didn't save you.

Chilton met them halfway, ducking under the yellow tape, sealing a clear evidence bag as he walked. "Single bullet through the heart. And check this out." He motioned for them to follow, all three careful of the numbered evidence cards littering the ground. "I don't think the victim even saw it coming. Looks like the bullet went through her back and out her chest to strike that tree." He pointed. Anticipating their next question, he said, "Bullet was removed before we arrived."

"Cool and calculated," David said.

"Yep."

"Anybody hear anything? See anything?" Elise asked, her eyes scanning the crowd.

"A couple saw a woman alone, but they didn't hear a shot. A mother and her two kids came upon the body." He winced upon mention of the kids, probably thinking of his own in such a situation.

"Silencer?" David wondered aloud.

"That'd be my guess," Chilton said. "I heard Lucille Bancroft launched her own investigation of the Remy case and was asking for tips on her website."

David wasn't surprised. "So maybe she was lured here. We'll see what our forensic techs can dig up. Did she have a phone with her?"

"Yep. Got it bagged. Marilyn has it if either of you want to take a look."

"There's Avery." Elise nodded. "I'm going to see how he's doing."

"Brutal," Chilton said once she was gone. "We didn't know who the victim was at first. Avery shows up thinking it's a routine homicide, or not so routine, depending upon how you look at it. Woman alone. I brief him, and we both figured she was killed by a boyfriend, or maybe it was a drug deal gone bad. We chat awhile; then one of my assistants turns the body slightly so we can see her face." Chilton shook his head. "Poor Avery goes white. I look closer, recognize her."

David knew what Avery was going through. He considered excusing himself to talk to him, but it looked like Elise had things under control. She was touching the detective's shoulder, and he was nodding, hand to his face. No need to intrude.

"How's John?" Chilton asked.

David was glad to be able to share some positive news. "Doctors think he has a chance of a full recovery with time."

"That's great. Shame about Mara, though. She was a sweet kid. But I sure as hell hope John gets back soon. That ass they sent down from Atlanta might be the end of me. She's around here somewhere, so watch out."

"I've had a few run-ins with her over the past couple of years. She seemed a tad too militant for Savannah."

"You're being generous. I've never been around anybody who speaks so little but still manages to be overbearing." Chilton held eye contact a little longer than he should have. "You okay? Because I have to say you look like you could use a good night's sleep."

David rubbed his face, surprised to discover he hadn't shaved. Again. "Not much sleep lately." The sleeplessness should have been due to their unsolved case, but in truth he was also worrying about Elise. Over what Strata Luna had told him and the attack in the parking garage. "In fact, I'm not sure when I last got a full night's sleep." He'd pressed Strata Luna about Elise's scars, wondering if the Gullah woman had misunderstood and Elise had been talking about the tattoo that covered her back. He hadn't mentioned that he'd seen Elise in her underwear and had never noticed any deformities. But Strata Luna convinced him that Elise had been talking about scars, big scars, deep scars.

Everybody had a tipping point. He could only guess that their return to Savannah and the police department, plus the attack on John and murders of Mara and Loralie had been Elise's. No wonder she'd finally decided to see a shrink.

It was his turn to scan the crowd. Elise was no longer with Avery. David spotted her talking to a tech, both of them looking at a clear evidence bag.

And Avery . . . Someone probably should have stuck with him, because he was flipping out in front of the press, shouting, gesturing wildly, unaware of an audience, basically out of his mind. Before David could intervene, Avery pulled out his badge, tossed it to the ground, and stomped away, all of it caught by cameras. As one who wasn't immune to public meltdowns, David internally applauded Avery's behavior.

Moments later, in what seemed an afterthought, Avery returned to find David. "I'm out," he said. "I hate to leave this mess with you and Elise, but I'm done. I can't do it anymore." He put a hand to his chest.

"Lucille was killed because I was dating her, because I've got a target on me. I don't know about you, but I'm going to go home and board up my house, booby-trap it, then sit facing the door with a loaded gun while I wait for that son of a bitch Remy to come for me." He stormed off. David picked up the discarded badge and stuck it in his pocket. Avery would be back. Then David and Chilton joined Elise and the cluster of crime scene techs in black slacks, blue polo shirts, and latex gloves.

Lucille had dropped in what was called a dead-man's fall, ankles crossed, pitched forward, probably dead before she hit the ground.

Crouched next to the body, Elise pointed with a gloved finger. "No sign of struggle. No bruising." She carefully lifted one hand, gently, by the wrist. "Nothing under the nails." She looked up at Chilton. "I think you're right. She didn't see this coming."

A crime scene tech moved close and bagged the victim's hands to keep any evidence from escaping during transport. "I think we're ready to roll and body bag her," she said.

Elise stepped back, and the crew stepped forward.

Dead bodies weren't easy to move, and Lucille wasn't a small woman. Three people rolled the victim into the bag. Then it was zipped and sealed and signed by Hollis Blake, John's replacement, who appeared out of nowhere, acknowledging Elise and David with a nod but no verbal greeting.

Elise snapped off her gloves. "I examined her phone," she told David. "Checked her e-mail, texts, voice memos, and Facebook. Nothing."

"Deleted?"

"That's my guess. I called in a subpoena so we can access her records."

"Why Lucille? She's no friend of Sweet's."

"Maybe Remy was sending a message to anybody who might be thinking of sharing information with us. Plus, he probably had no idea

Avery and Lucille were no longer dating. Speaking of Avery . . . I'm going to stop by his house and check on him."

"Need the car keys?"

"I'll take an Uber."

Seemed safe enough. "Text Avery before you approach his house. He's setting booby traps. And here, take his badge in case he changes his mind." He slapped it into her palm.

The other night, after she'd given him "the talk" in his apartment, David had thought moving to Ohio might be a good idea. Once this case was over he just needed to dive in and do it. But then that damn call from Strata Luna had come, and he'd slid right back to square one, thinking he needed to be here, to watch out for Elise.

His phone rang. A call from the hospital. He answered immediately, expecting a nurse or doctor, surprised to hear John's voice.

"You gotta get me out of here."

CHAPTER 38

David dropped the suitcase on his bed. "This'll work, right?" John stood watching from the doorway, looking shaky and pale. It was the day after Lucille Bancroft's body had been discovered, and John, dressed in pajama bottoms, a white T-shirt, and slippers, had just been released from the hospital—with his surgeon's extremely reluctant consent. On the way to Mary of the Angels, they'd swung by John's house, and David had gone inside to fill the suitcase with clothes and a toothbrush and anything else that looked like it might come in handy. Being there, seeing Mara's things, was tough. David understood why John had chosen to wait outside. And he wondered if his friend would ever be able to enter the house again.

The hospital release hadn't gone smoothly. John's parents had insisted he come home with them. "We've cleaned out your room," his mother said. "We have the backseat of the rental car ready for you, with pillows and blankets."

John had protested, reminding them that the memorial service was the next day.

"We can stay for it," his father had assured him. "We'll get a hotel suite. It'll give you time to rest away from a hospital environment before we head home."

On the surface, if they'd been anybody else, the plan would have seemed a solid one. Seeing the panic on his friend's face, David had intervened, letting them know in no uncertain terms that John would be coming home with him.

"I'm not going to take your bed," John now said, looking ready to pass out.

"Don't worry about it. I sleep on the couch half the time anyway." David fluffed a pillow. "Clean sheets, towels in the bathroom."

John pushed himself away from the wall and dropped to the mattress while David hung clothes in the closet and stuffed what remained in the top dresser drawer he'd emptied. Beside the bed went pain meds and sleeping pills, along with the antidepressant doctors hoped would get his friend through the next few months. David felt doubtful, but from experience he knew they helped. They made it possible to hang on to a certain and specific post-trauma numbness a little longer.

Suitcase unpacked, he helped John under the covers, returning to place a glass of water on the bedside table. "Isobel hates most people, so I don't think she'll bother you."

He'd barely spoken the words when the Siamese appeared and jumped lightly on the bed. "Make a liar out of me." David grabbed her, ready to remove her from the room when John stopped him.

"That's okay. She can stay."

David didn't think of Isobel as a particularly warm cat. In fact, "bitch" was how most people described her, but she further surprised him by plopping down on the mattress. Not close, but not so far that John couldn't reach her if he tried. Maybe she'd be good for him.

"Okay, yell if you need anything."

"I will. Thanks."

It was impossible for David not to think of the John Casper he'd first met upon arriving in Savannah. That electricity, his energy, the nervous way he couldn't seem to sit still. The two of them had immediately bonded over some stupid joke, both dropping into a riff that had annoyed the hell out of Elise. They'd been buddies ever since. David was pretty sure *that* John wouldn't be back. Someone would take his place.

Maybe someone with no light, maybe someone who was bitter and angry, maybe someone who was broken and could only move through the days in a fog.

David was going to miss the old John, but he would do his best to help this one.

His phone rang. It was the girl from Black Tupelo.

"Would you like me to come over tonight?" she asked.

David walked into the living room. "No, that's fine. And honey? Don't call me again, okay? The other night was nice, great, and you're a sweet girl, but it was a onetime thing."

She didn't completely fall for it and said something about coming whenever he needed her.

Before grabbing a couple of hours of sleep, David logged in to the LIMS to check for updates. He was surprised to see that both the baker and the piano teacher had dropped by for fingerprinting. Both passed, and an e-mail from Meg let David know that their stories held up. Marshall Hughes had indeed lived in Indiana and had indeed recently lost his wife. David called Elise to let her know, telling her to check them off her suspect list.

"That leaves the clown, the homeless guy, and the sports-store employee," David said. "It can't be the clown, right? That's too obvious, right?"

CHAPTER 39

Mara, for all of her love of dead bodies, had preferred cremation. *No box for me,* Elise remembered her saying. So there was no body to view at the memorial, just a photo on an easel, along with flowers and candles and sad music.

There had been some hesitation about a public memorial, because it was the perfect place for Remy to make an appearance, and some even worried about a repeat of the cemetery incident, and an all-out massacre. But John had insisted, saying it might be an opportunity to flush Remy out. He was right. And 75 percent of the attendees were involved in some sort of police work, all aware of the situation, all keeping their eyes open. Two armed guards stood at the door, screening guests as they entered, and the police cars parked in front of the church provided a visible presence. The press was not allowed inside, but that didn't keep them from setting up on the front steps and sidewalk.

Inside, people tried to be upbeat as they stood at the podium sharing stories about Mara. But it was impossible to bring the slightest bit of lightness to the occasion, no matter how hard people tried. Added to that was the underlying hostility carried into the room by Mara's parents. They would probably always blame John for their daughter's death and would always be convinced that he'd somehow sacrificed her to save himself. Elise knew the opposite was true. John would have died for Mara, but unfortunately loss often brought anger and pain. And she could see the extra dose of pain they were causing him. As soon as the service ended, she touched him lightly on the arm and whispered, "At least they live far away."

He was dressed in a suit and a tie she suspected David had knotted for him. She recognized the style. On his feet were the only things that looked like John—his red sneakers, something she also suspected had been David's doing. He was trying to remind John of who he was. The old John would have worn the sneakers.

John rewarded her comment with a small smile. "I'm staying at David's for a while."

"I heard." She nodded softly, approving. "I also heard Isobel has taken a shine to you. Believe me, that doesn't happen."

"She sees me as no threat."

His words were sad because they were probably true.

Others were waiting to speak to him, so she told her friend good-bye. "If you need anything, you have my number. Day or night."

Her words might or might not have registered. He numbly turned to the next person in the long line of attendees.

David emerged from the crowd. "I haven't seen anything suspicious."

"Me either."

"Be sure and stop by my place when this wraps up," he said. "Strata Luna is coming, and I think Sweet will be there. Maybe Avery. Just a small, private gathering of close friends." He scanned the crowd. "Once this place clears out. Maybe in an hour."

"How's he doing?"

"Physically he's coming around, but mentally . . ." David shook his head.

"If you need to hire someone to help out, don't forget what we talked about."

"Right now I think he's better off by himself."

Elise's phone vibrated. Her initial reaction was to ignore it, but a glance at the screen told her the caller was James LaRue. She answered.

"Got some interesting news," he said. "Something I think will surprise you."

"Not sure anything can surprise me anymore."

"This might."

"That kind of buildup almost always ends in a letdown."

"Okay, let's see how this plays out. Got a lead on someone who bought TTX from someone."

"A lot of 'someones' in that sentence."

"I can't divulge my source, and I want to stress again that I'm done with TTX unless I can get a grant to continue studying it."

She didn't have time to get into a long conversation with LaRue. "Who was the buyer?"

"Take a guess."

"I'm not going to guess."

"You're no fun."

"Just tell me, LaRue. I'm at a funeral."

David was watching Elise's frustration, curiosity on his face.

LaRue sighed. "The reporter. The woman who was recently found dead on the walking path."

"Lucille Bancroft?"

"That's the one. You sound surprised." He sounded pleased. "Please tell me you're surprised."

"How much confidence do you have in your source?"

"I wouldn't give him a hundred percent rating, but I'm ninety-five percent confident in the information."

"Can you share anything else, like when this was purchased?"

"Not if I want to live."

"Got it." She disconnected and looked at David. "Lucille Bancroft purchased TTX from a dealer."

David was surprised too. LaRue would have been proud of himself.

"I don't get it," Elise said. "Did Lucille have some connection to Remy? Is that why he killed her? She knew too much?"

"I'd be surprised to find there's a connection at all. I don't think the TTX had anything to do with Remy. Maybe Lucille just wanted to take you down."

CHAPTER 40

Medical examiner Hollis Blake wasn't thrilled about her temporary position at the Savannah city morgue, which was somewhat up and running again even though areas of the building were still partitioned off and under repair due to smoke and water damage. She might have been in charge, but she still saw the job as a step down, or at least a detour from her goal to become chief medical examiner at one of the most prestigious medical centers in Atlanta. Savannah was too small, too weird, and the coroner's office was a mess. The fire might have wiped out records and evidence, but she got the idea it had been a mess before. If a young woman hadn't lost her life, the fire itself could have served as a much-needed and thorough cleaning. Now Hollis was working long hours to try and organize what was left and try to make sense of the previous ME's record and filing system.

She'd thought of attending Mara Casper's memorial the day before, but had decided against it. It might have been awkward. She'd talked to John Casper on the phone a few times over the past couple of years, but they'd never met in person. She was beginning to hope they never would, because it was going to be hard to keep her mouth shut about his sloppiness.

That very sloppiness said a lot about the police department itself. They didn't seem to care. *Nobody* seemed to care. They didn't even have a chief of police. From what she'd heard, the position had been vacant for almost two months. Detectives had been fired and rehired. The city was a joke. And now she was here, working for that joke, missing opportunities in Atlanta that might come about only if she remained visible and did an excellent job.

She was all about excellence, and having to clean up someone else's mess, a mess that had taken years to make—it pissed her off.

Right now she was working late in order to upload the full autopsy report of Lucille Bancroft into the database. Expedient uploading of files was something she was adamant about, and it was also something John Casper had neglected to do, thus meaning important evidence had been lost in the fire. Proof that you shouldn't wait.

She heard a bang from the back of the building. Hands on the keyboard, she listened, waiting to see if it repeated. It wouldn't be unusual for criminals to return to the scene of the crime. She'd even been advised against working at night, and Detective Avery had suggested she carry a gun.

A gun.

Ridiculous.

But now, as the banging continued and it became obvious it was at the back door, the very door the criminals had entered when they beat up the previous ME and killed his wife, Hollis checked the industrial wall clock. After two. Maybe she should have looked into that gun. She hit some keys, still having the presence of mind to log out of the database before checking on the noise.

The soles of her sneakers squeaked on the tile floor. At the back door she found herself wishing for a peephole. "Who is it?" she shouted, wondering if her voice would carry through the solid-metal door.

The banging continued, and she imagined an angry fist pounding away just inches from her.

She shouted her question again, louder this time. And this time she got an answer.

"John Casper!"

She heard fumbling, like someone trying to open the door with a key.

They'd installed new locks after the break-in, and from what she understood, Casper hadn't been out of the hospital long. Common sense said this wasn't him.

"You're lying." She felt for the cell phone in her pocket. "I'm calling the police."

"Check the cameras."

It took her a moment to understand. She turned and strode down the hall to the office. A few key clicks brought up live images of the new cameras they'd installed after the attack. She moved the cursor over the frame of the man standing at the back door. She enlarged it to fill her screen.

The image was murky, but suddenly a driver's license appeared. She leaned closer and read the name. *John Casper.*

Moments later the license vanished, and she got a view of the back step and parking lot. He was alone. Not a car in sight other than hers.

She wasn't heartless. The man out there had lost his wife under the most horrific of conditions. And he'd survived. And it had happened right here. But she wasn't a shrink. And she certainly couldn't be a shoulder to cry on, if that's what he was looking for.

Calling 911 wasn't a solution, but she thought about contacting Elise Sandburg or David Gould. They were friends of his, and she vaguely recalled hearing that Casper was temporarily living with Gould. Maybe. She wasn't sure. She'd been so mad about her new position that she'd kept her head down, focusing on the tasks at hand while hoping Casper finally recovered so she could go home.

She returned to the back door. Silence. Had he left?

She listened, then, against her better judgment, unlocked the door. It flew open, slamming against the cement-block wall. A man lurched inside.

Everybody said John Casper was a sweet and gentle guy. She'd seen photos of him. Smiling, friendly, with wildly curly hair. This man was bald. Not completely bald. His head was covered with a shadow of new hair. And his face was not friendly. His eyes were deep black pits, and his skin was the color of paste. One hand was in a cast. Then she saw the red, swollen line across his skull. Evidence of a recent incision. The staple holes were still visible.

She'd heard Casper's injuries had required surgery to relieve pressure in his skull. What she hadn't been told, and what was beginning to seem apparent, was that he'd suffered brain damage.

He shoved past her, the door crashing closed behind him.

She followed, walking rapidly. "You can't be in here." Not true, but it was the first thing she thought of.

He swung around, his black-rimmed eyes boring into hers. "This is my place. *You're* the one who doesn't belong here."

"So right about that," she muttered.

Somehow he heard her. He stopped his dash down the hall and swung back around. "What?"

Now she took in more of him. Faded jeans, a thin white T-shirt with holes near the neckline. He smelled of alcohol, but she wasn't sure how much of his behavior could be attributed to that. Hostility radiated from him, and she took a step back, reached into her lab coat, and pulled out her phone. He slapped it from her hand. It hit the floor and shattered.

"Get out of here!" she shouted. "Get out of here now!"

He made no move to leave.

"I'm calling the police." She spun and ran for the office. He was right behind her, fast for a drunk man with a head injury.

She tried to slam the door, but he was too close. He shoved the door wider and followed her inside. She grabbed the landline phone. It was an old style, not portable, heavy, beige, with a coiled cord and a clunky receiver. Somehow it had survived the water damage. Too bad about that.

He ripped it from the wall. The receiver flew from her hand. He raised the base, his face contorted with pain and rage.

She put up an arm to deflect the blow, and then she shouted a terrified plea so pathetic she couldn't believe it came from her own mouth. "Don't kill me!"

The hand with the phone froze for a second before he threw it hard. It missed her by a yard, hit a filing cabinet, and let out a single loud ring. Without taking his eyes from her, Casper staggered away until his back met the wall. He slid to the floor, landing hard, and buried his face in his uninjured hand.

She had to get to another phone, a working phone, but he was too near the door for her to get past him. As she watched, his shoulders began to shake. And then he let loose huge, gulping sobs.

She'd seen men cry a few times in her life, but nothing like this. Nothing like this kind of unbridled anguish. She wasn't even sure she liked men, or even sure she liked people in general, but the sound of his pain cut her to the bone.

This is what love is like, she thought. *This is what it does to you.*

She'd had a dog once, and when it died she'd decided she never wanted another pet, because it had been too painful. Loss of a human must be a hundred times worse than that.

She approached him with caution. No longer intent on getting past him, she found herself lightly touching his shoulder. That touch evoked a wail and a long shudder. She jerked her hand away. Then she just sat down beside him, back to the wall, and waited.

* * *

David's phone rang, and he jerked awake, his neck stiff, a slight bit of drool on his face and arm, surprised and disoriented to find that he'd fallen asleep at his desk in the police department. He had a vague memory of telling Elise he'd go home in an hour or so to shower and sleep. Missed that train. Seeing the call was from the morgue, he blinked himself fully awake.

He expected a case-cracking report, or at least some news that might help them in the Remy case. Instead he heard the oddly hesitant voice of the substitute ME (because he would never accept that she was possibly permanent).

"I'm sorry to bother you this late, but we've got an issue. I'm at the morgue, and John Casper is here."

That seemed doubtful. "You sure it's Casper?" Last he'd seen him, John had been asleep in David's bed, Isobel curled up beside him.

"Oh, it's him. I don't know how he got here, but he's in no condition to drive. Can you come and get him?"

David checked the clock, confirming his suspicion of having been asleep for hours. "Be there in fifteen minutes."

At the morgue, Hollis Blake met him at the back door. Standing next to her was John, arms dangling at his sides, head down, looking like a child who'd been caught doing something wrong.

Behind them on the floor was a shattered cell phone.

"What happened here?" David asked.

Hollis gave him a look that said it would be better if they didn't discuss it in front of John. "Everything's fine." She jammed her hands into the deep pockets of her lab coat. "We can talk later if you like."

He read the scene. From the looks of things, he guessed John'd had a meltdown. Poor guy. "Thanks." He meant thanks for taking care of his friend. Thanks for being concerned about him. Thanks for not calling the regular police.

To John, he asked, "How'd you get here?"

"Uber," he mumbled.

Amazing that he'd been able to get to the morgue by himself. "Let's get you home."

John shuffled along beside him, docile, almost catatonic.

Behind them Hollis said, “If he wants to work part-time, that would be fine with me. It might be good for him. Once he’s stronger.”

In the past, David had found Hollis abrasive and devoid of humor, but now he cut her some slack. MEs tended to be a strange breed, most of them unlike John. At the same time, he was doubtful about John returning to the place where Mara had been killed and where they’d worked together. Memories would be everywhere. It probably didn’t help that Hollis Blake couldn’t be more opposite from Mara, even in looks. Older by several years, tall, reddish hair, a cross between severe and geeky. “I’ll see how he feels about that,” David said. Weird that she seemed to have more hope than he did, but then she’d never known the old John Casper.

CHAPTER 41

Simone Millett's phone rang. She adjusted the squirming baby on her hip, searched the diaper bag slung over her shoulder, dug out her phone, and answered her husband's call. "Can't talk now," she said. "I'm at the farmers' market, and it's crazy busy. I stopped to get homemade bread, but the damn bread guy isn't here."

The pacifier hit the ground. Juggling baby, phone, and bag, Simone picked up the pacifier, contemplated it as the baby's mouth opened wide in a silent wail. She jammed the dirty pacifier in her pocket, and the cry went live.

"Get some of that orange marmalade," her husband said, his oblivion and lack of empathy driving her irritation up a few more notches. The man didn't have a clue.

"Why should I get marmalade if we don't have homemade bread?" She looked back the way she'd come, at the wide sidewalk that ran from one end of Forsyth Park to the other, each side lined with vendors and shaded by live-oak trees and Spanish moss, the space between packed with people. "I thought the bread man was always here."

"Look what I got." Six-year-old Taylor patted her hip and lifted a bouquet of flowers.

Simone frowned. "Where'd you get those?"

He pointed through the crowd. "That man gave them to me."

"Oh, honey. He's blind. He wasn't *giving* them to you. He's selling them."

"Will you buy them?"

"No, give them back."

"Please?"

"No."

He stuck out his bottom lip and buried his face in the daisies.

"Go on. Take them back." She spoke more firmly this time, and he turned and stomped away. She'd be surprised if he actually obeyed her. He'd been testing boundaries ever since the arrival of his baby brother.

"When are you getting home?" her husband asked. She could barely hear him over the crying baby. People scowled as they passed. A few women shot her a look of sympathy, but she could also see what they were thinking: *Glad it's you and not me.*

"Aren't we having company for dinner?" he asked. "Or was that canceled?"

"Yes, we're having company," Simone said. "Traffic was backed up, and then Taylor was late getting out of school. And now the market's so crowded I'm about to lose my mind."

"I'm sorry. Take a deep breath."

It made her all the madder when he pulled that calm stuff on her. "I gotta go," she said. "Be home in forty-five minutes. Why don't you make a salad? Set the table? Pick up the toys? Give the bathroom a quick clean?"

"No problem."

His willingness made her feel bad about being annoyed. She put her phone away and realized Taylor was nowhere in sight. At first she was relieved, taking it to mean he'd actually listened to her and returned the flowers, but as time ticked away and he didn't return, she began to worry. Jiggling the still-crying baby, she squeezed through the throng of people and interrupted a flower sale to address the blind man.

"Did you see a boy?" She realized what she was saying and corrected herself. "Did a boy give your flowers back?"

"No, ma'am. You owe me ten bucks."

She watched the news. She knew it wasn't safe for anybody right now, especially young boys. But that kind of awful thing happened to other people.

Trying not to panic, she hiked the baby higher on her hip and dug into her shoulder bag, pulled out a twenty, shoved it into the man's outstretched hand, then ran off through the crowd, shouting for her son, her mother's heart hammering.

Her fear didn't go full blown until she saw the bouquet of flowers on the ground, stems broken, petals bruised. Along with the increase in fear, she experienced an inexplicable sense of denial. It felt as if someone had tossed a blanket over her, muffling her thoughts, protecting her from the possibility of something evil. Briefly she even imagined going home and preparing dinner, sticking to the script of minutes earlier. Later she'd tuck Taylor into bed, read him a story, kiss him good night. But while she frantically scanned the crowd, distantly aware of faces fading in and out and people watching her with concern and alarm, she knew deep down that something dark and serious and impossible was really happening.

With the baby shrieking in her ear, this time frightened by Simone's strange expression, she screamed Taylor's name.

CHAPTER 42

It was a kidnapping, not a homicide. Not their case, but the age and sex of the victim, along with the circumstances surrounding the abduction, made it something David felt merited their attention. Often kidnappings were treated as family abductions by the police department. David wanted to make sure that didn't happen. Speed was important. Sometimes it was everything. Life and death.

He and Elise arrived at the scene an hour after the boy vanished. The initial chaos following a missing-child report had died down. People were no longer running in circles, searching frantically, calling the boy's name. That was over. Now cops were scattered around the park, interviewing possible witnesses. A photo and description of the child, from weight and age to clothing, had been uploaded to the police-department website, and information was scrolling across squad-car monitors and television screens at that very moment.

They found the mother in shock, but responsive and helpful.

Elise made the introductions, and David pulled out pen and paper. "We're going to need the name, address, and phone number of the child's birth father," he said. "Often abductions are familial."

"It wasn't him." The mother, a tall woman named Simone Millett, hugged her folded arms to her as if she had a stomachache. In the distance, her husband cradled an infant while the baby sucked and patted a bottle. "And I already gave that information to someone else."

"Asking about relatives is procedure," Elise explained.

"Why haven't you issued an Amber Alert?"

"That requires a vehicle ID and plate number." David clicked his pen. "But we're feeding a photo and description of your son to police and the public right now."

"It wasn't Gerard. He's had nothing to do with Taylor, ever. He's never even seen him." She explained what happened. Elise and David shared a look.

The Florida abductions and later the abduction of Zane Novak had all occurred in a crowd. In a public place. Those old-favorite abduction locations like parking lots had lost popularity over the years. And with neighborhood watch groups and stranger-danger campaigns, the perpetrator cruising the street looking for victims wasn't as common either. Hide in a crowd. It was smart. That's what David would do if he were an evil bastard.

"But you're homicide detectives. Why are you here? Does that mean he's already dead?" Her voice rose on the last words, and she looked from David to Elise for reassurance.

"No," Elise said. David could see that the words of comfort she was trying to formulate were hard coming.

"We think this might be connected to a case we're working," he offered.

"That Remy guy."

"Yes."

The woman wasn't surprised. She'd been expecting it. David could see it in her face. "He brought me a bouquet of flowers." She pressed a shaking hand to her mouth. With red-rimmed eyes, she looked from one detective to the other. "I told him to take them back. If I'd only let him keep them. If I'd *bought* them, he'd still be here. Isn't it strange to think that an action so small and innocent could do such harm?"

"I'm sorry," David said softly. Parents always shouldered the blame. He knew that, understood that. Parents were supposed to protect their children. Protection was every child's right.

Simone wiped at her nose. "If it's that man, that Remy, what does he do to them?" she asked. "I know he kills them and stuffs them in walls. But I mean before that. What does he do? That's what I want to know."

"That won't help you right now," Elise said. "That kind of information would do you no good."

"I know, I know. Weird, isn't it?" She shook her hands as if trying to shake off water. "I can't stand the thought of him being afraid or being hurt. I'd almost rather he was dead."

Elise touched her arm and got the woman to look her in the face. Once she did, Elise said, "We're going to do everything we can."

Simone pulled in a quivering breath and stood up straighter. "I'm glad you're here." She glanced at David, then back to Elise. "Both of you. I saw the news about you and Chicago. And I don't care about that YouTube video." She waved it away. "What you do in your time off makes no difference to me. If you want to dance naked in the cemetery, that's nobody's business. You catch bad people. You kill them. You arrest them. So . . ." She nodded to herself, finding comfort in her acknowledgment of their presence. "I'm glad it's you. I'm glad you're here."

David could sense Elise's dismay, her hidden reaction to the responsibility of a child's life that had just been handed to them. He was feeling it too.

Right now things didn't look good. If it was Remy, did it mean he was falling back on his pattern of child kidnappings and killings? Was there a bigger reason for the abduction? Was it Remy at all? Whoever was behind it, David knew the child probably didn't have long, and he wasn't feeling confident about winning this round. But he and Elise were good at hiding reactions. They comforted the mother, offered her hollow words of encouragement, went through the motions, and gathered everything they could.

The mother turned her phone around so Elise and David could see the photo of her missing son. "He's beautiful, isn't he?"

The detectives agreed.

"Those eyes," David said.

"That's one thing he got from his deadbeat dad." Simone stuck the phone in her back pocket and looked behind her as she frantically scanned the nearby crowd for her husband, relief coming when she spotted him and their baby. David understood that she'd thought they might have vanished into thin air too. It made sense.

Their best chance of finding the boy was for a citizen to have spotted him, maybe when the abduction was being played out, or later. Maybe at a gas station, or as he was being moved from a vehicle to a place of captivity. The fact that the kid was strikingly beautiful would help. Dark hair, dark skin, and those brilliant blue eyes. He'd be noticed. People would remember him. Of course that might also be the reason he'd been grabbed in the first place.

David and Elise excused themselves to track down the flower seller, the last person at the scene to have had contact with the boy. They'd already been warned he was blind, so there would be no visual information he could give them, but hopefully he'd picked up on something a seeing person might miss.

As they walked, David offered Elise a bite of a cookie he'd grabbed from Parker's Market earlier.

Elise eyed it with suspicion. "What kind is it?"

"Oatmeal and peanut butter."

"That sounds horrible."

"It not too bad, actually."

"My father's method of justice is beginning to make sense to me." Elise took a bite of the cookie, didn't make a face, passed it back. "Not that I'd ever consider taking matters into my own hands the way he has, but I get it now." She chewed, swallowed. "The punishment really isn't about punishment. It's not about making bad people pay for the bad things they've done. It's about making sure they don't ever do anything bad again."

David finished off the cookie, wadded up the wrapper, and tossed it in a nearby trash container. "You might not agree, but I think your father is a brave man. He might not do things the way you or I would, but that doesn't mean the choices he's made are easy. He sees something that needs to be done, and he does it."

Elise and David introduced themselves to the blind man.

"Did you say your name was Detective Sandburg?" He was about seventy, with skin like leather. His clothes were tidy, and even though it was hot as hell, his white shirt was buttoned to his throat. He was a regular at the farmers' market and was known for pulling out a harmonica and joining some of the other musicians who sometimes busked in the park.

"Yes," Elise said. "I work for the Savannah Police Department."

The man reached into his pocket and produced a folded piece of paper. "I was told to give you this. I didn't understand at the time. Guy just came by, bought some flowers, and handed me this note. Said to give it to you when you showed up."

Elise looked at David, then took the folded piece of paper and opened it.

David watched her read the note, watched her face go pale. When she was done, her eyes met his, and she seemed startled to find him there. Without a word, she passed the note to him.

It was his turn to go white. He had an answer to his earlier question. This wasn't an unrelated child abduction. The message was from Remy, and he wanted to make a trade.

Someone jostled him. Like the mother just minutes ago, David looked up and experienced a brief moment of panic when he didn't immediately see Elise. She reappeared with an evidence bag. She handed it to him, and he stuck the note inside. Too late to worry about touching it.

They finished questioning the flower seller.

"He had a voice that made me think he was white and middle aged. I imagine people certain ways, just from their voice. I'm right about eighty percent of the time, even down to hair color, but when I'm wrong I'm really wrong."

While David looked on, heart still slamming, Elise thanked the man and gave him her card. He tucked it in the same pocket where the note had been. As if on cue, her phone rang. She checked the screen and answered it. As she listened, her expression went through a transformation that told him the identity of the person on the other end, a man who seemed to know everything about them while they knew nothing about him, not even what he looked like.

CHAPTER 43

As Elise stood on the edge of Forsyth Park, some distance from the abduction spot, sun beating down, the world shrank to nothing but the voice at the other end of the line. She moved away from anyone within earshot, hitting "Speaker" so David could listen.

"I want to make a deal," the man said. His words were muffled and distorted, and she had to strain to hear.

"Okay. I'll deal," Elise told him. "Whatever you want."

Beside her, David nodded, opened and tapped his "Record" app, and held it near Elise's phone. Recording the conversation was legal. Georgia had a one-party consent law, but if she'd used her own phone app to record, it would have alerted the caller.

"I'm calling from a burner phone, so don't waste your time trying to trace this. And I'm also not anywhere near my home base, so don't waste your time trying to triangulate the call. Within minutes of hanging up I'll be far from this location."

Which meant he was in a vehicle.

"I want confirmation that the child is alive," she told him.

The abductor put the boy on. Elise spoke to him, softly, assuring him that he'd be home with his mother soon. He cried. But at least he *could* cry. For now. She tried not to dwell on the likelihood that the recording of the conversation might very well be the last time his mother heard his voice.

"That's enough," the man told the boy, reclaiming the phone.

"What do you want?" she asked.

They might not be able to trace him, but the longer she kept him on the phone, the more likely he'd slip up and reveal something that would help them find him. A speech pattern, or background noise that might alert them to his vicinity. Anything.

"I want Jackson Sweet to suffer," he said. "I want him to turn and twist and lose his mind."

So it *was* Remy. "The child has nothing to do with this. Why involve him?"

He didn't answer her question. "You think I'm bad, but I'm not."

"I'd like to believe that." She wanted to point out the bad things he'd done. Instead she said, "If not, let Taylor go. Drop him off at a corner. Or in a park. We'll find him."

"Your father framed me. Did you know that? Framed me for a murder I never committed. He *ruined* my life."

"Let's talk about this. Let's discuss your options. Maybe we can get the case reopened."

He wasn't listening. "I had a girlfriend. I was engaged to be married. Had my own business. He took all of that away from me. If I'm a bad man, he made me one."

"So you didn't kill children before your incarceration?"

"I love children. Is that what he told you? I wanted children of my own."

John Wayne Gacy had professed to loving children too. "The house with the bodies inside. What do you know about that? And Zane Novak? I'd like to get to the truth, and if you know who's behind these crimes, we should talk. Can we talk? Face-to-face? Right now?"

"It's too late."

"What about Florida? Do you have any insight into the Florida cases? You might be of help to us."

"Just some crazy lunatic." He sounded distracted now. She was losing him.

Quickly, before he hung up, she repeated her earlier question, keeping her voice smooth as she attempted to placate him. "What do you want? What can I do for you? How can I help you? Let me help you."

"I want to destroy Jackson Sweet the way he destroyed me. And in order to do that, I want to destroy the person who means the most to him."

"Strata Luna," Elise said.

"I'm not talking about her. I'm talking about you."

No reason to correct him. This worked in their favor. "You'll have me," Elise said as David gestured frantically, trying to stop the direction of the conversation even though she had no intention of going anywhere with Remy. "Just tell me where and how. You can have me right this minute if you tell me where to meet you."

"You, for the boy," Remy said. "Downtown tomorrow night, during Johnny Mercer Day."

Like Remy's choice of an abduction site, downtown was a smart move. The noise and the confusion and the crowds would be his cover. And the area was a dark maze, with alleys and stairways and passages cut between stone. Such an easy place to vanish.

"The boy is your fault, Elise. I tried to meet you under different circumstances, but you wouldn't cooperate."

Criminals often saw themselves as victims, with everyone else to blame. "You're the one behind the goofer dust on my porch," Elise said.

"Not me."

"How about the tainted apple?"

"That wasn't me either. If it *had* been, we wouldn't be having this conversation right now. I would have snagged you the night you walked to the cemetery."

Was he telling the truth? Had David been right about the apple and the goofer dust having no connection to Remy? Was the information she'd gotten from LaRue accurate? "But you were the one tailing me," she said. "And you attacked me in the parking garage."

He ignored her question, and she could sense he was growing more agitated. "I have something for you," he told her, jumping to another topic. "A gift."

"I'm partial to jewelry."

"You don't wear jewelry. You're just trying to keep me talking. Let the present be a surprise. Tomorrow night," he said. "Stroll west on River Street through the middle of the crowd. I'll find you."

"And you'll have the boy."

"I'll have the boy. If anything goes wrong, he'll be killed. I don't want to do it, but I will." His voice shook with what seemed excitement. "I'll torture him; then I'll strangle him. And it will be your fault. I'll even record it so the mother can watch over and over."

CHAPTER 44

Once David failed to talk Elise out of the exchange, he turned his attention to making sure nobody got hurt, especially Elise. They'd go through the motions of Remy's game, catch him, and it would all be over.

He e-mailed the recording to digital forensics to see if they could pick up any background noise or lift the muffle from the voice. Somebody else was researching green sedans registered in the county, state, and beyond. Once again they were asking for help from the public, and the tip line was ringing off the hook. A few people were prioritizing the calls, and officers were knocking on doors and conducting interviews, but David had the feeling it was all an exercise in futility.

"This can't happen," Sweet said. After hearing about Remy's demands he'd driven straight to the police station, frightened and intimidated the officer at the security checkpoint, then stormed into David and Elise's office. Avery was also on board, leaving his barricaded home to be part of the operation.

They were braced for what had to be done, but none of them were quite prepared for the storm that was Jackson Sweet.

"Remy, and I'm sure it's Remy, isn't going to let that kid go." Sweet paced while Avery sat on the corner of Elise's desk, nervously rubbing his face and staring at the floor. He obviously didn't want to be there, but he was back to support Elise.

"Can't talk her out of it," David said. "I tried."

But Sweet was right. David wasn't going to fool himself. He knew there was a good chance the boy wouldn't survive. There was a good chance he might be dead already, but David tried not to think about that. "We have to go into this knowing we might fail and the boy might die anyway," he said. "Remy likes to kill kids, and it seems unlikely that he'll release this one."

"He might," Elise said. "Since we're promising him something he wants."

"I don't see that we really have a choice," David told Sweet. "Not if there's any chance of saving the boy, no matter how slight."

Sweet stopped in front of him, and for the first time David saw the full-blown persona Elise had told him about. "You always have a choice." The friendly grandpa was gone, his face replaced with cold, calculating eyes and an overall aura of emotionless brutality that sent a chill up David's spine. That brutality was now directed at David. "Don't drag Elise into your do-over. You're trying to make up for your own failures by backing this dangerous plan."

"What are you talking about?"

"I'm talking about your kid. The older we get, the more we try to fix our mistakes, mistakes that can't be fixed. You want to save this kid because you couldn't save your own."

Elise stepped forward and tried to urge Sweet away, but he jerked his arm from her hand and refused to break eye contact with David, unaware of the daughter he was defending. "You can't bring your own child back," Sweet said. "You can't make up for not noticing you were married to someone who was a danger to that child. Don't use this stage to try to make yourself feel better about your life and your loss."

"You son of a bitch."

Sweet's words were basically the same words Lamont had spoken to David not that long ago. And David had knocked the ex–FBI agent on his ass. It took everything to keep him from punching Sweet.

Sweet saw David's attempt at restraint and smiled. Even his smile was chilling. "You'd like to hit me, wouldn't you?"

"If you weren't so old and feeble and pathetic, I would."

Sweet finally broke eye contact and swung around, faced his daughter, but his voice still held that cold edge. "Don't do this, Elise." It was spoken as an order. A parent telling his child she could not, must not, endanger her life.

"If we're going to talk about the psychology of our own behaviors," Elise said, "then let me point out that the reason you're protesting is because of the guilt you'll feel if anything happens to me. Remove yourself from the equation for a moment, and think about the right thing to do." She stared back at him, cold eyes to cold eyes, waiting for a response.

He said nothing.

"I didn't think so," she said. Her father dismissed, Elise addressed the others in the room. "I don't want to hear any more talk about why we shouldn't do this. That's a waste of valuable time. Let's focus."

The next two hours were awkward, but they formulated a plan, coordinating with their sniper team, all of them knowing no exchange would actually take place. Elise would not be going with anybody. She'd wear a tracking device in the off chance they lost her in the crowd. They'd have police positioned in various locations. Snipers on roofs.

"You'll walk through the crowd," David said. "When you reach Remy or the boy's handler, you grab the kid and drop. We'll take Remy out." He glanced at Sweet, then back to Elise. "I know you'll want to go after Remy, but your one and only focus will be to shield the child and protect yourself. We'll do the rest. We'll have people stationed up and down the street, people on buildings. Remy won't get out of there."

Elise nodded, then blinked as she received a text. She pulled her phone from her pocket and checked the screen.

David was on full alert. "That him?"

Elise stuck her phone back in her pocket. "It's nothing." She excused herself and left the room while David watched her go.

* * *

Down the hall, Elise made sure the restroom was empty, pulled out her phone, and read the message again. Further instructions from Remy for the exchange, these meant for her alone. If she didn't comply, if she didn't follow the instructions to the letter, the child would die. If she told anyone else, especially her partner, the child would die. She leaned against the wall, eyes closed, head back, heart pounding, legs weak. Could she risk being captured? For the child? Coming to a decision, she called James LaRue. "I need to meet with you," she told him.

"Where? When?"

"Right away. And LaRue? I want you to bring something."

"Can't imagine what that would be, but shoot."

"TTX."

"I already told you, I don't mess around with that stuff anymore."

"Don't lie to me."

"I had nothing to do with that incident with you in the cemetery."

He sounded a little too adamant, and she was beginning to wonder if he'd tricked them again. Had *he* supplied Lucille with the drug? That would be just like him. "I didn't say you did. This isn't a bust. I don't want to arrest you. I don't want to pry into what you're doing. But I need TTX."

He thought about it, then said, "Okay."

She told him to meet her outside the market and gas station just around the corner from the police station. He agreed.

"I don't know what you're going to use this for," LaRue said thirty minutes later. He sat across from her at a small table in the blazing sun, eyes unreadable behind dark glasses as he pushed a small white envelope to her. "I cut it so it wouldn't be so potent, but this small amount is still enough to kill a grown man." His voice held concern. "More than enough."

Or kill a grown woman.

She picked it up, folded it, and stuck it in her pocket.

He took a long suck from a straw and leaned back in his chair. "Can I get you some sweet tea?"

"I've got to go." She stood up. "But thanks."

Remaining seated, head tilted back, he said, "Sorry about that time I drugged you. I'm not really a bad guy, you know."

"Sorry about that time I sent you to prison."

"Would you go out with me sometime?"

The straightforward innocence of his question caught her off guard. "I don't think so." She didn't add that she might not be around much longer.

CHAPTER 45

Everything was ready for the exchange, the setup and positioning to take place in several hours. There was nothing else Elise could do but pace and wait.

She wanted to go home. Just for a while. When she voiced that desire, her father said he'd sit at her front door with a gun, and Strata Luna said she'd send her driver and bodyguard. But Elise didn't trust Sweet or Strata Luna right now. Sweet was so adamantly against the plan that she wouldn't put it past him to hold her captive until the evening was over and the child was dead.

In the end, David went with her.

Everyone experienced those fleeting or not-so-fleeting moments of dread and something that felt like a solid and trustworthy and impossible-to-ignore portent of the future. Some came true and some didn't. When those events happened, when the dreaded thing occurred, Elise always wondered about the how. Did thinking about it put it out there in the world? Make it happen? Was time somehow more flexible than people knew? Had she already lived it, and the reason it resonated more than déjà vu was because it was something bad, very bad?

This time she understood the sense of finality she felt about the day and about her life. She caught herself thinking that this could be the last time she unlocked her front door, the last time she stepped inside to the scent of old and new. In the living room, she inhaled and let the space calm her, soothe her. She needed this house in this moment. And as much as she'd convinced herself she'd gotten the home for Audrey, Elise understood that she'd also bought it for herself. It calmed her. It centered her.

David had been quiet on the drive. Too quiet for David.

"I don't want Audrey to know about this until it's done, until it's over," she told him.

He nodded.

She wanted to lie down in her own bed, for just an hour, maybe two.

David followed her upstairs. In her bedroom, he pulled a chair close. "I'm sitting here until it's time to go."

Once she was in bed and the light was out, she whispered in the softened room shadowed by the light from streetlamps seeping in around the shutters. "Come lie down beside me."

He did, with a sigh, arm behind his head as he stared up at the ceiling.

She turned to him and put a hand to his unshaven jaw. Had she ever touched him like this? She didn't think so.

No spells. No mojos. Nothing that was false or forced. Nothing that didn't feel right. It wasn't fair to David, coming to him now, but it also seemed the only way she might ever come to him, on a night that could very well be her last.

What would a shrink have to say about that?

Their time together was measured and sad—the removing of clothing, the exploration and memorization of muscles and curves. Like that other time in his apartment, David trembled and his breath caught. She found herself soothing him, shushing him, whispering to him, words she didn't even realize she was saying until they were spoken.

She wanted to tell him she loved him, but that would be too cruel. It was bad enough that she'd given in during the final hour. If she were to die, if she were to lose her mind, he'd have one more thing to face. So, as they wrapped themselves around each other, as they held on tightly, she whispered, "This doesn't mean I love you." The lie was a gift for him.

His breathless reply was equally unromantic, his forehead resting against hers. "I know." Spoken as if to reassure her, to let her know it was okay that she didn't. That maybe his love was enough for both of them.

They dozed a little, and talked a little, and made love again. Two hours after arriving at the house, they dressed in silence.

She didn't try to hide her scarred body. Let him see it now in these last hours. But she kept her head down, not wanting to witness his revulsion. She was brave, but not that brave.

Once they were dressed, she forced herself to look up and saw longing and confusion in his eyes. He wasn't repulsed. That's how much he loved her. He swallowed, broke eye contact.

She trusted him. He was strong enough. He would hold it together for as long as he needed. Save the child. He would save the child. Because Sweet was right. Funny that Sweet had called him out about putting a child before her when her father had admitted to framing Remy for the very same reason. To save children.

They gathered their things. Avery called to let them know the team was setting up along River Street.

She disconnected.

David was watching her with an intensity she'd never seen in him before. And he looked like hell, or at least as much like hell as David Gould could look. His hair was wild and over his forehead, his shirt buttoned incorrectly. She reached for him, began to redo the buttons. "It might be okay. Everything might be okay."

He put his hands over hers. "This was good-bye. I know good-bye when I see it."

She finished with the last button and repeated herself. "It might be okay."

"There's something you aren't telling me. What aren't you telling me?"

"You know everything I know." She watched his face, could see the exact moment he believed her lie.

He spun away, his back to her, hands at his waist. She watched his shoulders rise and fall as he looked down at the floor and pulled himself together. He slipped his Smith & Wesson from his belt and checked the magazine. "Don't do anything stupid just because you couldn't possibly deal with the awkwardness of seeing me every day after this."

She almost laughed. He knew her so well.

He looked over his shoulder. "If you want me to forget about it, I can do it. I'm good at forgetting." He slid his gun back in the holster. "If everything goes the way it should—and it will—I'll pretend sex between us never happened."

She had bigger concerns right now. And he was talking as if she'd return, as if there would be a tomorrow. She wasn't sure if she'd come back from this. Physically or mentally. She didn't tell David that.

She felt a stab of terror, then thought about the envelope from LaRue, and a calm came over her. The things that had made the psychologist cry? Nobody would ever do those things to her again. She would be in control of her own life. In control of her own death.

CHAPTER 46

The towering brick and stone warehouses of Savannah's River Street had been built on a bluff, with the lower floors opening to wharves for the loading of cotton and rice onto cargo ships docked in the port. What remained of those days were dark and narrow passageways and tunnels—places where the roots of the city, good and bad, could still be felt.

Today it was a place where history and tourism collided, and the riverfront, with its eateries, hotels, and bars, smelled like taffy and fried food, cigarettes, cigars, and beer. Now, near midnight and just minutes from the time the exchange was to take place, boats were anchored in the Savannah River waiting for the fireworks to begin, and the street was crammed with thousands of people, most of them drunk. Girls in short dresses stumbled along the trolley tracks, snagging their heels in the deep spaces between the cobblestones as they screamed with laughter.

River Street was for tourists, not locals.

"Don't do anything heroic," David had told Elise thirty minutes earlier as he'd tightened the Velcro of her bulletproof vest. "When you're close to the boy, grab him, duck, and run. We'll do the rest." A simple plan.

David, Sweet, and Avery, along with strategically positioned sharpshooters, were on roofs. At street level, plainclothes cops were in the crowd, keeping an eye out while Elise stood in an alley, her back to a wall, waiting for her cue.

David's voice came through her earpiece. "Nod if you can hear me." She nodded, knowing he was watching her through binoculars.

"Okay, say something."

She spoke into her chest. "A woman just pulled down her pants in front of God and everyone and is peeing in the street."

He laughed.

The sound relaxed her, but only for a moment. A loud report echoed off the warehouses and bluff to roll across the sky, announcing the start of the fireworks and the signal to begin her walk.

"Be careful," David said. "If it comes down to the kid or you, choose yourself. I mean it, Elise."

The undulating crowd on River Street was like a current she just had to move with. People were shoulder to shoulder, and occasionally she felt a hand grope her ass. She didn't react. She wouldn't allow anything to distract her.

As she walked, David spoke in her ear. "Anything?"

"No," she said. "I'll keep moving west."

It seemed impossible, but the crowd thickened. It was like a rock concert, people shoulder to shoulder, nowhere to move. With a discreet gesture meant to look like the stroking of her hair, Elise ducked her head and removed the earpiece to let it fall to the ground, where it was immediately trampled. Under cover of the crowd, she unclipped the mic from her shirt and dropped it too, completing the process by untaping and ditching the tracking device. It would take a while for David to notice. Hopefully she'd be long gone by then.

The crowd surged forward. She spotted an opening, cut through, and ducked into a bar. Inside, she worked quickly, stripping off her dark shirt, pulling a black cap from her vest, slapping it on her head. That was followed by aviator glasses. She peeled back the Velcro and removed the vest, uncovering a baby-blue top. All so her own men wouldn't spot her when she emerged on the other side of the building.

Like many riverfront businesses, the bar had a back entrance. She walked through the establishment, climbed three flights of stairs, and exited high on Factor's Walk, where it was relatively quiet compared to the crush of the lower street.

Head down, she moved quickly along the sidewalk, crossing a park-like area as she put distance between herself and the river. Behind her the sky exploded and people cheered. On Bay Street, just as she'd been told, a black van waited. When she was even with it, the side door slid open, the interior dark and foreboding.

She stopped. "The boy."

In a move that took her by surprise, a child was shoved out the open door. He fell to the ground like a broken doll, silent and still. She didn't know if he was alive or dead.

"Leave him," came a voice from the darkness. "I have a gun on his head, and I'll shoot if you don't get in the van."

She got in the van.

***

While the team fanned out to search for Elise, David scrambled down the fire escape, dropping several feet to the street below. He ran, shoving his way through the crowd, taking the path she'd been on before communication had failed. He ducked inside the bar where he'd lost visual, and immediately spotted a black shirt and Elise's bulletproof vest on the floor in the corner.

Not equipment failure. She or someone else had removed it. He suspected Elise herself and now understood her uncharacteristic behavior earlier and why her actions and her demeanor had been one of acceptance of defeat. She'd been preparing for this. While they'd been making plans, Elise had been following her own script. Or rather a script likely provided by Remy.

He shouldered his way through the bar and took three flights of stairs to the main street, ducking out the door. He ran down the sidewalk, his eyes searching for anything out of the ordinary. He stopped a couple, asked if they'd seen a woman. "About five foot seven, dark hair?" He spotted a group of people looking at something on the ground. He ran for them, shouting Elise's name. When he got close, he saw that the shape was too small for Elise.

A child.

Approaching, he pulled out his phone, called 911, and gave them the location. Then he broke through the onlookers to crouch next to the boy. In the light of the fireworks exploding overhead, David recognized Taylor Millett, his eyes red and filled with tears, his mouth covered with silver duct tape. Bruised arms were secured behind his back.

"I'm a cop," David said softly. "I'm here to help you." Carefully, knowing it would hurt, he removed the tape from the boy's face. Taylor didn't react—probably in shock.

"Anybody have a knife?" David asked.

A guy stepped forward and handed him a pocketknife, blade open. David cut the tape from the child's wrists. Without taking his eyes from the boy, he passed the knife back.

Taylor's mouth opened wide, and sobs erupted.

"You're okay." David pulled him into his arms and hugged him to his chest, burying his face against the boy's sweet and sour hair, remembering the scent of his own child. "You're okay now."

The boy clung to him, small hands gripping David's shirt, clinging to his tie. It shouldn't have gone down this way, but the child was safe. And David knew this had been Elise's plan.

Sirens wailed, and an ambulance pulled to a stop on Bay Street. Doors flew open, and flashlight beams cut erratically through the narrow strip of park.

The boy didn't want to let go, and the young female medic had to pry him away. "You'll be okay," David said. "You get to ride in an ambulance. And you'll see your mother very soon."

Once the child was gone, David could still feel the imprint of his body like an echo of David's old life. Ambulance and siren fading into the distance, David called Taylor's mother and told her they'd found him.

"Is he hurt?" Panic in her voice.

He answered the question she couldn't bring herself to ask. "He's alive." Taylor had lived through something horrendous, something that could have had a much worse outcome. But thanks to Elise, he was free and would be home soon. "Medics are taking him to Candler," David said. "You can see him there, in the ER."

"Thank you."

David disconnected and looked up at a sky still bright with fireworks, thinking about the price Elise had paid and the eerily prophetic words he'd spoken to her just hours ago. *I know good-bye when I see it.*

CHAPTER 47

Getting into the van on Bay Street, Elise had been hit with a Taser, bound, and gagged, the battery removed from her phone and the device smashed for extra measure.

Two men. Probably the same men who'd shot up the cemetery and attacked her in the parking garage. Black ski masks, one driving, one who'd pressed his knee to her spine to further immobilize her.

She'd tried to keep track of the route—the passing of minutes, the turns—but whenever she grew too still or too alert, the man with the knee on her spine Tasered her again.

And now here they were. She was tied to a chair, hands behind her back, ankles secured to the chair legs, mouth covered with duct tape.

One of the masked men positioned himself in front of her, arms crossed, legs spread wide. He might have been Remy, might have been the man on the phone. She got the idea he was the leader of the pair, and the other person, no longer in the room, was his henchman, his follower.

"I have somebody I want you to meet," the man said.

They were in a warehouse. Where, she wasn't sure. Brick walls, wooden floors, a building that was vast and cavernous, that echoed when the man walked and talked. Few windows, and well over a hundred degrees inside. Her shirt was soaked with sweat, and Remy, if it was

Remy, was sweating profusely too. If she could have spoken, she would have advised him to remove the mask before he suffered heat stroke.

"I met a friend of yours some time back," he said conversationally. "Wait here while I get him. I wanted to surprise you both."

She'd made a lot of enemies in her career. What cop hadn't? He could be talking about anybody. So why was her heart pounding faster, and why was she sweating more?

The man walked down the center of the vast, open warehouse to disappear around a corner. She heard his footsteps fade, followed by the distant sound of awkwardly shuffling feet, then his return. More than one person this time. Moving slower this time.

Three men appeared in the distant gloom, the room so vast she watched them approach for what seemed minutes as they grew from something small enough to crush with her fingers to full-size men. As they drew closer, she understood the cumbersome sound of their steps. One of them was attached to a long pole, the kind used to control vicious dogs, or mental patients years ago. The third man, the man she figured for the henchman, followed along behind, a video camera in his hand. His mask was gone, but he was no one she recognized. White, thirties, dirty and skinny, with meth sores on his face. She kinda wished he'd put the mask back on. Maybe not a Remy convert after all. Just a junkie working for his next fix. As he walked, he kept an eye on the flip-up camera screen in his hand.

"He's normally pretty easygoing and does what I tell him to," the masked man said about his charge. "But I thought I'd take extra precaution, because I wasn't sure how he'd react to seeing you in person."

The man attached to the pole appeared docile—until he was close enough to get a good look at Elise. Then all hell broke loose. He lunged and roared, and the masked man had trouble keeping him under control, fighting like someone bringing in a sailfish.

Her "present," her surprise, didn't look human. A large part of his face was *just gone*. He had a raw crater in the center where a nose should be. But the eyes . . . She recognized those eyes.

Atticus Tremain.

Now she understood what John had been trying to tell them the first time he woke up. Tremain was alive—or whatever this existence could be called, because it couldn't be living. She'd been willing to sacrifice herself, but not like this. In her darkest nightmares she could never have dreamed up anything like this.

He lunged again, his hands raised like claws, his mouth agape, jagged and broken teeth bared.

Behind the tape, Elise screamed, and the man holding the pole laughed while the meth head got it all on camera, the documentation of her fresh torture at the hands of Atticus Tremain another gift of Remy's, this one no doubt for Jackson Sweet.

CHAPTER 48

"We need to get an ID on the body that was left in Remy's grave," David said, addressing the other men in his office. "That's an important lead and could be the break we're looking for." It was early morning, and Elise had been gone six hours. As usual, they were enlisting the public's help, hoping for a vehicle spotting, but so far nobody seemed to have seen anything. They'd probably had their eyes on the fireworks. "I'm convinced the switch took place in the funeral home."

"The search for the identity of the body in the casket proved a dead end," Avery reminded him.

"Maybe we didn't go wide enough." David had been up all night, and his skin felt too tight for his body, but he was focused. "We were looking in Chatham County, but the body might not have come from here."

John Casper surprised him by offering to help. "I'll check out the library microfilm." He'd arrived not long ago, looking weak and trembly and unfit to be out of bed, let alone involved in a murder-and-kidnapping investigation. "I'll concentrate on missing persons around the date of the burial," he said, his voice not much above a whisper. "And I'll go broad."

David didn't have the heart to tell him to go home instead. But then again, the kind of research he was talking about wouldn't be physically taxing. It might even be good for him to feel he was doing something to catch the man who'd killed his wife.

"Okay," David said.

"It's your fault." The accusation came from Sweet, who stood with his arms crossed, staring a hole through David. He'd entered the room with that expression, and it hadn't changed in the hour he'd been there, silently listening to their brainstorming while adding nothing.

"If you don't have anything to contribute, leave," David said.

"You could have stopped her."

"Nobody can stop Elise."

"She would have listened to you."

"You're wrong."

"You don't know what you've done."

"We saved a child. Your daughter saved a child's life. Try to appreciate that for a moment."

"I'd appreciate it a lot more if she was safe."

"She will be soon," Avery said.

"You're delusional." Sweet finally broke eye contact with David. "You're all delusional. The best we can hope is that he kills her fast. But that's not going to happen. A mercy kill isn't what this is about. Her death will be slow, and it will be painful. And if by some chance she does survive, she'll never be the same."

"So you're giving up?" David knew his question would light a fire under Sweet, and he also knew Sweet would never give up. He'd just dropped in to lecture them on their stupidity.

"I'm hitting the streets to see if I hear anything," Sweet told him. "Let me know as soon as you have any new information, and I'll do the same." He left.

David took off a few minutes later, heading to the hospital in hopes of questioning Taylor Millett. He was relieved to find the boy looking healthy, all things considered. David sat down on the edge of the bed and pointed to a box of crayons. "Mind if I do a little coloring?"

The boy pushed the box at him without a word. David tore a page from a blank tablet, pulled out his badge. While the boy watched, David chose a bright-blue crayon, placed the paper on top of the badge, and ran the crayon over the rough surface, making a copy. It was something his son used to do.

"I know you probably don't want to talk about this," David said, "but I need to ask about the man who abducted you." Abducted. A big word for a kid his age, but he'd be hearing it a lot and there was no need to water it down or make it something cute.

David pulled a flyer from his pocket, unfolded it, and showed him the composite drawing of Remy. "Have you ever seen this man?"

Taylor gave it a glance, then went back to coloring. "Don't know."

David tried another tactic. "Did you know the man who took you away from the park?"

"No."

That eliminated acquaintances. David asked him more questions. About where they'd gone, what kind of vehicle the man drove. Was it a truck? A van? A car?

Taylor gave him nothing more. "Did he tell you not to say anything?" David asked.

The crayon stopped, then started again.

That was it. He was afraid to share what he knew.

The boy began to rock back and forth. "I'm gonna add stars too. Mommy says stars are out in the day; we just can't see them."

Out of the mouths of babes.

Remy was working and living in plain sight. David was sure of it. He thought about the short list of suspects Meg had put together. Outside the hospital, without slowing his stride, David called Sweet. "Since you've proclaimed yourself to be the eyes and ears of the Savannah underbelly, see if you can find anything new on the panhandler from our suspect list." He gave him the name of the homeless shelter where the man might be found. Before Sweet had a chance to chew him out again, David disconnected.

CHAPTER 49

John wanted to help find Elise, and finding Elise also meant finding Mara's killer. For the first time since regaining consciousness in the hospital, he felt a spark of purpose. At the downtown Live Oak Library, he began by viewing newspapers in neighboring towns, then expanding his search to include places like Hilton Head, South Carolina. After two hours of loading plastic reels into the microfilm machine, his head was pounding and he needed to rest. He eyed the marble floor and wondered how it would work as a bed. Eyes burning, arm shaking from full-body weakness, he loaded another reel, this one from the *Charleston Post and Courier*, Charleston being a short two-hour drive from Savannah. He threaded the film under the glass, then watched the monitor.

He was halfway through the second article when his hand paused over the "Advance" button. He read the piece again, about a man named Brian O'Connor, who'd gone missing on a business trip two days before Remy was buried.

He zoomed in on the headshot and adjusted the focus. Then he slipped a quarter into the slot and pushed "Print." Beside him, a copy machine spit out an enlarged photo. Another quarter and he had the full article.

He called David's cell. "I think I might have something." He gave him the information, adding, "The accompanying photo looks like our John Doe, but I can't be certain without a dental match."

"That would take too long. You're the coroner. You performed the autopsy. What do you think?"

He was talking forensic anthropology. Not John's thing. "I don't know."

"Get a copy of the newspaper image to me, and I'll forward it to Hollis Blake. She can compare it to photos she took of Doe after his acid-melt. She can at least check bone structure."

John stared at the microfilm machine. "I don't think I can make a digital image." Times like these, he could really tell his brain wasn't working right, and it was especially evident when he got tired.

"Take a photo with your phone."

"It'll only be seventy-two dpi."

"John."

"Okay, okay."

He took a photo of the print and sent it to David.

"In the meantime," David said, "I'll get Meg Cook on this. But what's your opinion? Don't think too hard. Don't second-guess yourself."

"This isn't at all scientific or professional."

"We don't have time for scientific or professional."

"Are you going to trust the opinion of a guy with a head injury?"

"Absolutely."

"I think it's him."

"Okay. Go home and rest. Hear me? You sound exhausted. I'll keep you updated."

John packed up the film and tucked it back in the labeled canister and told the librarian thanks while she tried not to stare at his bald head and cast.

"Car wreck." He didn't know why he lied. Maybe the story of him and Mara was too personal to speak of to a stranger.

"I recognize you."

"Well shit." He headed back to David's apartment.

* * *

David called Meg Cook and told her to find out everything she could about O'Connor. Thirty minutes later he heard back from Hollis Blake. She agreed with John.

"This isn't at all scientific," she reminded David over the phone.

"So I've heard."

"Let's put it this way. When I compare the morgue photo to that of the newspaper, I see nothing in the images that tells me these two people cannot be the same person. But why don't I forward the JPGs to an acquaintance of mine in Atlanta? He's an expert in forensic facial reconstruction and should be able to make a more accurate and confident assessment."

David agreed to the plan, but his mind was already made up. It was the same guy. He was telling her good-bye when he got a call from Meg.

"O'Connor was a salesman from Florida," she said. "He had a wife and two kids."

Florida.

"I need to talk to the wife, if she's still alive."

"Already checked. She is. She lives in California now, pretty much as far away from Florida as a person can get. Her name is Tracy O'Connor."

"Good work."

"There's something else. Her kids? A few years after O'Connor vanished, they both died under what were considered suspicious circumstances. After that, some even suspected she was behind her husband's disappearance. The DA tried to prove the kids were victims of Munchausen by proxy, but the mother never wavered in her innocent plea. She got off eventually, although it sounds like she was pretty much ostracized after that."

"See if you can set up a Skype call. I need to talk to her."

"Will do."

An hour later David sat at his computer monitor introducing himself to the woman who used to live in Florida. She had bleached hair and a sad face. He could see she'd attempted to apply makeup.

"What's this about?" she asked.

"We have reason to believe your husband's disappearance thirty-six years ago was somehow tied to Frank J. Remy, a convicted killer in the state of Georgia. Have you heard of him?"

"I've seen articles about him in my Facebook feed, but I don't know what that has to do with my husband."

"Are you aware of the recent child killings in Florida and Georgia?"

"Are you really a detective?" She looked ready to bail. "You sound more like a reporter. I don't talk to reporters. I've been lied to by reporters. I moved to California to start over and get away from them."

David held up his badge.

"You could buy one of those online."

He tucked the badge away. "Guess I could." He was dangerously close to unraveling, thinking of the ticking clock and Elise, but he forced himself to maintain, dredged up his charm while appealing to the mother in Tracy O'Connor, hoping she hadn't been behind the murder of her own kids. "I'm not a reporter, but I'd like to ask you a couple of questions about the deaths of your children." She blanched, and he continued, quickly getting to the point before she could end the call. "I understand the killer was never caught, and I'm trying to determine if the recent Florida and Georgia murders were perpetrated by the same person. His capture won't bring your own children back, but it will keep other ones from losing their lives. And it will clear your name."

His straightforward approach worked. She gave in and described the deaths of her children. Asphyxiation, same as the Florida murders. Same as Zane Novak. Same as Mara and Loralie.

"Can you think of anybody in your area, a neighbor, someone at school, a teacher, anybody who might have wanted to harm them?"

She shook her head. "I've been through this again and again. You aren't asking me anything new."

"Were you dating anyone?"

"I dated, of course. I mean, I wasn't old."

"Who were you dating at the time of the deaths?"

"It couldn't have been Franklin."

Franklin. David fought the urge to lean forward as he tried not to appear too desperate.

"The kids loved him, and he adored them even though they weren't his own."

"The killer might very well have been charming and loving. Psychopaths are charming."

Tracy suddenly seemed eager to share her story. There were probably few people she could talk to about the darkest period of her life. "We started seeing each other shortly after my husband went missing. Franklin was wonderful, thoughtful, just what the boys and I needed, but we broke up after their deaths. It was too much for Franklin. He had such a soft heart. And even though he never said it, he suspected me. I could see it in his face."

It would have been hard enough to lose her kids, but to be blamed for those deaths by the very people who should have been supporting her . . . And how sick would it be if Remy had searched out the widow of the man whose body had replaced his in the coffin? It seemed that might be exactly what had happened. It would also explain why Remy went to Florida rather than farther away from Georgia.

His motive for the cemetery fiasco? The identity of the body would have led them straight to Tracy O'Connor and her murdered children.

"Franklin could do anything," Tracy said. "Sing, play the piano, clean house, cook. He was Mr. Mom, always baking cookies and cupcakes. Even doughnuts. He made the most amazing doughnuts."

CHAPTER 50

"Time to ramp this up," Remy said. "You're getting desensitized to him, and we're not getting good footage."

Hours had passed since Elise had been introduced to Tremain, and she'd quit reacting. To remedy that, Remy had removed Tremain from the room a few times, hoping each reintroduction would produce some epic video, but none would ever be as satisfying as her initial response. The fact that Remy still wore his mask told her he felt some twisted measure of shame, because she was sure he had no intention of letting her live so she could ID him.

"Camera on?" he asked.

The meth head nodded.

"Don't miss anything. You're only going to get one chance."

"Under control."

Remy hit the release mechanism on the restraint pole, then lifted the looped end over Tremain's head, freeing him. It took Tremain a few moments to realize what had happened. When it finally sank in, his dead eyes lit up, and he charged at Elise, shouting her name. He ripped her shirt open and dropped to his knees in front of her, his hands on her thighs while the other two men stood feet away.

Before the horror of the scene could fully sink in, he bent his head, opened his mouth—and bit into her upper stomach, just below the breast. She screamed and bucked in the chair. He lifted his head to look at her face, smiled a bloody smile, and came at her again.

This time he ripped the tape from her mouth and pressed his face to hers. She thought he was going to bite off her lip, but instead he plunged his tongue down her throat while his filthy, clawlike hands kneaded her hips.

Unsatisfied, he pulled away and stood up. Never taking his eyes from her, the smile never fading, he fumbled with the zipper of his pants while Remy moved even closer for prime viewing.

Her stomach a raw pit of pain, her mouth free of the tape, Elise ducked her head. Using her teeth, she reached into her bra and pulled out the packet LaRue had given her. The contents were meant for her, but instead of biting it open, she spit it out. It dropped to the floor in front of Tremain.

He was never going to rape her again. No matter what it took, even if it meant killing them all, herself included.

Elise moved her chair forward—two rapid hops. With the final hop, a chair leg burst the packet open, white powder exploding. In a final attempt to survive, she held her breath and pushed herself backward, the room turning. She heard the sound of splintering wood as the chair shattered, felt the crack of her head hitting the floor. She dug in her heels, scrambling away from the cloud of tetrodotoxin, tried to get to her feet, tripped, collapsed, crawled, and kept crawling, leaving a trail of blood behind.

* * *

"We have to coordinate this," Avery said in David's office. "Brief a SWAT team, bring in a hostage negotiator. Maybe some people from Atlanta."

"Set it up. But I'm not waiting around." David fastened the Velcro on his bulletproof vest.

The baker had somehow falsified his prints. Not a hard thing to do today. Hell, there were probably YouTube tutorials on it. On top of that, Meg Cook was taking the news hard because her research had removed Hughes from their short list of suspects, but she couldn't be blamed. He *had* lived in Indiana, and his wife was dead. He'd just left out the part about visiting Florida before moving to Savannah.

On the phone in Forsyth Park, Remy had tried to convince them of his innocence when it came to murder. David hadn't fallen for it, and Remy's connection to the O'Connor children supported that. Many child killers never confessed no matter how much evidence was stacked against them.

David strode from the building, not seeing anybody, almost crashing into Sweet outside the main entrance.

"The panhandler is not our man," Sweet said.

"I know."

"But he was telling me about a meth head who claimed to know Remy."

"Forget the meth head." David didn't slow down. He unlocked his car from across the parking lot. "I've got a strong lead."

Seconds later, Sweet in the passenger seat, they roared down the street. David ran red lights and cut across medians to get around cars waiting at intersections. He ignored the honking horns and finger gestures. At the vast warehouse, he slammed the car into park and cut the engine. Inside the bakery, David held his badge high above his head. "Everybody out."

Chairs scraped. Mothers grabbed children. Within seconds the place was empty except for the young girl behind the register.

"Where's Hughes?" David demanded.

She'd seen too many cop dramas, because she locked her hands behind her head. "I don't know."

"When did you last see him?"

"Y-yesterday. I opened today, but he wasn't here." She stumbled against the counter as David shoved past her, heading for the kitchen. One quick sweep was enough to tell him it was empty. He returned to the girl. She had a cell phone in her hand and was running for the door.

"Stop!"

She stopped.

"Are you calling 911?"

"Yes."

"No cops."

"You're scaring her," Sweet said.

He was right. She was shaking and trying not to cry. Hell, she was just a kid, no older than Audrey. Wearing clothes she probably detested—a pink ruffled apron and white sneakers.

"Don't call the cops," David said in his kind and charmingly persuasive voice. "Got it?"

The girl nodded and ran out the door.

David called Avery and told him they were checking the entire warehouse.

"You need backup?"

"Be ready. I don't want anybody coming in with sirens blaring."

"Got it."

Down a narrow hall of old brick, they found a freight elevator with a metal accordion door. The lift had stopped on another floor; David could see the cables and gaping shaft.

They both pulled their weapons. Sweet pointed. "Stairs."

The building was maybe five stories tall. The second floor turned up nothing. David was getting nervous, thinking this was a waste of valuable time, when they stepped onto the ancient third floor.

The warehouse space was vast and dusty and dark, but not so dark they couldn't make out four bodies. Weapons braced, David and Sweet moved forward until they were close enough to see that three of the bodies were men. The fourth was Elise, unmoving, a trail of blood behind her.

David swallowed the despair in his throat.

Sweet's hand lashed out. "Don't move." He nodded toward a dusting of powder on the floor.

"TTX?" David asked.

"Maybe."

An imaginary clock ticked down seconds that felt like minutes as David visually processed the scene. With chilling acuity, David realized Elise had most likely had the TTX on her. She'd planned to kill herself, which explained her actions and behavior the previous night. Instead she'd taken them all down, herself included. The scene in the warehouse played out in his mind, the sequence of events that had led to the men on the floor and to Elise and the shattered chair. Beside him, Sweet was eerily silent.

David wanted to drop to his knees and cradle his head. He wanted to vanish. Disappear. Forever, completely, because the pain was too much.

Instead, moving slowly and cautiously, he gave the powder a wide berth. The slightest waft of air could send the poison their way, and Elise might still be alive. When he reached her, he knelt down, hand shaking as he pressed two fingers against her neck, first lightly, then harder when he didn't get a pulse, finally picking up a faint rhythm. That was all he needed to know.

He stood, put his hands under her arms, and dragged her backward, a safe distance from the powder. He had to make a decision. Leave her there and wait for an ambulance, or risk further injury and carry her to fresh air. He chose fresh air.

He hefted her into his arms. "Call 911." David headed for the elevator but heard no movement or conversation behind him. David glanced over his shoulder to see Sweet frozen in place, a look of anguish on his face. Maybe Sweet had screwed up over the years, but it was obvious the guy was crazy about Elise.

"Call 911," David repeated.

Sweet jerked to attention and made the call, including a cautionary warning about the powder.

Elise let out a moan, and David's heart jumped in his chest. This was what hope felt like.

Two minutes later they were outside in the blinding sunlight, temps over a hundred. He placed her in the shade of a pitiful excuse for a tree, noted that her skin was ice cold. Maybe due to the blood loss. Maybe the inhaled TTX. Maybe both.

"Lie still," he said when she struggled to sit up. "You've been shot." He could hear the ambulance getting closer.

"Not shot," she said faintly, the fresh air seeming to bring her around. "He bit me."

Holy hell. David moved the fabric of her shirt aside to get a better look at the wound. Reassured that she didn't have a bullet in her, he wiped a finger across her bloody lips.

"And kissed me."

Her words sent a chill through him.

"Is Tremain dead?" she asked.

Tremain? She was delirious.

The ambulance arrived, followed by coroner Hollis Blake and crime scene personnel, who began pulling on hazmat suits and respirators. The emergency medical tech said Elise's veins were as flat as tapeworms. Finally, after too many pokes, she was hooked up to an IV and placed on a gurney. They were ready to take her away when she stopped them with a firm command, followed by an explanation. "I'm not leaving until I know he's dead."

To placate her, David called Hollis, who was now inside, and asked about the men.

"One person is still alive," she said.

"Do you have an ID on him?"

"No, but he's a skinny guy with meth sores. He was a little farther away from the powder. Strangest thing. There's a man here with half his face gone. I can't believe he lived with that kind of destruction. Looks like a gunshot injury to me."

David tried to keep his voice level. "Recent?"

"Within the last year or two."

"Run his prints as soon as possible."

"I can do it right now with a fingerprint app."

He heard footsteps; then she was back a minute later. "It pulled up a twenty-point match." Her voice sounded strange. "And you're not going to believe this."

"Try me."

"Atticus Tremain."

Watching Elise, David told the coroner thanks and disconnected. "Twenty-point match." And then the words she was waiting for. "Tremain. And he's dead."

She let out a relieved breath. He'd tell her about Remy later.

"I suppose this means things are going to be really awkward between us now," he said as the EMTs loaded her and the gurney into the ambulance.

Elise closed her eyes and smiled. "Undoubtedly."

CHAPTER 51

"Jump on my back."

"I'm not going to jump on your back. Complete it without me."

"Come on." David braced his hands on his knees. "We only have a half mile left."

"I don't think it counts if someone carries me."

"I'm not going for a gold star here. I just want us to cross the finish line together."

Elise and David stood in the middle of the street while Run for the Animals participants with numbers on their chests moved past them. Avery was long gone. Elise figured he'd finished at least thirty minutes ago. They'd jogged and walked over twelve ungodly miles, and David didn't even seem tired.

"I don't know why I agreed to this," she said.

It had been only two weeks since Atticus Tremain had tried to make a meal of her. Certainly too soon for something so strenuous. The healing bite on her stomach burned, and her leg was screaming. And David was still bent at the waist, waiting.

She laughed and shook her head—then jumped on his back. It wasn't really a jump. Kind of an awkward clamber. He grunted and hefted her higher, his hands braced under her legs while she linked her arms around his upper chest, her chin resting on his shoulder.

Before the race he'd told her he wasn't taking the job in Ohio. And right now the team was back. Elise, David, Avery, and John. Evidence had been found at the bakery and Remy's house, unequivocally proving his guilt. The weirdest thing? He'd won a posthumous award for his Johnny Mercer doughnuts. And knowing Savannah, the doughnuts wouldn't die with Remy. Elise expected knockoffs to begin showing up at tourist establishments around the city.

"This is ridiculous," Elise said.

"I'm here to entertain."

The day after the warehouse incident went down, Elise had insisted upon going to the morgue to see Atticus Tremain. She'd touched his cold skin, stared at him, taken photos that she'd no doubt pull up whenever she experienced a sick sense of dread and need to reassure herself that he was really and truly dead. Her father had checked out Remy in a similar way, muttering something about the bastard being dead for a second time.

No one was quite sure how Remy and Tremain had met. The meth head, if he could be believed, thought it had been at a halfway house where Tremain had lived for a while after being medically treated as a John Doe.

So far Elise and David hadn't talked about their night together, but they would. Sometime. Maybe when she got back from her visit to Seattle to see Audrey.

They crossed the finish line.

Sweet, Strata Luna, Avery, and John Casper were there, clapping and cheering. She and Sweet had somewhat reconciled. David had related her father's reaction when they both thought she might be dead. Whatever their painful history, it was obvious she meant something to him. Maybe someday she'd even move him to her short list of people she cared about most.

David eased Elise off his back and turned around to steady her with both his hands. Then, before she saw it coming, he smiled and kissed her in front of the whole damn world.

ABOUT THE AUTHOR

Photo © 2012 Sharyn Morrow

Anne Frasier is the *New York Times* and *USA Today* bestselling author of more than twenty novels that range from thrillers to memoirs. She is a RITA winner for her romantic suspense books and a recipient of the Daphne du Maurier Award for paranormal romance. Her thrillers have been featured by the Mystery Guild, the Literary Guild, and the Book of the Month Club. Her memoir *The Orchard* received a B+ review in *Entertainment Weekly*, was an *O, the Oprah Magazine* Fall Book Pick, was named an American Library Association "One Book, One Community" read, and was singled out as a Librarians' Best Book of 2011. Her most recent novel, *Truly Dead*, is the highly anticipated fourth installment in the Elise Sandburg series.

Frasier currently divides her time between Saint Paul, Minnesota, and her writing studio in rural Wisconsin.